BENOTRIPIA
The Complete Trilogy

MCKENZIE WAGNER

Sweetwater Books
An Imprint of Cedar Fort, Inc.
Springville, Utah

Cover illustrations by Rachel Sharp
Inside illustrations for *Benotripia: The Rescue* by Tera Grasser
Other illustrations by Rachel Sharp

ISBN 13: 978-1-4621-1751-2

Published by Sweetwater Books, an imprint of Cedar Fort, Inc.
2373 W. 700 S., Springville, UT 84663
Distributed by Cedar Fort, Inc., www.cedarfort.com

Library of Congress Control Number: 2015943027

Benotripia: The Rescue previously published in 2012
Benotripia: The Stones of Horsh previously published in 2013
Benotripia: Keys to the Dream World previously published in 2014

Cover design by Rachel Sharp and M. Shaun McMurdie
Cover design © 2015 Lyle Mortimer
Edited and typeset by Melissa J. Caldwell

Printed in the United States of America

10 9 8 7 6 5 4 3 2 1

Printed on acid-free paper

Contents

Sweetwater Books
An Imprint of Cedar Fort, Inc.
Springville, Utah

Contents

Prologue

IT WAS A CHILLY NIGHT—CHILLY FOR THE TROPICAL ISLAND of Benotripia. There were no clouds, however, and no cold winds swept the air.

Under the starry night sky, a woman made her way cautiously across a white, starlit beach. The waves lapped gently against smooth, gray rocks, and the moonlight glinted in the woman's silky honey-colored hair.

As soon as she reached the water's edge, she stopped. There was complete silence—save for the waves continuing their tireless routine of rolling in across the beach. A few tiny waves of water reached the woman's ankles, but she took no notice.

The woman sighed. It was a beautiful night. She wished her husband could be here to see it. But then, he could be looking at the stars right now also. She only wished she knew where he was.

Heavy footsteps sounded through the darkness, shattering her thoughts, and she looked around apprehensively. A tall red-headed man appeared almost instantly by her side, and she sighed with relief.

"I'm glad you could come," she whispered. "Especially after the tragedy that happened this morning." Even in the darkness, the woman could see the look of utter confusion on his face. She was surprised he didn't know.

"What are you speaking of?" the man whispered back with concern.

"Magford. He's gone."

"What?"

"Gone. Without a trace."

"Do you have any ideas how it . . . ?" He trailed off as a noiseless crystal tear trickled down the woman's cheek. "Leader Danette, we will find him. I promise. You will not be the only leader of Benotripia for long," the man vowed.

The woman nodded with a weak smile and hastily wiped the tear off her cheek.

"How is Roseabelle?" the man whispered, referring to her two-year-old daughter.

"She doesn't know yet—she's too young to understand," the woman answered. "Losing a parent is a terrible fate."

The man nodded again. "It is probably better that she doesn't know. I will aid your daughter in any way I can. She will need help as she grows."

"Thank you. For everything."

Without another word, the man slipped away into the shadows of the slightly swaying palm trees.

CHAPTER 1
Roseabelle

"Roseabelle, it's time for training," Danette called up the stairs. "If you don't hurry, you'll be late."

Roseabelle quickly sat up in bed.

When Benotripians reached eight years old, they started school at one of Benotripia's many power training academies. Every student had his or her own personal trainer, and since Roseabelle had been at the Central Power Training Academy for two years, she had developed a personal bond with Shelby, her trainer.

She hastily dressed into her crimson sports dress and slid her feet into black slip-on shoes. After brushing her long, auburn hair and pulling it back with a red ribbon, she zipped downstairs and grabbed her water bottle.

"Train hard," Danette encouraged.

"I will," Roseabelle answered.

As Danette exited the room, Roseabelle strode to the shadow falling behind the wooden steps. When she was nine years old, she had learned to shadow tumble. Shadow tumbling was one of the uncommon powers that Roseabelle had since she had Meta-Mord. Meta-Mord was extremely rare, and it bestowed Roseabelle with many unique powers.

The required actions of shadow tumbling were to fully immerse yourself in a shadow and picture a place where you wanted to go. You could travel through the shadow and arrive at the place you had pictured—or at least in a shadow nearby.

Roseabelle stepped into the shadow. She pictured Central Power Training Academy and thumped her foot. She felt herself being whisked away, and before she knew it, she had landed smoothly on the soft soil.

She opened her eyes and saw herself standing next to the magnificent structure of Central Power Training Academy. She saw kids piling in through the front doors. Memories flooded back to Roseabelle. Here at the academy she and her friends had learned how to use and fight with weapons and had studied more about their powers.

Among the crowd of students, Roseabelle spotted Jessicana and Astro, her best friends.

Jessicana had long blonde hair and aqua-blue eyes and was wearing a bright red and orange shirt, lemon-yellow tights, and a short green and blue skirt. Her shoes matched her eyes.

In contrast, Astro had spiky jet-black hair and alert green eyes. He was wearing a black T-shirt with waves of blue on it and a pair of jeans. Matching blue and black flip-flops completed his outfit.

Jessicana and Astro each had one power. Jessicana could shape-shift into a parrot, and Astro could shoot lightning bolts from his fingertips.

"Hey, Roseabelle! Over here!" Astro called. Roseabelle streaked past the throng of people.

"How's it going?" Roseabelle asked earnestly.

"Fine, I guess," Jessicana said.

"Come on. We had better get checked in," Astro said.

They entered the academy. It really was a stunning sight. The entire building was built out of polished white marble. With its 244 rooms and its majestic balconies, the Central

Power Training Academy was one of the grandest Academies in Benotripia.

Roseabelle, Astro, and Jessicana signed in on the register and turned to find Shelby, Polly (Astro's trainer), and Asteran (Jessicana's trainer) waiting for them.

"Better get going," the three friends muttered simultaneously. Shelby led Roseabelle to a large room on the fourth floor, labeled "Creature Care." Shelby opened the door and beckoned for Roseabelle to come inside.

The room was filled with all sorts of animals—ordinary and magical. Cages lined the walls, containing toucans, red-eyed tree frogs, and boa constrictors. Tanks full of water housed various kinds of colorful fish and crabs. A small fence surrounded a creature with meaty legs, a tall oval body, sharp five-fingered claws, and a round pudgy face with a snout and three beady eyes.

Shelby turned to Roseabelle. "You might know that Meta-Mords have the ability to sense animals' emotions and feelings. Today we will work on this," Shelby explained.

"First, we will start with the mottel on the window over there." She nodded to a window with a flat wooden board attached. On it rested a bird with a soft middle and round, bumpy toes. It had a sharp beak, two round eyes, brightly colored feathers, and large rounded wings.

Roseabelle knew a little about mottels. They were native birds that spoke messages. A person would tell the mottel the message, and then the small bird would fly off to the person who was to receive the message. The mottel would repeat what it had heard and then fly away. Roseabelle knew that Jessicana's mother kept some for pets.

Roseabelle ran over to the window and was shortly joined by Shelby.

"Put your hand on the mottel," Shelby instructed. Roseabelle did. "Now block out every little bit of sound you hear. Pretend you are alone with the mottel. No one there. No one," Shelby said hypnotically.

Roseabelle tried her best and put all her focus on the mottel, which was watching her curiously.

"All right, are you getting anything?" Shelby asked. Roseabelle closed her eyes. Nothing so far. She didn't feel anything different.

Roseabelle started to get a little jumpy and eager. She wanted to get up and move around. She had to! Something was holding her down. She didn't want that. But what was it?

Suddenly Shelby's voice broke through her thoughts. "Are you feeling any peculiar emotions?"

Roseabelle opened her eyes. "Yes," she said. "I'm feeling like I need to move around. I want to but something is holding me down."

Shelby nodded. "That is probably what the mottel is feeling. The something that is holding it down is your hand. You did good, Roseabelle. Which animal do you want to try next?" Shelby questioned.

For the next hour or so, Roseabelle practiced feeling the emotions of other animals. She gradually and naturally excelled at it. When she asked Shelby if she could practice on the ugly animal locked in the fence, Shelby turned white and hissed, "No!"

Roseabelle was surprised. "Uh, okay," she said, slightly taken back.

Instead, she walked to a spotted juddle—a mammal with leathery skin, almond-shaped eyes, and sticklike legs.

At lunchtime, Shelby dismissed her, and Roseabelle fled down the stairs. She sped into the bright cafeteria and quickly spotted Astro in the back of the lunch line. She grabbed a lunch tray and joined him.

"Have you seen Jessicana?" Roseabelle asked.

"No," Astro said simply.

But it wasn't hard to find Jessicana in her bright clothing. The parrot-girl soon walked into line.

"There you are," Roseabelle said with relief. But Jessicana didn't respond. She was staring at Asteran, her trainer, with concentration. Although puzzled, Roseabelle decided not to disturb Jessicana.

When she reached the food bar, Roseabelle piled butter onto her potatoes, took a fruit cup, and dished herself some yogurt. She then sat down at one of the large lunch tables. All Jessicana took was some fruit and nuts. Astro heaped plates of salad, bowls of soup, and glasses of water on his now heavy tray. He sat next to Roseabelle and began to eat ravenously.

When Astro had finished the last of his soup, Jessicana whispered, "Look at Asteran. Doesn't he seem a little secretive?" Roseabelle looked to where Jessicana was pointing. She was right. The tall trainer was looking around cautiously and clutching his arm. "I'm going to see what he's up to," Jessicana whispered. She started to rise from the table, but Astro took hold of her sleeve.

"What are you thinking? People don't like you prying into their business," Astro urged quietly.

Jessicana shrugged. "I don't think it will hurt. After all, I am his trainee," she reasoned. Astro and Roseabelle shared a look and there was a long pause.

Jessicana tapped her foot on the marble floor, sending an echo across the large cafeteria. "Oh come on, Astro," she said impatiently.

She tried to rise again, but Astro grabbed her sleeve for the second time. "Jessicana, no! What are you thinking?" Astro said, shaking his head.

"Astro," Roseabelle half whispered. "The Darvonians haven't taken any action since m-my father disappeared." Roseabelle took a deep breath at the thought of her father and paused for a minute. "You know what they're like. Their reputation is silence for a few years and then suddenly revealing a well-planned, brilliant scheme. Nothing has happened for eight years. They've had plenty of time to plot something against Benotripia," Roseabelle said. "I just think we should be on our guard about anything suspicious. That's all I'm trying to say."

Astro looked at Roseabelle and sighed. Then he groaned. "All right, all right," Astro said, "but I'm coming with you."

"Me too," added Roseabelle. The three friends rose from the table, placed their dirty lunch trays on the counter, and walked with quick, short steps toward Asteran.

The dark-haired trainer was leaning against the wall, his eyes darting around the cafeteria. Astro, Jessicana, and Roseabelle stood casually next to a slight break in the wall, which hid them from Asteran's view. When Asteran made sure no eyes were looking his way, he slipped out the lunchroom door.

Roseabelle led her friends out of the cafeteria. She saw Asteran turn into another hallway and then disappear. The trio walked to the end of the hall and turned down the same hall. They followed Asteran is this manner, making sure that they weren't seen.

They had traveled through several hallways when Asteran reached a small side door that led outside. He opened it and walked silently through. Asteran closed the door behind him and disappeared from the kids' view.

Jessicana transformed into a parrot and rose into the air. "*Awk, awk*, he's up to something," she squawked firmly.

"Why don't you see what he is up to?" Roseabelle asked.

"*Awk*, I will," Jessicana replied. Astro opened the door for her and Jessicana flew in pursuit of Asteran. Astro closed the door.

"Well, we had better get to our trainers. I hope we haven't been gone long," Roseabelle remarked. At that moment, the two heard footsteps.

CHAPTER 2
Followed!

ROSEABELLE GULPED. POLLY APPEARED IN THE HALL. "Astro, there you are! And Roseabelle. I'm sorry, dear, but Shelby unexpectedly left. Haven't got a clue of where she went. Your mother will be informed of this. You may go. Now, Astro, back to the weather room," Polly said apologetically.

She beckoned for Astro to follow her. When Polly turned away, Roseabelle mouthed, "Meet me at my house." Astro nodded and walked away with Polly.

Roseabelle opened the door and walked out. She looked around for any sign of Jessicana before marching home. She didn't feel like shadow tumbling right now because thoughts were swarming in her head like a hive of angry bees. She knew it would be a long walk home, so she decided to jog.

Halfway home, she spotted a dark figure hiding behind a tree. A second later it vanished. Chills ran down Roseabelle's spine. She was being followed!

Maybe shadow tumbling was a good idea. She ran into the shadow of a large boulder and closed her eyes. She pictured her house and stomped her foot. She felt her body glide through air and land on the soft dirt. She opened her eyes.

Her amazing home was looming in front of her. Astro liked to call it "the tree palace," and Jessicana's name for it was "the fairy hideout." It was built on six oak trees and was made entirely of wood and thick vegetation. The windows were made out of sea glass, and the door was solid brass. A thick ladder made of vines hung from the door.

Roseabelle leapt onto the ladder and climbed up. She pulled open her door and hurried upstairs. Roseabelle raced along the corridor and flung open the first door on the left, which opened up to her bedroom.

Her walls were light blue and the carpet was leafen grass—a type of Benotripian plant that never withered. Her bed had a silken bedspread and an elegantly carved wooden headboard.

On her twig dresser rested a leafy pouch her mother had given her for her seventh birthday. She still remembered the words Danette had spoken when she had presented the pouch to her. "Never forget that in time of need, this case contains something that will give you great aid. Only open it if I am not here to help."

Roseabelle looked out her window. Danette was probably out in Benotripia somewhere, fulfilling one of her many duties as an honorable ruler. Her mother was not always home, but she promised that her trips would never take longer than two days.

Roseabelle looked at the mango tree leaning against her window. She opened the window and edged herself onto the sill, then jumped onto the tree and sat on a strong limb. She picked a mango, peeled it, and bit into it. Roseabelle wiped the juice that was dribbling off her chin with her hand and gazed out on Benotripia.

From her window she could see Bright Shore Beach. If you took a boat and rode for a long time, you would eventually get to Darvonia. Roseabelle took another bite of mango.

Where was Astro? Training would be about over by now. Was Jessicana okay? Had she found something about Asteran? Her thoughts were interrupted by a scream that came from the beach. "Roseabelle, help! Help—"

The shout was cut off. Roseabelle couldn't see who had made

the noise, but that didn't stop her from jumping off the tree and sprinting to Bright Shore Beach. There was no one in sight. Who had screamed, then? She squinted out to the ocean. Not even the smallest boat was out there. Her heart was beating three times faster than usual. The voice had been familiar. Who was it?

The undergrowth that signaled the entrance of Frogipani Jungle rustled a bit. Curious, Roseabelle bent to it and pushed back some foliage to see inside. No one. *Well,* she thought, *it could have been a gold-striped frog.*

Gold-striped frogs were fairly common in Benotripia. They liked to rest in dense places and were quick as an arrow.

"That's probably what it was," Roseabelle tried to convince herself. But then if that had been the situation, who screamed?

Confusion filled her mind. She wished that Astro would come soon.

Roseabelle looked at her home. She walked back to the mango tree, climbed it, and hoisted herself up into her room. Roseabelle skittered downstairs and looked out the kitchen window. Outside sat a parrot looking around wildly.

"Jessicana, is that you?" Roseabelle called out.

The parrot squawked excitedly and Roseabelle opened the window so her friend could fly through.

In a split second a blonde-haired girl stood in the parrot's place, clutching a rather creased raven feather. "Oh, Roseabelle," she said, sounding relieved. "There you are. I have a bundle of news for you."

"Where's Astro?" Roseabelle asked. Jessicana's face paled.

"He's not with you? I thought training was over," Jessicana said, panicking.

"Don't worry—we'll find him," Roseabelle soothed.

At that moment, a "Look out below!" came from the roof. There was a loud crash and then silence.

"Astro!" Jessicana and Roseabelle cried out at the same time. Roseabelle dashed out the door and leaped upward. Her hands clasped on a panel of wood, and she began to slide down. Roseabelle scraped at the wall, searching for a crack that she could hold on to. There were none and she began to fall. Roseabelle spotted the kitchen windowsill and lunged for it. She missed and started to plummet downward.

She pressed all her weight on the wall, and much to her surprise, her fall was halted. Roseabelle looked up. Astro was dangling from the roof, his hand clutching hers.

"Astro," Roseabelle gasped. "What happened?"

"Save the questions for later," Astro said as he pulled Roseabelle up on the roof. "Roseabelle, something fishy is going on, and I don't like it. I'm a little worried. Okay—make that really worried. I need to tell you something. I saw—" Astro began, but he was cut off by a pineapple soaring through the air straight at him.

He snatched it by the leaves and flung it away. "I—" Astro started again, only to see a jagged piece of silver zooming toward him. He simply grabbed it from the air and pocketed it.

"As I was saying—" the lightning boy tried again, but a porcelain bowl headed toward him. He shot a lightning bolt at the bowl and it shattered.

Astro sighed. "Never mind," he said.

"What was that?" Roseabelle said, gaping.

"Uh, nothing," Astro said conspicuously. "Let's just forget about it, okay?"

Roseabelle studied her friend carefully. Astro looked extremely twitchy and nervous, like he wanted to tell Roseabelle something but couldn't.

"Um, all right," Roseabelle said uncertainly.

"Good," he said.

"How do we get down?" Roseabelle asked.

Astro shook his head. "I was going to ask you," he stated.

"Great," Roseabelle groaned. "This is just great."

"Well, can't you shadow tumble or something?" Astro questioned.

"Yes, but you wouldn't be able to," Roseabelle answered.

"You could catch me."

Roseabelle looked at him incredulously. "Yeah, like I could catch you." She chuckled. Then she stopped. "Oh Kinetle's cloak!" she exclaimed. "I guess I could."

Before she knew it, Roseabelle had plunged into a shadow, pictured the brass door, and stomped her foot on the roof. She felt herself glide through the air and then land on the wooden platform next to the door. She climbed down the ladder and took a deep breath.

She knew what Astro wanted her to do, but she was extremely nervous. It, of course, had to do with her Meta-Mord, being another unusual power: fur beam.

Yes, it often sounded ridiculous—but the power actually came in handy at times. On the underside of her elbow was a sickening yellow spot. When she exposed the spot to the sun, her body would sprout fur. She would become stronger, more muscular, and fearsome.

Roseabelle truly disliked to perform fur beam, but right now she had no choice. Roseabelle twisted the spot to the sun and watched as a beam of light hit it. She felt herself twist upward and grow taller. She saw strands of brown hair grow on her arms and she hoped that no one besides Astro and Jessicana were watching. Her whole body ached, but Roseabelle just gritted her teeth—which had now grown a little longer. Roseabelle looked down at her legs. She was hairy!

"Astro," she growled. "Jump!" The boy jumped from the roof and Roseabelle caught him with her now large hands. He gave a lopsided grin.

"I thought I would never see you like this," he said as he gave a mock sigh. In return, Roseabelle set Astro down and revealed her furry elbow in the sun. She felt her fur, teeth, and body shrink back to their normal size.

A few minutes later, Roseabelle was completely normal. "Whew," she said. "I'm glad that's over."

Astro bit his lip, obviously trying not to laugh.

"Hey, you guys, come on up! We have some matters to discuss," Jessicana called from above.

Roseabelle climbed up the ladder and reentered her home. Astro followed. When they were all inside, sitting at the bark-made table, Jessicana spoke up.

"After I left you, I traced Asteran through Benotripia. He made some interesting stops. He traveled into Bird Song Jungle. There was a little wooden shack next to a palm tree, and he slipped inside. I followed him. It led to an old bar that served a lot of delicacies like coconut soufflé and banana cream pie.

"I was a little amazed by the special treats when the pub was in the middle of the jungle and totally rundown. Asteran sat down and ordered some food. He ate it both exuberantly and hastily.

"After he paid the bartender with a few bronze hadhadile coins, he set off.

"Asteran wound through the jungle and took a shortcut I had never noticed before. It led out of Bird Song and to a dirt path. He walked with quick steps to a small clearing with a large boulder. He trotted out, and I went after him. But the clearing led back to dense underbrush.

"I searched and searched, but I couldn't find him. I checked back in the clearing—even behind the boulder—but it seemed like he had disappeared. I went through the underbrush nevertheless and found myself on Bright Shore Beach. There was no sign of him. Disappointed, I went to your house and waited on the branch, and here I am!"

"Nice adventure, Jessicana, but may I ask, what's with the raven feather?" Astro questioned.

"Well, while I was tracking Asteran, this fell out of his pocket," Jessicana answered.

"Can I have a look?" Roseabelle asked. Jessicana handed the feather to her. Roseabelle took it. She quietly pored over it with great care. When she felt the middle of it, she cringed and moaned. Her entire body went rigid, and Jessicana watched in horror as Roseabelle squirmed out of her seat and fell to the floor.

CHAPTER 3

The Dream World

"WHAT'S GOING ON?" JESSICANA CRIED. ASTRO LEAPT to Roseabelle's side and saw that she was clutching the feather tightly. His eyes quivered with fear, and he reached for the feather. Roseabelle rolled over.

Astro tried to snatch it a second time, but Roseabelle violently kicked her legs in the air. Her eyes were now closed and she was completely out of control. "Kinetle," she groaned. "Kinetle."

* * * * *

WHEN ROSEABELLE TOUCHED THE CENTER OF THE RAVEN feather, she instantly felt nauseated. Her head was light, and she had only the slightest idea of her surroundings. She saw Jessicana's expression turn fearful, and felt herself slip and land with a thud. She tried to get back up, but she didn't have the strength. Roseabelle was beginning to black out now. The last thing she saw was Astro bending over, his eyes full of concern.

* * * * *

"WHO'S KINETLE?" JESSICANA WONDERED OUT LOUD.

"I don't know," Astro replied, still struggling to get the feather.

"Darvonians, Darvonians," Roseabelle muttered. "Darvonians."

"Did you hear that?" Astro asked as he lunged on top of Roseabelle to get the feather. Jessicana nodded. "Well, if we're ever going to get this feather out of her hand, you're going to need to help," Astro said.

Jessicana bent down and said, "I have an idea." She whispered something in Roseabelle's ear. Roseabelle paused for a moment, giving Astro the opportunity to grab the feather from her. Roseabelle began to open her eyes.

* * * * *

SOMETHING AROUSED ROSEABELLE FROM HER FAINT. SHE WAS lying on the ground on a rocky shore. By the looks of it, the land did not seem to match up with Benotripia. There were mountains, caves, boulders, and pieces of sharp rock. A figure with a black cloak strode to her. "Rise," a harsh voice commanded.

Roseabelle struggled to her feet. "Have you got her?" the figure asked.

Roseabelle was confused. "Um, what do you mean?" she asked.

The man took in a quick breath. "Imposter!" he bellowed. "Do you not know who I am?" Roseabelle, a bit frightened, shook her head boldly.

"I am Ugagush, son of Kinetle, and leader of the Darvonians!" Ugagush shouted. "And you will not escape. Never shall you leave this state."

Kinetle? Roseabelle had heard about her. She was merciless, greedy, and cruel. Her son must be equally so. Roseabelle had to get free.

She turned to run, but an invisible wall blocked her. She heard Ugagush howling with laughter.

Suddenly she heard a voice: "Roseabelle you are in the dream world. Don't worry—we're coming." It was Jessicana's voice. Roseabelle was comforted, and she stopped struggling and trying to run.

Then everything began to black out again. The last image before she became unconscious was Ugagush shrieking, "*Noooo!*"

ROSEABELLE SAT UP. SHE WAS BACK IN HER HOUSE WITH ASTRO and Jessicana kneeling beside her. "Whoa," she muttered. "That was weird."

"Roseabelle!" Jessicana cried out. She embraced her friend. "What in the name of Danette happened?"

Roseabelle told them all about the sensation with the feather, what happened, who she saw, and how she ended up back here.

"I'll say that is quite an adventure," Jessicana remarked.

"Jessicana, what were you talking about when you said the 'dream world'?" Roseabelle asked.

Jessicana's expression turned grave. "Roseabelle," she said, her tone quavering. "It's an ancient myth. Before I didn't believe in it, but now I do. According to the legend, the dream world was created by an IB."

"What's an IB?" Astro asked.

"IB stands for *Imitation Benotripian,"* Jessicana answered steadily. "And they are as rare as Meta-Mords. They are born into the Darvonian race, but they look nothing like their parents and could easily pass for a Benotripian. IBs are very intelligent, and so far, none of them have been on the good side."

Astro and Roseabelle were staring at her openly. "How in Benotripia's Beauty do you know all this?" Roseabelle asked her.

Jessicana blushed and shrugged. "Just research in the library, I guess. Anyway," she continued, "the dream world was a sort of place where Darvonians communicated with their own kind. They also trapped Benotripians into a terrible motionless state."

Jessicana paused, waiting for a reaction. Astro was looking eager for her to go on, but Roseabelle was sitting on her chair, keeping her gaze on the floor. "Roseabelle, what's wrong?" Jessicana asked.

Wordlessly, Roseabelle went to the door. She traveled down the ladder and walked as if in a trance to Bright Shore Beach. Astro and Jessicana shared a look and then scrambled after her. At the beach, Roseabelle squatted down and touched the flower that she had pushed back earlier.

She pushed it back again and called, "You guys, over here!" Astro and Jessicana came to her. "When you were gone this afternoon, I heard a scream. It sounded familiar, but now I know exactly who it was. My mother is in trouble. I came to the beach and checked the bushes. Stay here. I'm going to see again," Roseabelle said.

Astro looked worried as did Jessicana. Jessicana put an arm on Roseabelle's shoulder. We're coming with you," she said firmly.

Without another sound, the threesome crept into the bushes. It was dense, and Roseabelle could barely see. She tried hard not to stumble blindly. When they had gone a long distance, Roseabelle stopped in her tracks.

In front of the auburn-haired girl were footprints. Three pairs, in fact. One was sleek and elegant, one was heavy and clumsy, and the other was thin and long. Roseabelle studied the sleek pair. It seemed like those footprints were uneven, as if the person they belonged to had been dragged.

The footprints continued for a few short paces, then vanished. The other footprints kept going. Roseabelle noticed apricot juice dripping from a leaf. She picked up the leaf, and her eyes widened. She nudged Astro and Jessicana. "Look," she whispered. It was an intricate, delicate message written in apricot juice!

"Read it," Astro urged. Roseabelle cleared her throat, then, "*Help! This is Danette, leader of the Benotripians. The Darvonians have kidnapped me, and I don't know where they are taking me. If you are reading this, warn my people and tell them to prepare for the enemy's invasion. Do not come after me. Tell my daughter, Roseabelle, to look inside the place where only she will know what I mean. Remember what I say. Tell Roseabelle that Shelby is a—*" Roseabelle read. "It stops there," she said quietly.

No one spoke for a while. Finally Jessicana broke the quiet aura in the trees. "Danette kidnapped? This isn't good, Roseabelle. We have to do something. What does she mean *the place where only she will know what I mean*? It could help us."

Roseabelle didn't reply.

"A—are you all right, Roseabelle?" Astro asked. Roseabelle lifted up her face.

Tears were dripping from her eyes. She hastily rubbed her face on her sleeve and turned to the beach. "Astro, Jessicana, the thing that she wants me to know. It's at my house. Let's go."

CHAPTER 4
Fight for the Pouch

When they arrived back at her house, Roseabelle leapt up the ladder and opened the door. She ran in the house, up the stairs, and into her room.

On her dresser was the little leaf pouch Danette had given her. She grabbed it and jogged back downstairs. Roseabelle scampered on the sand back to her friends and showed Astro and Jessicana.

"Open it," Astro said.

Roseabelle was about to lift the green flap when a deep voice growled "Stop right there." The three friends whirled around.

Three figures in black robes were standing in front of them, armed with different weapons. One beefy man held a Trapita, a long rod with three sharp blades on the sides. One man bore a Thepgile, a round disk with spikes on the edges and a wire attached to the middle. The other end of the wire could be clipped on your wrist. The last figure looked female. The figure was clearly the leader and was clutching a Dragocone Ray.

Dragocone rays were part fire, part sunlight, and part magic. If you got hit by one, you would be knocked down with the force of a wild animal and experience some painful burns. The only substances they didn't affect were silk and latick, a kind of precious metal. You had to wear silk gloves to safely hold the weapon.

The third figure was wearing silk gloves. "Darvonians," Roseabelle whispered.

"Hand over the pouch," the first man commanded.

"Umm, let me think about that," Astro said. "How about this: no way."

It happened so fast that Roseabelle and her friends didn't even see the Darvonians coming.

The Darvonian with the Dragocone Ray swung her ray and charged the three friends. The other two figures went after her.

Roseabelle's first instinct was to use one of her powers. But which one?

She turned to look at her friends. Jessicana was still, her face pale. Astro was like stone for one second, then just as the dark ones closed in, Astro lifted a finger, and a sharp lightning bolt erupted from it.

It knocked into the cloaked man with the Trapita and sent him flying. The other uninjured figures didn't pause for a second.

The Darvonian with the Dragocone Ray reached Roseabelle first. She tried to snatch the pouch, but Roseabelle quickly dove under her arm and backed away. The Darvonian headed for her again, this time raising her Dragocone Ray.

Roseabelle remembered the dark figure with the Thepgile and whirled around just in time to see the weapon spin right to her. Roseabelle sidestepped it and yanked the wire where it was attached to the deadly weapon. Her movement sent the Thepgile zooming into a tree trunk.

Roseabelle quickly turned back to face the sinister figure. She was just in time, for the Darvonian had just wound her ray and the weapon was inches away from her arm that held the pouch.

Roseabelle immediately decided that now was the time to use some of her powers. She turned to the Trapita that the Darvonian had been holding. It now lay untouched beside the large man. Using one of her more common powers, Roseabelle performed telekinesis. In a quarter of a second, Roseabelle lifted the weapon with her mind and levitated it into her waiting hand.

Roseabelle turned to block the ray. She was in time to stop the ray from hitting the pouch, but she couldn't stop it from hitting herself. The ray hit her shoulder instead, and Roseabelle was sent tumbling right into Jessicana. The blow was so great that Roseabelle lost her vision for several moments.

She saw Astro shooting lightning bolts at the two figures before them. Since the man was so large, the bolt hit him easily, but the leader was a more difficult target. Astro shot bolt after bolt, and finally one of the lightning bolts hit the third figure's arm.

The now-crippled Darvonian cried out in anguish and the ray flew out of the third's hand. Roseabelle was able to stand. She ran to the ray and took the third's gloves and slid them onto her own hands. She picked up the ray and turned to the third trespasser.

"Besides the fact that there are multiple Benotripian homes in close range that I can signal for help, you and your men are injured. I can assure you that Benotripians will not tolerate your presence here. Go while you still have the chance. Leave."

The figure gave her a piercing, withering, defeated look. The leader growled. Roseabelle looked the dark Darvonian in the eye.

"Go," she commanded.

The Darvonian made a series of grunts and growls, then stood and pulled her henchman up with her good arm. Together they limped to the beach.

"Jessicana, make sure they leave, will you?" Roseabelle asked. Jessicana transformed into a parrot and flew off.

"That was generous," Astro commented.

"Astro," she replied, "they're our ticket to reach Darvonia. They probably need to get a boat, right? I suspect they got here on a one-way trip. Perhaps the pouch provides transportation. Anyway, they'll have to build or take a boat. Either will take some time. We open the pouch, get prepared, and go after my mother."

Astro nodded. "Good idea," he said. A minute later, Jessicana returned in her human form.

"They're at the beach, all right," she said. "And they are starting to make a tiny raft. According to my judgment, they should be finished in two days."

"Good," Roseabelle said lightly. "But now let's go inside and open the pouch." Together the three friends boarded the rope ladder. The sun was beginning to set and they sat at the kitchen table.

Astro eyed the pouch. "Your honor," he said. Roseabelle took a deep breath and lifted the green flap. She reached inside and pulled out a withered piece of trutan—a parchment-like substance that Benotripians used for writing. The house was quiet.

"I-is that it?" Jessicana asked, looking at the trutan.

"I don't know," Astro replied, his voice unbelieving. It appeared blank, but there was something unusual about it.

"It's almost dusk, you guys," Roseabelle said. "So why don't you go to your homes and get some sleep?"

Jessicana shivered. "My parents are on vacation on the north side. I don't want to go to the house alone. Can I spend the night with you?" Jessicana asked with hope.

Roseabelle nodded.

"Uh, yeah about that, Roseabelle, as you know my dad is busy with his job and everything, and, well, my mom is on a cruise, so could I stay too?" Astro asked. Astro's father worked for *The Tropical Times* and was usually all over Benotripia doing what a reporter does.

Roseabelle sighed. "I guess so," she said. Astro let out a whoop.

"All right, where do I sleep?" Astro and Jessicana asked at the same time. Roseabelle thought for a moment. Her home had six rooms. Downstairs was the kitchen. Upstairs was her room, Danette's room, the guest room (it had once been Magford's "working room"), Danette's study, and the tower room—they called it—which was sort of a mini library.

"Jessicana, you can stay in the tower room. It has lots of books, so I think you'll be happy there. Astro, I think the guest room will suit you," Roseabelle offered.

Jessicana and Astro bobbed their heads and hurried up the stairs. She turned back to the parchment. She then walked up the stairs and went to her mother's study.

She sat down at the large desk. Roseabelle took a small bottle of ink made out of papaya juice. She randomly doodled a raft on the trutan, and then after finding some blankets and pillowcases in the laundry for her friends, she trekked to her room.

She laid the trutan on her dresser and climbed into bed. She closed her tired eyes, not noticing something expanding from the trutan.

CHAPTER 5

Midnight Raft

ROSEABELLE WOKE UP AND YAWNED. WAS IT TIME FOR training yet? Any minute Danette would call her down for breakfast, urging her not to be late.

But then Roseabelle remembered. Her mother had been kidnapped! The pouch—the trutan! Roseabelle turned over to her dresser and shrieked. "Astro, Jessicana!" she shouted. "You have got to see this!"

On her very own dresser sat a long wooden raft. It was made out of tree trunks lashed together with bamboo. Roseabelle swore that if she laid horizontally on the craft, it would take five of her to cover all of it. Jessicana came in, then Astro.

"How did that get there?" Jessicana sputtered.

Roseabelle picked up the trutan that she had drawn on last night. There was not a spot of ink to be found.

"No way," she murmured. She turned to her friends. "Guys," she said. "I drew a picture of a raft, and a raft came out of the trutan! This is no ordinary trutan, for sure. It's an extraordinary gift."

"Whoa," muttered Jessicana.

"Cool," Astro said enthusiastically.

Roseabelle sighed. "I think we should prepare today. Astro,

scout from the beach. If those troublesome Darvonians come back or if you see a ship on the horizon, let me know right away."

"Got it," he said.

"Jessicana, go to your house and bring me two mottels. Loyal ones," Roseabelle instructed.

"I'll be back," she said.

"I'll stay here and *pack*. More like draw. Anyway, let's plan to leave tomorrow," Roseabelle said. Jessicana transformed into a bird and flew out the window. Astro went out the door, climbed down the ladder, and set off for the beach.

Roseabelle turned back to the trutan. She went up to Danette's study and drew three large backpacks complete with ice coolers, water bottles, solar hand warmers, Dragocone rays in silk bags, and, for some strange reason, potted plants.

Roseabelle decided to get a snack. She poured herself some water and ate a banana. She then went to her room and pulled on jeans and a green T-shirt.

When she went back to her mother's study, the backpacks were already starting to form. She looked out the window and saw Jessicana running to the house, followed by two gentle-looking mottels. One mottel was brown with black specks in its feathers while the other one had white and black stripes.

The two mottels flew through the window while Jessicana raced to the ladder and entered through the door. "Got them?" Roseabelle asked.

Jessicana nodded, breathless.

"I hope Astro's holding up with those Darvonians," Roseabelle said.

"Me too."

"Follow me," Roseabelle invited. She showed Jessicana the trutan. The top half of the backpacks were protruding from it. "Jessicana, after they're fully formed, could you strap them onto the raft?" Roseabelle asked.

"I could do that," Jessicana said. They waited for about

an hour, spending it by reading about Darvonia in the tower room, something Jessicana thoroughly enjoyed.

She has always been the smart one, Roseabelle thought.

Afterward, Roseabelle went to check on the backpacks. "They're ready," she announced to Jessicana.

The parrot girl found straps on the raft and clasped them around the backpacks. Meanwhile, Roseabelle drew a pile of blankets and other supplies. *Well, we do have to be prepared,* Roseabelle thought.

As Roseabelle picked up her book from the tower room, she read, "The government of Darvonia is uncertain. Kinetle is the leader. Her husband, as far as we can tell, is either dead or lost. She has seven children: two twins about twenty-five, a twenty-year-old son, a seventeen-year-old daughter, a fourteen-year-old son, an eleven-year-old son, and a young daughter of age four. It is rumored that one of these children is an IB."

"An IB?" Roseabelle said out loud. This was not good news. She recalled someone following her from school. Could that person be a spy for Darvonia?

When the supplies were done, Roseabelle carried them to Jessicana. The blonde girl placed them in the packs. Roseabelle took a few books from the tower room and put them in the backpacks. She drew oars on the trutan and waited.

Jessicana came to her. "You can go to bed, Roseabelle. I'll send a message to Astro," she said. Sleep sounded refreshing, so Roseabelle went up to her room and collapsed onto the bed.

CHAPTER 6

Sea Voyage

"ROSEABELLE, WAKE UP! IT'S TIME. THE DARVONIANS are leaving. I packed clothes and food and the trutan. Let's go!"

Roseabelle opened her eyes. Jessicana was standing above her dressed in a slender blue wrap dress and a gray jacket. "I'm coming," Roseabelle sleepily muttered.

She stood and, when Jessicana left the room, dressed in a peach shirt with sleeves that went down to her elbows, light orange leggings, and pale sandals.

Roseabelle took two small bottles of cherry ink from her dresser in case they ran out. She wanted to make certain the trutan was accessible.

Roseabelle slipped a small sparkling ruby pendant into her pocket for good luck.

When she went downstairs, Jessicana was at the front door in parrot form. "Follow," she squawked.

Jessicana flew to the beach and Roseabelle ran after her. Astro was standing at the beach, the raft next to him. The two mottels were sitting beside him. "Hurry," he said. "We're losing them."

He pointed to the sea where a small raft was holding up three figures. Jessicana turned back into a girl and they scrambled onto the raft. The mottels fluttered and landed on the watercraft.

"I'll paddle," Jessicana offered.

"Me too," Roseabelle said.

Each girl took an oar and started to row. It was tiring and Roseabelle's muscles were sore, but still she pushed on.

"I'll take Jessicana's place," Astro said. He took hold of an oar. They made sure that they didn't lose sight of the Darvonians. They pushed on and on.

Jessicana switched places, and Roseabelle, relieved, let go. At noon Roseabelle pulled out a canteen of coconut juice. She handed some to Astro and Jessicana, then drank some herself. It began to get extremely windy.

"Roseabelle," Jessicana said. "Could you make a sail? The trutan is in my backpack." Roseabelle pulled it out and took some cherry ink from her pack. She drew a pole with a sail attached.

The lines started to get bolder, and Roseabelle said, "I'll row for you, Astro. Watch the trutan."

She took hold of an oar and pushed. She thought about her powers. There was one power that wasn't as unusual as her others. She could transform into a dolphin. It might really come in handy. She had a feeling this was going to be a long trip and doubted that it would be windy the entire time.

She kept pushing and pulling, pushing and pulling.

Soon Astro took Jessicana's place. The sky turned to dusk. She was grateful when Jessicana took her load.

It was windier than ever, so she checked on the sail. It was ready! She hoisted it up, and Astro and Jessicana stopped rowing. The raft picked up speed.

Roseabelle pulled out three mangos from a backpack and handed two to Jessicana and Astro. She ate one herself then dug out some water from her pack and passed it around. They decided that one should keep watch during the night and make sure that they were in range of the Darvonians.

They pulled out two blankets. Jessicana would keep first watch. Roseabelle sat back against her blanket and quickly fell asleep.

"ROSEABELLE, YOU HAVE LAST WATCH," ASTRO WHISPERED. Roseabelle's eyes opened. She gave her blanket to Astro and went to the front of the raft. The raft was losing speed; the wind was dying down. She took down the sail and then checked in her backpack for rope. There it was. She tied it around her waist, then attached one end of the rope to one side of the raft and the other end to the other side.

Roseabelle took a deep breath and jumped into the water. She pictured a dolphin in her mind, and when she glanced down at her body, it was smooth and slippery. She flicked her tail, and Roseabelle and the raft sped on. Roseabelle swam on and on as fast as she could.

As dawn approached, Astro and Jessicana began to stir. She heard a deep sleepy voice: "Where's Roseabelle?"

This time another voice, "Here, silly—" The voice cut off. "Where is she? Astro, this isn't a joke!"

"Hey, I asked you first."

"Astro, this isn't funny. Are you hiding her?"

"Sure I'm hiding her. Whatever! How could I hide her on this open raft?"

"Do you think she went overboard?"

"Hey, why is the sail down?"

"Who cares about the sail?"

"Why are we going so fast?"

"I don't know, I—"

Just then Roseabelle let out a squeal. Both Astro and Jessicana looked down at the dolphin.

"Roseabelle?" Jessicana asked. Roseabelle thought hard of her human form and then changed. She grinned up at Jessicana, the rope still clinging to her waist.

"That's me." Roseabelle laughed.

"Seriously, what were you trying to do? Scare us?" Jessicana scolded.

"No, the wind was dying down, so I transformed to speed us up," Roseabelle said.

Astro laughed. "You never told us you could turn into a dolphin." He chuckled. "This is totally great!"

"Well," Jessicana admitted. "It is pretty fortunate. Good thinking!"

Roseabelle grinned. "Well, we had better not lose those Darvonians," she cried out. Roseabelle dived back into the ocean and thought of how good the water felt on her. Without even realizing it, Roseabelle transformed and began to swim forward.

Roseabelle swam for a while, but when the Darvonians stopped, Jessicana told Roseabelle to have lunch. Astro and Jessicana would row. Roseabelle transformed and pulled herself out of the water. Jessicana found a long cloth that served as a towel and handed it to Roseabelle, who dried herself off.

Roseabelle discovered a few oranges, and she ate them hungrily. She thought that they should have enough food and water for another couple of days. Soon they would have to break out the trutan. Roseabelle untied the rope and stuck it in her pack. She pulled a blanket from the raft, curled up, and caught a few hours of sleep.

CHAPTER 7

Scythterrian

ASTRO ROWED ON WITH JESSICANA BY HIS SIDE. THEY were keeping up a good pace, but the Darvonians were starting to disappear into a thick fog ahead of them. It wasn't any ordinary fog either. There was something mystical—something mysterious—about it.

"Wake Roseabelle up," Jessicana urged. Astro reluctantly put his oar on the raft and shook Roseabelle gently. She sat up and rubbed her eyes.

"Oar duty?" Roseabelle asked sleepily.

"No," Jessicana said. "But you have to have a look at this."

"Hold on a minute," Roseabelle said. She peered ahead. "Strange," she muttered. She reached inside her backpack and pulled out a thick scroll titled *The Known Secrets of Darvonia*. She unrolled it to the table of contents and scanned the page. "There it is!" Roseabelle exclaimed.

She traced her finger on "Travails of Darvonia." She then unrolled to the chapter. She read, "*Only spies for Benotripia know this important information.*" It listed a bunch of coordinates and directions that, to Roseabelle, were meaningless. Roseabelle continued: "*On the way there stands a thick fog. You have to go straight through it. Do not try to avoid it, for such could get you lost. It is there for a reason.*" Roseabelle and Astro looked at Jessicana.

"Go straight through," they chimed together.

"I would if one of you would row with me," Jessicana said.

Roseabelle took the oar and rowed as hard as she could. A current was tilting them sideways. She and Jessicana struggled against it, but it was too strong.

"Help us, Astro," the girls cried out as the raft nearly capsized. Astro fastened his grip to Roseabelle's oar. Together they pushed and pushed, but it was no use. The current was taking them away altogether.

"Here," Roseabelle said. "Stay here." She took the rope from her pack and tied it around her waist. Then without another word, she plunged into the icy cold water. Astro and Jessicana looked around wildly, and they pushed and pulled with the oars. They were both thinking the same thing. "Hurry, Roseabelle!"

Roseabelle pictured the smooth texture of a dolphin. When she looked at her hands, they were no longer hands. Flippers had taken their place. She propelled her tail forward and only forward. She tried to balance herself out, shifting right then left. It was working! The raft was floating forward slowly but surely. With the current it was hard work. Roseabelle gracefully swished her tail back and forth.

When they got past the current, she sighed with relief. She pictured her human form, and in a minute she could no longer hold her breath underwater very long. She rose to the surface and put her hands on the raft.

She boosted herself onboard and then removed the rope. As soon as she got on, her friends cheered and almost upset the raft by jumping up and down. Now that they had entered the fog, they could hardly see anything. The white mist curled around their feet as Jessicana and Astro rowed through.

Roseabelle was busy reading the chapter "Travails of Darvonia." She read quietly, "*Once past the mist, you will enter*

Blackwater Sea (which is actually an ocean). These waters are the most dangerous you will ever enter. Sea monsters lurk beneath the murky waves, seeking their next meal, and carnivorous fish bite into water-born crafts, causing them to sink."

Roseabelle shuddered. She put the scroll away and was about to tell her friends when their craft broke through the fog. Roseabelle's heart sank. They were in Blackwater Sea.

It was the scariest thing Roseabelle had ever seen. The black waters churned and bounced up and down. Waste and garbage littered the surface, and she heard Jessicana yelp.

Roseabelle thought about doing just that. She saw the Darvonians up ahead sailing smoothly along. Then the Darvonians' craft stopped. Since the sun was beginning to set, Roseabelle decided to stop too.

"Let's get some sleep," she advised. She curled up on her blanket. Astro took watch. Within a few minutes, Roseabelle was temporarily dead to the world.

VIOLENT ROCKING OF THE RAFT WOKE ROSEABELLE UP. SHE looked around. No one was on watch! Jessicana and Astro were both snoring away. Roseabelle peered in the distance. Not a craft in sight. The Darvonians! Where were they? She shook her friends awake.

"Wake up," she hissed. They sat up. "Who fell asleep during their watch? The Darvonians are gone."

Astro turned bright red. "Er, sorry," he said.

"Sorry?" Jessicana bellowed. "Sorry? Is that all you can say? We've lost the Darvonians and the tiniest, slimmest chance of finding Roseabelle's mom. It's all your fault, and all you can say is sorry? Come on!"

"Roseabelle, Jessicana, I'm really sorry," he said.

Roseabelle sighed. Astro looked distraught. "It's okay, Astro," she said.

She tugged on her oar and started to row. Astro took the other one. They moved in silence, secretly debating which direction they should head. Suddenly Jessicana sat up straight.

"What's that noise?" she asked uneasily.

Astro and Roseabelle shared a look. "Are you okay? I don't hear anything," Roseabelle stated.

"Did you hit your head?" Astro joked.

"No seriously, the water's vibrating."

Roseabelle hated to admit it, but now she felt it too. "Guys," she asked. "What's going—"

A huge bellow came from the water, and a monstrous shape erupted from the icy depths. A wave the size of a tsunami swept the raft to the sky. They all screamed.

The raft smacked against the water, and then Roseabelle realized what was happening.

It was a sea monster—as tall as five stockfish (a type of fish as big as a blue whale). It had sickly green scales with a yellowish tint, two crests on its bumpy head, sharp claws, a mouth full of teeth—just one tooth was the length of Roseabelle from her shoes to her hair—and a terrible tail. The tail was long and covered with spikes and at the very end was a nasty point hiding beneath layers of giant needles.

From her short research, Roseabelle recognized it immediately. "Scythterrian," she whispered. The three friends were paralyzed with fear. The monster began to strike again. It lifted its tail, and then, quick as a flash, it came at them. Roseabelle saw it in slow motion.

Jessicana screamed for the second time and pointed to her backpack. Somehow Roseabelle understood. She zipped it open and found a silk bag. She tore it open. Inside was the Dragocone Ray. Next to that lay a pair of silk gloves. Roseabelle knew what Jessicana wanted her to do.

She pulled on the gloves and grabbed the ray. The tail was hurtling toward her at the speed of lightning. She raised the ray and—*thwack*—the monster went flying. It catapulted into the air and then plummeted back down again. "Look out!" Astro called.

They dove underwater just in time. It was chaos. The impact made thousands of tons of water fly everywhere. The Scythterrian might've hit the bottom of the ocean because a giant whirlpool began, and everything was being sucked into it, including the raft, which was right next to them.

They struggled with the raft, but when it started to drag them underwater, they let it go. Roseabelle suddenly had an idea. "Get on," she instructed.

She handed the gloves and the ray to Jessicana and jumped into the water. Roseabelle soon transformed into a magnificent dolphin. She pulled the craft, but the whirlpool was still hanging on to it. She needed help. Desperate help. She looked down and saw the Scythterrian.

Its deep, meaty mouth was hanging open, ready to catch his prey. *Well, all right then*, she thought. *If I can't get out, I'll have to go in.*

She transformed back to human and let the whirlpool pull them in. The three friends held their breath as the raft pulled them under the surface of the water. The Scythterrian looked triumphant. The raft dragged down and down, faster and faster. The craft got so close to the monster's mouth that Roseabelle could practically reach out and touch one of the sharp teeth. Astro closed his eyes. A string of bubbles escaped from Jessicana's mouth that could have been a whimper.

Roseabelle grabbed the ray from Jessicana and swung it, hitting the Scythterrian's tooth. This time the blow was weaker, but the sea monster was pushed back all the same.

Wow, Roseabelle thought. *He must be strong. Two blows with a ray are usually deadly.*

This time the Scythterrian couldn't recover. It lay motionless on the ocean floor. Roseabelle dragged the raft and her friends to the surface before taking another gulp of air and diving deep. Roseabelle crept up and climbed up the monster's scaly chest. Its eyes were closed. Doubtful, she leaned over. Its claws snatched at Roseabelle, but she swam up just in time.

Gasping for breath, she reached her watercraft and accepted Jessicana's outstretched, pale hand.

Astro started to say, "Is it gone?" but the answer came instantly.

The monster rose above the surface of the water, a red glint in its eye. But his tail was spotted with burns, and when it opened its mouth, Roseabelle saw that two of his teeth were missing.

After what had happened, Roseabelle had expected that the monster would be smart enough to back off. Apparently she was wrong. The monster leapt at her so quickly that Roseabelle wasn't prepared.

From behind, Astro pushed her, causing her to free fall into the water. The monster clawed the air where she had been floating and bellowed with rage.

She managed to swim underneath its belly, veering to the side. When Roseabelle got to the side, she carefully hoisted herself up and somehow climbed onto its back. She took her ray and plunged it into the sea monster's scales.

It howled and flew up. It flipped back and forth, and Roseabelle fell off.

She started to plummet down. It was happening so fast. Roseabelle blacked out when she hit the water.

CHAPTER 8
Darvonia

BREATHE, ROSEABELLE, BREATHE. I HOPE SHE'S ALL right."

"Stop fussing, Jessicana. She's waking up."

Roseabelle's eyes fluttered open. Jessicana was in front of her, holding a maroon bottle and a glass spoon filled with a fine peach powder. "You're awake," Jessicana cried. She shoved the contents of the spoon into Roseabelle's mouth. It tasted like orange with a touch of sourness and a sprinkle of saltiness.

When Roseabelle had swallowed, she asked Jessicana frantically, "What happened? Is the monster dead?"

Jessicana nodded. "For good," she said. "You took quite a plunge. Astro swam out there and pulled you back to the raft. I flew and checked to see if the sea creature was dead. I transformed back and landed on his stomach. Nothing happened. I told Astro, and we set sail again." Jessicana paused to feed more powder to Roseabelle. "The wind picked up, and we put up the sail. Soon we saw a small dot in the distance. We caught up, and well, we think it's Darvonia! I know you will go crazy over this, but you've been out for six days."

Roseabelle nearly spit out the medicine. Six days! They had been at sea for more than a week. Roseabelle sat up. Astro was digging in his pack. "We haven't been eating a lot," he explained. "I think this is a good time."

Roseabelle looked around. Sure enough, a dot was in the distance. But now it was less of a dot. It was growing bigger every minute. Astro handed her a handful of honey-covered nuts, which were considered a type of delicacy in Benotripia. Roseabelle downed them quickly.

Jessicana pulled out a handful of hadhadiles, machegh's (black gold coins and a type of currency), and kierteks (white gold coins and the most valuable currency in Benotripia).

"What's that for?" Roseabelle asked. Jessicana shrugged. "Darvonians use precious metals for melting them down and them reforming them into their own currency," Jessicana said. "You never know when you might need a coin."

She put them away and asked if Roseabelle could take the first watch because the sun was setting. Roseabelle nodded. She took a piece of wraptook (a flat bread) from her backpack and began to chew.

Roseabelle was extremely tired, but she had learned her lesson not to fall asleep thanks to Astro. She watched as Darvonia came closer and closer and closer. After eating another loaf of wraptook, she tapped Jessicana and Astro on the shoulder as they began to pull up on the shore.

Roseabelle and Jessicana pulled on the oars. The beach looked deserted, but they still made sure that they were safely hidden from prying eyes. As soon as they reached the shore, Roseabelle gagged. Darvonia was terrible! The land was dirty, dark, and scorched. Tree stumps lay in every direction and trash was everywhere. The land was quite mountainous, so when they dragged the raft on the island, Astro ran off to find a place where they could sleep, while Roseabelle and Jessicana crept off to a boulder for a temporary hiding place.

Astro came back. "There's a cave nearby," he panted. "Come on."

The three friends discreetly hiked up the rocky terrain.

Astro led them to a small crevice in the rock, which led to a cave. "Perfect," Roseabelle whispered.

She set the raft down along with their other belongings. "Someone will need to guard this at all times. We can switch," Roseabelle stated.

Astro and Jessicana nodded. "Also," Jessicana piped up, "we need to be ready for a hasty exit. Let's not unpack entirely."

The others agreed, and then they began to set up camp. Jessicana laid two blankets down, and Astro set out the hand warmers. "I'm going to check out Darvonia," Roseabelle said.

Astro shuddered. "Be careful," he said.

"I will," Roseabelle replied.

She crept out of the cave and set off.

ONCE ROSEABELLE WAS BACK ON THE SHORE, SHE STARTED off into Darvonia. It was a long walk. She didn't see any Darvonians. Then she heard some commotion.

Roseabelle crept along stealthily. She looked ahead. There was a high metal gate that joined a stone wall. The wall wrapped around a large area. Roseabelle figured it must be a village. She looked at the gates. They were firmly padlocked. She looked at the wall. It was several feet high.

Roseabelle put her hands on the wall. It was jagged and rocky and had many places where she could find holds for her hands and feet. She began to climb. It was difficult work. Roseabelle knew that if she fell, well, she didn't want to think about it.

When she was at the top, she peered cautiously over the side. It was a village. At the front were two guards making sure no outsiders got in. *It's a clever strategy,* Roseabelle thought. *It appears on the outside as if someone could climb over the gates and just walk in.* Sadly, that wasn't the case.

Further off was a large campfire. Young girls were dancing around it using their hands to show expression. All of them had ghostly skin and dark hair. The black marks behind their ears signaled their own culture mark. Beyond the campfire were many huts constructed of mud and burnt wood. The houses kept going and going, then stopped at a large building. Two guards with solemn faces were standing in front of it, one armed with a long sword and shield and the other with a brutal Thepgile. She considered climbing to find out why they were guarding it when the girls stopped dancing and bowed.

"Archery," a male voice called. The boys pulled out bows and quivers of arrows and aimed for the wall. Roseabelle ducked down and hoped that they hadn't seen her. She carefully scaled down the wall and ran off. She couldn't help thinking about the building. When she got to the rocks, she began to climb. Finally she reached the cave. Jessicana and Astro looked up, their faces shining.

"What did you find?" Astro asked. Roseabelle told them about the village and the events that had occurred. After some silence, Jessicana spoke.

"Do you think that's where your mom is, Roseabelle?"

Roseabelle pondered it for a moment.

"Perhaps," she decided.

"The sun is going down," Astro said promptly. "I suggest we eat and then get some sleep. Since Roseabelle went on that expedition, she can give out the watch schedule for tonight."

They all looked at Roseabelle. "Jessicana, you watch till about midnight. I will guard until four in the morning. Astro, you'll watch till eight." Roseabelle said.

They all nodded. Jessicana took a knife encrusted with pearls from her bag and went to the front entrance. Roseabelle lay down on her blanket. It was harshly cold, so she put on her hand warmer.

She could hear Astro snoring next to her. She desperately needed some sleep. It was all such a shock to her.

She recalled her mother's message they had found. The last part was "*Tell my daughter Roseabelle that her trainer Shelby is a*" and then it had cut off. What was Shelby? Was she truly a

Benotripian? But she couldn't possibly be a Darvonian! She bore no resemblance to one. Her tired state soon lulled her to a deep sleep.

JESSICANA SHOOK HER AWAKE AT MIDNIGHT. ROSEABELLE SAT up. Jessicana whispered softly in ear that she couldn't use the Dragocone Ray because it might attract attention.

"I have some weapons in my bag," Jessicana whispered, "so take your pick."

Roseabelle gave her blanket to Jessicana and then reached inside her friend's bag. Next to the ray was a Trapita and two rusty Thepgiles. Roseabelle wasn't the expert at Thepgiles, so she settled with the Trapita. Seizing it, she walked out and readied her weapon. The trees rustled, but no one came.

Four hours later, Roseabelle was about to get Astro when a dark shape streaked across the rocks. Roseabelle gasped and readied herself, drawing into the shadows. Not a peep. Sighing and assuring herself it was probably her imagination, she tapped Astro on the shoulder.

He woke up, and Roseabelle motioned for Astro to choose a weapon. She set down the arrows in Jessicana's bag and then curled up on a blanket.

CHAPTER 9

Distraction

"Let's get going," Astro said in her ear. Roseabelle shot up and bolted from the cave floor. She changed into a green long-sleeved shirt and a pair of green and brown pants with leather boots.

After everyone was ready to go, Roseabelle led them down to the village. It was quiet when they got there. Astro boosted Roseabelle up to the wall.

The campfire was gone, but the cloaked guards were still at the gates and in front of the building. "We have to get in there," Roseabelle reasoned, "but how?"

"Wait here," Astro whispered. "Give me a boost, Jessicana."

When Astro was up, he winked and scampered away. Jessicana and Roseabelle shared a look and rolled their eyes.

On the far side of the wall, Astro took a deep breath and then whistled. He ducked.

The guard looked at where Astro had been and frowned. "Who's there?" he growled. He stalked over to the wall. Astro flattened himself against it. The cloaksman shrugged and walked away. *Not the brightest of guards,* Roseabelle thought.

Then Astro whistled again.

"Who goes there?" the cloaksman roared. He stalked over again, his face contorted with confusion.

Astro snatched a spare robe from the ground and pulled a hammer from his backpack, which was on his back. He banged the top with the hammer, hoping to attract attention. The cloaksman marched closer.

Astro banged it a second time. The Darvonian was nearly to Astro.

Astro banged it a third time, also accidently releasing a lightning bolt that hit the wall. The top part crumbled. The guard shouted with fury, and Astro pulled the robe on so he could pass for a Darvonian, then fled.

The cloaksman jumped over the now-crumbling structure and chased after him. When the other cloaksman realized what had happened, he also followed after Astro.

"That was brave," Roseabelle said.

"Should we drop down?" Jessicana asked.

Roseabelle nodded. "The other cloaksmen are too far away to see us. Let's make a move before they come back."

Jessicana changed into a parrot and flew down. Roseabelle smiled. Jessicana had it too easy. She took hold of a log protruding upward and clung to it. The weight caused it to come down with a thud. The cloaksman closest to the building watched his perimeter.

Jessicana quickly turned back to her human form and pulled Roseabelle down behind the log. The cloaksman stared past them. Jessicana breathed a sigh of relief. They stood up and crept around the houses. Roseabelle peeked inside one of the mud-formed windows.

A Darvonian mother was sitting in a burnt wooden chair, carving a wooden sword sheath while three little boys were playing around her feet with a waxy ball. One of the boys stood up, and Jessicana tugged on Roseabelle to continue.

They walked through the village, all the way hoping that no one would spot them. More than a few feet away, the

Darvonians were staring straight ahead. The girls were hidden at the side of the building. Roseabelle carefully studied the door. It didn't look locked, but Roseabelle decided she was going to find out what was in the building, locked or not.

She put a hand in front of Jessicana to signal for her to stay put and watched the Darvonians carefully. Roseabelle raced to the back of the building. Once again it was jagged and crooked, so Roseabelle climbed it with ease.

She scaled the mud walls and hoped that the cloaksmen would be clueless enough to fall for her trap.

* * * * *

ASTRO WAS SCARED. THERE WAS NO HIDING IT. THE Darvonians were gaining on him, and if they got their hands on him, they would surely realize that he was a Benotripian, not just a troublesome Darvonian kid.

He was getting tired now and didn't know where to go. Running to the cave would lead the guards to it, so he crossed out that idea. Circling around wouldn't be much help. All the weapons were at the cave, so he couldn't fight back.

Astro charged up some rocky land. A cloaksman went after him. He staggered up and up. He then saw a tiny opening in the rock up ahead.

He sprinted using all his energy and turned the corner. He bent down and slid inside. It gave him enough room to squeeze in. Astro heard the heavy footfalls catching up and held his breath. Then they passed him. He breathed a sigh of relief.

* * * * *

ROSEABELLE WAS ON THE ROOF. SHE CREPT CAREFULLY across. When she was at the edge, she dipped down. The guards were about three feet away from the door. Roseabelle leaned over the side and motioned for Jessicana to come up.

She heard a flap of feathers and then a squeal and a flurry of steps. A few minutes later, Jessicana was at her side.

"Don't tell me you flew." Roseabelle said. Jessicana sheepishly nodded. "Come on," Roseabelle hissed.

She pointed at the guards, then pantomimed herself climbing down the wall behind the guards and opening the door, then running. Roseabelle motioned that the guards would notice and run after her.

Jessicana looked at her like she was crazy. "Then what?" she mouthed.

Roseabelle motioned that Jessicana could sneak in and hide. The cloaksmen would be busy chasing Roseabelle. She motioned for Jessicana to stay put inside the building. Roseabelle would then get out and then come back in. Jessicana was staring at her like she had lost her mind. Roseabelle sighed and mouthed, "Get ready."

She went to the edge and carefully turned around. She put her foot on a jagged spot, then found a round stone to place her hand.

She continued to her put her hands and feet in good positions. When she got down, she couldn't believe her plan was working. Her back was to the Darvonians. They hadn't even noticed she was there. Carefully she lifted the latch on the door and opened it.

It creaked.

Roseabelle hurled it open and charged down a narrow passageway, which led to a hall with seven doors.

Roseabelle threw open one door and ran through, not even caring to shut it. It led to another hall with six doors. She opened one of the doors and ran through, this time shutting it. It led to a room with five doors. She opened the nearest one and sprinted in. That led to a room with four doors. She pushed open one. It led to a hall with three doors. She tore through it. Inside was a room with two doors. She opened one. It led to a room with one door. Roseabelle reached for the knob and . . . it was locked.

Roseabelle gulped and then raced to a shadow in the

corner of the room. She pictured the cave and then stomped her foot. She felt as light as air and whisked past drifts of cold and warm air.

Then she landed in the stony cave that she and her friends were staying in. Roseabelle sat down and desperately hoped Jessicana went along with the plan.

* * * * *

JESSICANA WAS CONFUSED. WHAT IN THE WORLD WAS Roseabelle aiming to do? It didn't make sense. Then Jessicana remembered that Roseabelle was Meta-Mord. She was likely to use one of her special powers. The very thought made Jessicana feel better as Roseabelle climbed down the wall.

She was terribly brave to do that. Roseabelle was taking every risk to save Danette, Jessicana thought in admiration.

If Roseabelle wanted her to do something, then she would do it. When Roseabelle opened the door, Jessicana watched with bated breath.

She watched as her friend flung open the door and raced inside. The Darvonian guards whirled around and shouted something that sounded like Daronese, the secret Darvonian language. Jessicana had been learning the basics and she translated it:

"There's a bee in my skirt!"

Jessicana was sure that that was not what he meant. As they chased after Roseabelle, shouts came from the building. "There's a bee in my skirt. There's a bee in my skirt!"

When the shouts diminished, Jessicana placed a hand on a rock and began her climb down. When she was on the ground, she cautiously went inside. She reached a hall with multiple doors.

Jessicana chose one on the far right and went through. It was empty except for a tall wooden cabinet and a small worktable. Jessicana opened the cabinet and prepared to step in when she realized that the cabinet had no floor.

She peered inside and saw that it was a long way drop. Jessicana turned into a parrot and descended.

Jessicana continued to fly down, all the while wondering if the tunnel ever stopped. Shortly after her feet brushed against stone, Jessicana turned back into a girl.

She looked up. Even at her present state, the usual floor line was several feet above her. Jessicana looked down. It was too dark to see anything. She brushed her hand against what seemed like a floor. It was smooth with the exception of a little notch sticking up. She pulled on the notch. Jessicana gasped. *I have to tell Roseabelle. But how?* she thought.

It was a hidden trapdoor. Jessicana's mind was racing. What could it lead to? Another village? Where Kinetle lived? Perhaps a secret meeting place? Could it have something to do with Danette? Where was Roseabelle?

She wished she would get here right away. This was a truly important discovery.

* * * * *

ROSEABELLE WAS SITTING ON THE CAVE FLOOR, PONdering her next action. She wanted to help Jessicana, but what if she ended up with the Darvonians? She had to wait, though she did not like it at all. Deciding to do something useful, she pulled the trutan out of her pack and started to draw.

Soon Roseabelle was standing in front of three black robes. She put one on. She found one with just the right fit. She saved the other two for her friends, putting them in Jessicana's backpack.

She sat down and ventured to a shadow and thought hard of the hallway with seven doors. She stomped her foot.

Roseabelle landed in the hall. She passed the door that she had entered earlier and opened a different one. Empty.

Roseabelle tried another door. Dust and dirt but nothing else.

She opened another. It was filled with empty crates and boxes.

A different door had cans of a thick, creamy paste behind it. Roseabelle pocketed a small jar.

A different room held a few binders filled with folders. She tucked one in her robe. The last door she entered had a table and a tall cabinet. The cabinet door was ajar. Roseabelle walked over to it and peered inside. There was no floor.

She scuttled inside, keeping her hands on the wall. She was slipping but kept her grip tight. One arm slipped off the wall. Roseabelle clawed frantically at the stone.

She fell, screaming all the way down. Then shaky, skinny arms broke her fall. Kind aqua-blue eyes stared into hers. "Jessicana?" she asked weakly.

Then everything went black.

Roseabelle sat up. Where was she? What had happened? Then she remembered. Jessicana had saved her! Through the darkness Roseabelle saw Jessicana bending over her, pouring water on her forehead.

"Roseabelle," Jessicana cried, "you're awake. I need to show you something." Jessicana pointed to the panel. "Look," she said. "It's a secret entrance."

Roseabelle's heart leaped. What if it led to her mother?

* * * * *

ASTRO WAS IN THE ROCK CAVITY, TRYING TO NAVIGATE where he was. He had seen a patch of rocky land close to both the cave and the village. Maybe that was where he was.

He hoped his desperate action had been enough for his friends to get to the building. The question was where would he go next? The cave would be too risky. The village was out of the question. But he couldn't just stay put! He had to think of something. He sighed, wishing he could escape without a trace.

A few hours later, Astro was bored. It was dark, and he was hungry, thirsty, tired, and uncomfortable, and his throat was parched and sore.

He knew he should leave soon. The cloaksmen must have given up by now. They were most likely guarding the city. How would he get in? All these questions.

Just then, a few pairs of large, pounding footsteps went by him, and Astro curled up against the wall. He realized that two Darvonians were talking to each other, grins on their faces. "I'm the one who followed her daughter!"

"And what's the significance of that? I actually captured her!"

"Don't forget, I'm the one who put up the defenses in the castle. I had to construct the maze in front of the dungeon."

Astro's ears perked up. Could these two Darvonians be talking about Danette? He went through what they had mentioned; a castle, a dungeon, and a maze. His heart lifted. Could that be where Danette was being kept?

Mustering up his courage, he stepped out of the opening. The coast was clear. He set off for the village.

* * * * *

"I think we should go in," Roseabelle said eagerly. "Wait a minute. We need to wait for Astro. He'll help us."

Roseabelle threw up her hands. "Astro. I forgot about him. Don't worry. I'll be back."

She ran to a shadow in the corner and pictured the village wall. She stomped her foot, and flashes of sky and land passed by her.

When she opened her eyes a boy was coming to the wall. He stopped. Roseabelle tried to get a better look. The boy had spiky black hair and green eyes. Astro ran to Roseabelle.

"Come on," she whispered. "Jessicana and I found something. Oh, yeah, one minute. Wait here."

Roseabelle retreated into the shadows and pictured the

cave and shadow tumbled. A few moments later she was standing next to Jessicana's backpack. She hefted all the blankets in her own pack and then pictured the wall and shadow tumbled. As she came out of the shadow next to the wall, and seeing Astro, she said, "Let's go."

The cloaksmen were still out looking for him so they weren't back yet. They both scampered up the wall and then dropped down. They ran to the building. Voices were muttering inside.

Taking a deep breath, Roseabelle and Astro draped the robes over their shoulders and opened the door.

Heavy footsteps were coming their way. Roseabelle pulled Astro through the passage and to the hall. One of the doors was starting to open. Roseabelle opened a door and threw herself inside. Astro followed her. They had just closed it when they heard footsteps clomping out.

They waited until the footsteps were gone. "Here," Roseabelle whispered. She turned around and pointed to the cabinet.

"Roseabelle, Astro, is that you?" a voice called from below.

"Yes," Astro announced.

"Come on down," came the reply. "Roseabelle, there is rope in my pack," said Jessicana.

Roseabelle pulled it out and tossed one end down. It tightened as Jessicana grasped it. It slacked a bit as Jessicana tied a loop in her end and fastened it around a large stone protruding from the inside.

Up above, Astro tied the rope to his waist. "Here I go," he said nervously. He pushed off from the cabinet and disappeared from view.

"Are you down?" Roseabelle called.

"Yep. That was cool, but remind me to never do that again. That must have been what, a sixty-foot drop? It was still a thriller though."

"Whatever," Roseabelle muttered.

The rope came back to her, and she caught it. She looped it around her waist and pushed off. She was plummeting straight down. Roseabelle seriously thought she was going to hit the floor. When she landed, she instantly tore the rope off her.

"You don't need to remind me to never do that again," she said shrilly. Jessicana stood up.

"I showed Astro the trapdoor," she said.

Roseabelle nodded. "Good."

"I think we should go," Astro said excitedly.

"Quick, let's find out where this leads."

He was already lowering himself down. Roseabelle followed him, then Jessicana.

CHAPTER 10

Moformi

It was a dark passageway. The friends had to crawl low or hit their heads on the ceiling. It became wider with every step and soon it was a clearing.

They sat down to have lunch. Or dinner. Or breakfast. Roseabelle had no idea what time of day it was or how much time had passed.

As Astro and Jessicana ate their honey nuts, Roseabelle decided to creep ahead. The clearing led back to a passageway.

The passageway then split into two.

"Astro! Jessicana! Come here!" Roseabelle called. There was some rough scuttling, and then her friends appeared.

"What?" they asked.

"Which way should we go through?" Roseabelle asked.

"That way," they said, pointing opposite directions.

Roseabelle sighed. The left-hand passage had a set of steps going down. Roseabelle shook her head. How many feet below were they?

The other passage went a few feet out and then came to a halt at an iron door.

"Split up," she ordered. "Jessicana and I will go down the steps. Astro, you can go to the door."

They trotted obediently to where they had been assigned. Roseabelle went to the stairs with Jessicana.

She stepped on one.

It became jellylike and squirmed around. Roseabelle quickly withdrew her foot. The red substance squirmed to the other step, which turned jellylike too. The substance combined and squirmed to another step. That turned into red jelly too. Roseabelle backed away.

Whatever it was, she was certain that it wasn't Benotripia's strawberry jam.

The jelly was on the tenth step now and almost to the bottom.

Squirm, swish. Squirm, swish.

Five steps left.

Swish, swish.

Three steps left.

Squirm, squirm.

Two steps.

Swish, squirm.

One step.

Soon all the steps were red jelly. The jelly started to bubble and hiss. It grew and grew.

"Run!" shouted Jessicana.

They tore out of the passage and to Astro. He was pounding the door. He turned to them. "Locked," he said simply.

"Locked!" Roseabelle screamed. "Look what's behind us!"

Astro swiveled around. His face paled. "Guys, let's get out of here!" The jelly substance had formed into a monster. It had a wide forehead, squinty eyes, a large nose, and a huge, gaping mouth.

It started toward them, its mouth wide open. "Jessicana!" Roseabelle shouted. "Give me your backpack!"

Jessicana threw it at Roseabelle, too stunned to speak. Roseabelle ripped open the pack and pulled out silk gloves and the Dragocone Ray. She pulled on the gloves and took the ray.

"Astro," she said, "blast open the door. Get to safety. Read Jessicana's books and see if there's anything that tells us how to fight a jelly monster. Go!"

Roseabelle swung the ray at the monster. It hit its enormous belly and the jelly broke apart for just a minute. Roseabelle took the opportunity to slash at the monster. Its mouth and eyes fell away from its body. They quickly squirmed back together, this time forming a slug with a huge mouth. The slug snapped at Roseabelle, but she dodged it and struck again with the ray.

It caused the shell of the snail to detach, but the monster rejoined itself, this time into a dragon. The dragon blew jelly fire at her.

Roseabelle sidestepped out of the way, but some of the curling red mass brushed her shoulder. It began to spread, causing searing pain.

"Astro," she cried, "is there anything on it?"

"Hold on, Roseabelle. Hold on." The pain had spread down to her hand and now was inching its way up to her neck. Roseabelle gritted her teeth and swung again.

The dragon hissed another spurt of the flame, but Roseabelle batted it away with her ray. The dragon pounced on Roseabelle, and she leaped out of the way.

"Astro," she called, "I need info on this now!"

"I have some," he replied. "This is a creature called 'Moformi,' or a jelly creature. You might find it as a harmless metal shape but once touched it will turn to its true form. It can morph into any shape. The jelly it is made out of can be poisonous. After a while, it will start to harden and become metallic. If it hardens in a shape of a monster it will be invulnerable. To defeat it will require us to morph it to an everyday shape such as a small toy or a tool. If done, it will only awaken again if a living hand touches it," Astro read.

"Uh-oh," Roseabelle said, glancing down at the red fluid flowing on her body. "I'd better defeat this guy quick." She looked up and saw the dragon's head turn gray and hard. She gulped. "Let's do this thing," she said.

She charged the Moformi raising her Dragocone Ray and then bringing it back down again. The monster swiped a claw at her but not before separating its body from its head. She slashed at its body again and again. She chopped with all her strength, and soon curvy pieces of jelly were squirming around.

Every time one tried to rejoin, Roseabelle slashed it up into tinier pieces. Soon one piece was pure metal. Then another. And another. Roseabelle worked hard until every last strip of jelly was metal once again.

She sighed with relief. But then she looked down at her body. The jelly was nearly down to her heart. She ran to Astro. She pointed at it. "The slime won't turn back into metal until it is off my body. It's poison."

Astro gulped and jostled Jessicana who had been emotionally petrified by the sight of the Moformi. She blinked then said. "W-what?" she asked shakily.

"You're the medicine girl," Astro said. "Roseabelle has poison coursing through her veins. You have to help."

Roseabelle was feeling woozy. She swayed on her feet. She couldn't hear what Astro was saying. She saw Jessicana reach over and pull something out.

She frantically went over to Roseabelle and shoved something that tasted like sour syrup in her mouth. Roseabelle gagged and spit it out, but Jessicana shoved some more in. Roseabelle let herself swallow it.

Her focus got a little better. Jessicana gave her more of the stuff. Soon Roseabelle was back to normal.

"Jessicana," she coughed. "What was that medicine? Only expert healers can get their hands on that kind of medicine. Wait . . . are you a healer? I thought you could only become a healer once you were old enough to do the training."

"Well, you know when you're twelve and you graduate from Power Training Academy, you go to an ESOK Academy."

"Yes, Jessicana, I know that," Roseabelle said impatiently. "It stands for 'Expert Schools for Older Kids.' But why are you a healer?"

"Because my mom was. I wanted to be her apprentice by helping her with her tasks. I did them so well that she let me try a simple concoction. It worked perfectly. I performed greater tasks until Mom decided to talk to your mom, and she confirmed me a healer. When Danette saw my talents, we had a proper ceremony, and I got my certificate. My dream has always been to be the Head Healer in Benotripia," Jessicana explained.

Roseabelle shook her head. "And I never knew." She nodded at Astro. "How'd you find out?"

Astro shrugged sheepishly. "I walked in on her while she was preparing a mixture for delirium. She had no choice but to explain."

"And when was it that you found out?" Roseabelle asked.

"When we were all eight, thirty days after I received my certificate," Jessicana said. "Anyway that isn't important. You know the truth, so let's move on."

They all looked at the dark way forward. They pulled on their backpacks and trooped on.

The passage got thinner until it stopped. Above was a blank wall. Instinctively Roseabelle pushed on it.

CHAPTER 11

Cart Ride

THERE WAS A RUMBLING NOISE AND THE WALL MOVED. The way was now clear, up to ground level. Roseabelle gave them a "stay put" sign and climbed up.

The room was made of stone and had a single oil lamp glowing on a small table. She beckoned for them that the coast was clear.

Jessicana and Astro climbed up.

"Come on," Roseabelle mouthed.

She led them to a stone door. Roseabelle pushed on it tentatively.

It opened up to a wagon. The back of it was facing them. In front was a short Darvonian with his back turned to them.

They dove into the back. It smelled of straw, and Roseabelle saw a group of crates filled with black fruit of all different shapes and sizes.

The straw was enough to cover Roseabelle and her friends. They felt the cart jostle and then move forward. It was a long ride. It seemed to be endless.

When Roseabelle peeped her head out of the cart, the sun was rising. She was hungry, so she took a mango from her pack and ate it.

She thought that they really needed to draw on the trutan. They had illustrated a bit when in the passage, but since then they hadn't taken a pen to the trutan.

The cart came to a stop. Roseabelle shared a look with Jessicana, which showed they were thinking the same thing: *We need to get out of here!* Roseabelle saw Astro embedded in the straw.

He was pawing at it and raising his head to the surface. "No, Astro," Roseabelle hissed, but before she could take action, he had risen to the air.

His head came back under. "Get out," he whispered urgently.

"How?" Jessicana hissed.

"Just go," Astro whispered, "his back is turned. Go."

Roseabelle and Jessicana scrambled at the straw and rose to the surface. Astro had been right; the old Darvonian's back was turned.

They got out of the cart and stepped onto black pavement. They ducked behind the old wheelbarrow. The old Darvonian man turned around, and Jessicana peered over the side.

She leaned back to Roseabelle and whispered, "He's loading the fruit onto another cart. Astro's still in that one. If the man pulls out enough crates, he could be exposed."

"Let's hope Astro gets back out soon," Roseabelle whispered.

When the old man was loading a fat crate of fruit, Astro leaped out and came tumbling down right on top of Roseabelle.

"Ouch," she grunted. Jessicana pulled Astro off and gave him a *you-don't-always-have-to-be-such-a-show-off* look.

Luckily the man who was loading the fruit hadn't heard Astro. He absentmindedly carried fruit back and forth from his cart to the other.

When he was done, he began to steer his cart around. The friends clung to the back, and when it was facing the opposite cart, they dove in.

Astro pumped in the air and silently slid into the straw. Roseabelle and Jessicana did likewise.

A few hours later, Roseabelle looked above the straw to see where they were going and saw the scenery for the first time. They were in a sea of dry tree trunks tangled and matted together, their branches sharp and pointy. They had no leaves or buds or fruit. They were just bare. Up ahead Roseabelle spotted a valley. They were heading toward it.

She was wondering if they would ever find her mother. She sank back into the straw and fell into a tiresome sleep.

ROSEABELLE WAS HAVING A WEIRD DREAM. SHE WAS ON A boat on Blackwater Sea traveling to Darvonia. She had no idea why, but the voyage seemed very important.

On the boat was a Darvonian. He was following her every command. It was a little strange, but she didn't mind until he started saying, "Yes, Sheklyth." "Of course, Sheklyth." "May I help you, Sheklyth?" "Is there anything you require, Sheklyth?"

Roseabelle realized she was wearing a black hood. What was going on? She pulled up her long sleeve. Her skin was pale and her fingers were too long.

"Slow down," she barked at the Darvonian. Her voice was different. She leaned over the side of the boat and looked at her reflection in the black water. It was hard to see, but it was there.

When she saw her reflection, Roseabelle was looking at the face of her trainer, Shelby. "What? I'm Roseabelle," she exclaimed in Shelby's voice. "This isn't right!"

The wind howled as if with laughter, the waves splashing in her face. Then she woke up.

Roseabelle started fiddling with some straw.

What had been going on in her dream?

She had been Shelby, for sure. But had the Darvonian known she was Shelby?

What did it mean? If he had known that Shelby was a Benotripian, well, any Darvonian would have hurled a Benotripian overboard immediately.

But the Darvonian had been calling Shelby a different name. What was it again?

Shirley?

No, that wasn't it.

Seklt?

No, that didn't seem right either.

But how could Shelby have concealed her identity? It made no sense. Maybe it had just been a silly dream with no meaning.

But all the same, Roseabelle had a terrible nagging feeling that Shelby wasn't exactly what she seemed.

* * * * *

ASTRO WAS LOOKING AT THE STARS. THEY WERE STILL THE same as they were in Benotripia.

He thought guiltily of his parents. Astro's mother had been due back home a week from the day they had left for Darvonia. She was surely frantic by now.

And his dad—well, he was too busy with his job to worry about Astro.

Astro was an only child like Roseabelle. He knew that while Jessicana always complained about her two sisters and three brothers, she was truly lucky to have them. They had gone with her parents on vacation since all of them had graduated from ESOK and were much older.

Astro wished that his parents could see him now. He was no longer the gawky ten-year-old who told jokes and funny stories to get him through the day, no longer the person who was always picked last in every activity and skipped classes because he was tired.

He had grown mentally and physically, putting others before himself and learning to work hard and endure hardships. He had been at sea for more than a week!

And he had Roseabelle to thank for it. He couldn't help admiring her bravery and her determination to find her mother.

She could have turned back on the sea voyage or the first step she took on Darvonia. But she held fast and fought with all her might, not losing hope of finding her mother.

And there was Jessicana with her mighty brain. Her talent was extraordinary, and Astro had complete faith in her.

He wanted to help the two girls that were with him. He was occasionally teased at school for hanging out with girls, but he didn't care because he knew secretly the other students were envious. Besides, he would rather hang out with them than anybody else. Roseabelle and Jessicana were different than others. Truly they were.

* * * * *

JESSICANA PUSHED HER HEAD THROUGH THE STRAW. THE cart was moving slowly. And up ahead was a castle. Jessicana blinked. It was still there, and they were moving toward it. It had an enormous drawbridge, which was now closed. She could see three towers that loomed above and five turrets all constructed out of latick. They didn't have castles in Benotripia. Almost everyone was treated as equals.

Though Jessicana still wanted to overlook the castle, she could see a quarry up ahead and since it was light, many Darvonians were probably mining in it. She ducked down into the straw, not knowing what she was facing.

The cart came to a quick halt the following morning. Roseabelle was drawing in the trutan. She put it away. She dug into the straw sideways and found Astro, arms behind his head and snoring loudly, and Jessicana, stretching her arms and yawning.

"Jessicana, I'll wake Astro. Go see what's going on," Roseabelle ordered gently.

Jessicana, now fully awake, popped her head out of the straw, and Roseabelle shook Astro. He woke, and they waited for Jessicana to give them a report. When she dipped down again, she told them, "We're at a castle. I saw it yesterday and I forgot to tell you. There's people everywhere—it's pandemonium."

Astro raised his head a little out of the straw and then said, "They're selling and trading all sorts of stuff." He looked hopefully at Roseabelle. "Can we go?"

"No," she said.

"Come on," Astro complained, "we have those Darvonian robes and some Benotripian money. We can get Darvonian money from the trutan or maybe trade something we have for things we need. We might even be able to get in the castle. Please?" he added.

"Astro, the whole point of this mission is to rescue my mother. I'm not going to risk some market trip for her freedom. Got it?" Roseabelle said fiercely.

"Didn't you hear what I just said? This might be our free ticket to the castle. I'm almost positive that Danette is here!" Astro argued.

Roseabelle sighed. "Fine, but honestly we have to find out what Darvonian money is before we draw. Astro, you go!"

Astro pulled on his black robe and carefully leapt from the cart.

"I hope this works," Roseabelle muttered to Jessicana. A few minutes later Astro was back, rolling his eyes. "What is it?" Roseabelle demanded.

"Sorry," Astro said with a note of sarcasm, "but I just can't believe it. They have twenty-five kinds of money! I can only remember one. It's half latick and half gold. Talk about exquisite! They can't even build properly, yet they have all this fancy currency."

Roseabelle took the trutan, a bottle of boorsh-berry juice from Benotripia, and a small twig. She took the twig and began to draw a large sack, including heaps of half latick and half gold coins within the sack, onto the trutan.

The three friends then gathered to wait, not noticing the cloaked figures chuckling to themselves outside of the cart.

CHAPTER 12

Dust Draining

WHEN THE COINS WERE COMPLETE, JESSICANA AND Roseabelle pulled on their cloaks, and Roseabelle tied the sack of money to her waist. They scrambled out of the cart. No one was facing them. So they carefully moved to the stone pavement.

Roseabelle gaped at the sight. How could anything be so horrifying and amazing at the same time?

There were stalls and booths in every direction, and cloaked figures were selling their goods behind them. One booth was selling weapons, including swords, daggers, spears, bows and arrows, trapitas, Thepgiles, and Dragocone rays. Another was trading stories written on trutan.

Astro picked a trutan up and, after reading a few lines, turned green and put it down. He shuddered. "Who would ever want to read that?" he muttered filled with distaste.

One booth was selling *A Journey,* apparently Kinetle's autobiography, while another sold dried skins and furs. Darvonians were selling food, water, political guides, and even some things that Roseabelle thought she would get sick over.

"Let's get what we need and go," she whispered to Jessicana. "I'm getting restless to go to the castle."

Jessicana nodded and told Astro.

Roseabelle went to a weapon stall and asked the Darvonian how many she could get if she paid him a coin. He replied gruffly that it was a cutthroatine coin and with it she could buy nine swords, three spears, five quivers of arrows, two crossbows, one Trapita, and a Dragocone Ray.

Roseabelle was flustered and said she would only take a dagger, a crossbow and quiver of arrows, and a spear. He gave her two handfuls of pure silver coins in change and told her to move it. She slipped the coins in her sack and bought a sheath for her dagger.

After purchasing a leather belt, a canteen of lukewarm water, and a red robe, she met her friends at some other stalls.

Jessicana had gotten *A Journey* and a political guide.

Astro had purchased a few Benotripian birds that had clearly been stolen (and he planned to set them free) and a small Dragocone Ray.

A few minutes later, they stood in front of the drawbridge of the castle.

"So Mister let's-go-into-the-castle-and-everything-will-work-out-fine, what's the plan?" Roseabelle asked, her voice low.

Astro gulped. He cleared his throat and said loudly, "We would like to speak with Kinetle immediately."

The bystanders didn't hear, but a magnified voice rumbled, "What is the cause?"

This had better work, Roseabelle thought.

"Uh, for EFID," Astro confirmed.

Roseabelle and Jessicana gaped at him. How did he know what to say?

"Come in," the voice said.

The drawbridge lowered. Once in the courtyard, Roseabelle whispered, "How did you know that?"

"Hush, there's no time to explain," Astro said quietly.

They crossed the courtyard and went up to the castle

looming above. The friends looked back at the drawbridge. It was up again. They shuddered as the large castle door in front opened by itself. They stepped inside and viewed their surroundings.

The windowless room they were in was built of dark, sturdy stone. They didn't have time to notice much more because Roseabelle's face turned bright green, Jessicana's legs slipped under her, and Astro had to lean onto the wall for support. A horrible stench was filling the room and drenching the three friends in disgusting odor. Roseabelle gasped for clean air. The smell was a thick mixture of spoiled meat, rotten eggs, garbage, and wet wool.

Jessicana and Astro gasped continually. "Can't . . . breathe," Jessicana coughed. She was on her knees, clutching her throat. Her eyes rolled back into her head and she collapsed against the stone floor.

Astro was starting to cough too. "Roseabelle . . . you're Meta-Mord . . . do something," he whispered weakly. He too slumped onto the floor.

Racking coughs filled the air as Roseabelle thought about her powers. What could she do? The smell was making them lose consciousness. Suddenly it came to her. She knew she could drain and dissolve things into thin air.

She had only done it once because it took tons of energy from her, but now it was her only option. Just as dizziness nearly overcome her, Roseabelle opened her mouth wide and sucked in the air.

The smell began to diminish and the particles vanished completely. Roseabelle scrambled to Astro's side and shook him. Astro sat up.

"That was the most terrible event that's happened in my life," he muttered. He turned to Roseabelle. "What did you do?" he whispered. Roseabelle explained. "That is an incredible power," Astro remarked quietly. "What's it called?"

"Dust draining," Roseabelle answered. "Come on, let's

wake up Jessicana. Whatever you told them, Astro, it worked. Enough to get us into the castle, at least," Roseabelle said.

When Jessicana was up, Roseabelle led them forward into the deep bowels of the castle. She realized that they had just entered a minor sitting room. When she opened a heavy stone door, it led to a fork of passages. One led to higher ground, while the other went down. There were a handful of other doors, but Roseabelle saw all different kinds of smoke coming out from under the doors. She didn't have the strength to dust drain again.

"Maybe we should split up," Astro suggested.

"No," Roseabelle said sharply, remembering the jelly creature. "We stay together. This is most likely Kinetle's palace, remember? I say we go up."

"Why?" Astro asked.

"Well, look at the other doors," Roseabelle explained. "See how they're built into the wall? There are so many of them that none of them could have a complicated maze inside. Besides, I don't think my mother is going to be in the very front of the castle. She'd be too easy to get to. And the passage that goes level, well, if you look ahead, it doesn't go far either. That's why we should go up." Roseabelle looked up. "Well, what do you think?" she asked.

"Well," Astro said, "it's a good observation, and it's the only plan we have. We can always go back if something goes wrong or if we reach a dead end." Jessicana nodded her head. "Well, let's continue then," Astro said encouragingly.

Jessicana smiled, and then together they tiptoed up the gloomy passage.

THE PASSAGE SEEMED TO LEAD ON FOR WHAT SEEMED LIKE hours, and then they came to a halt in front of a door with gruesome images carved on it.

Before Roseabelle peered through a crack in the door, Astro noted, "Darvonians don't have the best sense of decoration, do they?"

He chuckled weakly, but no one laughed back. Roseabelle saw a stone floor through the crack, and standing on it were four table legs in the shape of poisonous snakes. Nearby was the grand base of an ornate pot.

Hearing no sounds, Roseabelle cautiously pushed the door open. As she had supposed, a large desk stood in the middle of the stone floor of the room. Beside it was a black pot containing a withered plant. There was a soft chair made of a velvety substance (something Roseabelle guessed was moon panther fur) and a jar of black ink with a pen.

Roseabelle saw that there was a piece of trutan on the desk. On it was written,

S,

What is taking you so long? You have deliberately failed me. Unbelievable! You, my eldest child, of all people! I tell you, that girl is suspecting you. You're not even careful. The little Benotripian was bound to know she was being tricked! You have disgraced me! I want you to come to the castle right away. That girl and her friends need a little talking to. See you soon!

—K

Roseabelle reread the letter with interest. What did *K* mean by "that girl"? Could it be talking about herself? But that was impossible! *K* was obviously a Darvonian and the Darvonians didn't know that Roseabelle and her friends were here. Well, at least that was what she thought.

Then she recalled the name of the leader of the Darvonians. *Kinetle.* Could Kinetle have written this and then forgotten to send it?

Roseabelle gulped and made sure the trutan was positioned in the place where she had found it. She bent down and studied the ink. By the look of it, the ink was wet, which meant Kinetle had written the letter quite recently.

Roseabelle shivered. What if Kinetle was in the palace? "Come on," she said to Jessicana and Astro. "Let's move it. I have a creepy feeling about this."

There was another door at the front of the room, and Astro opened it.

Before them stood a maze of passageways, tunnels, and dead ends.

CHAPTER 13

Maze of Danger

"Wow," was all Astro could utter. "We're supposed to go through there?" Jessicana asked, her voice strained.

"How?" Roseabelle groaned.

She was about to take a step forward when Astro shouted, "Stop!"

"Astro," Roseabelle hissed, "the castle isn't deserted. There's probably someone here. Now we'll be discovered."

He put a finger on the maze floor. It shuddered, and then a huge chunk of it fell into a deep, dark abyss. Roseabelle looked at Astro.

"Well, it's good you came along. That was one cruel trap."

Astro shrugged. "Darvonians are full of those kinds of things."

Roseabelle tried to think of a solution. She reached inside her robe and pulled out the folder she had taken from the building where the passage had been found. Nothing that could help them there. She plunged her hands in her robes, twisting and grabbing for something. Her hands then closed around a small vial full of black creamy paste.

"I got this from that building," she exclaimed.

She turned to Jessicana. "Do you know what this is?" she asked. Jessicana eyed it quizzically and then pulled a heavy book out of her pack. She flipped pages through the book and then motioned for them to listen.

"Here," she announced, "listen up." Then Jessicana began to read. "*This substance, scientifically called Aphrotykkiedle, or otherwise known as Lypith, is very dangerous. It is a black, thick liquid/paste that can be used to heal or wound. For healing, spread it over the wound and wait. To cause damage, toss it in cold water and it will solidify. Touch it with a small bar of gold and throw it. It will soon explode. If you pour it on latick, it becomes as heavy as a full-grown man. The full powers of Lypith are yet to be uncovered.*" Jessicana looked up. "Does that help?" she asked.

"Yes," Astro said. He turned to Roseabelle. "Jessicana can fly over the gap. She can fly but not land. Jessicana, you can have a squirt of this Lypith. Let it fall on the latick floor. If it breaks the floor, it means the floor won't support our weight, so fly back over here to help us. If it doesn't, land and help us get across the abyss," Astro ordered, taking charge.

"How?" Jessicana asked.

"Well, you could perhaps drag us along."

"Yeah, and drop you along the way," Jessicana said.

"Oh, so you got a better plan?" Astro asked. Jessicana was silent. "That's what I thought," Astro said.

He poured a little Lypith onto Jessicana's hand, and Jessicana transformed. She flew to the other side and let the black liquid drip from her wing onto the stone. It didn't break and Roseabelle breathed a sigh of relief.

Jessicana flew to Astro and turned back into a girl. She grabbed his shirt and turned into a parrot. Her claws were grasping his shirt. Roseabelle watched with her fingers parted over her eyes. Jessicana flew out onto the trench of blackness.

Roseabelle saw that Astro was weighing her down. She watched in horror as her friends started to slip down. This wasn't going to work. She turned to her backpack and rummaged through it, trying to find something that could help them.

Her hands closed around thick rope. Roseabelle slapped her hand against her forehead. Rope! How could they have forgotten?

She tied it around her waist and flung one end of it to Astro. He caught it and looped it around his wrist. Roseabelle reeled him in like a fisherman reeling in a fish.

When he was safely in the room, she said, holding up the rope, "Forget this?"

Astro's face turned red.

"Sorry," he mumbled.

Roseabelle sighed and removed the rope from Astro's wrist. She flung it to the maze and it caught on a patch of stone. Roseabelle dropped and was going down into the trench. Then she stopped in midair. The rope was working. She climbed up it and reached the other side of the maze. She held it out to her friends several feet away.

Jessicana got the message and flew to her. She clutched the rope in her beak and brought it to Astro. Roseabelle watched as Astro tied it around his waist and swung to her. Jessicana flew over. Roseabelle was holding the jar of Lypith.

"Good thinking, Roseabelle!" Jessicana cheered.

"Totally," Astro approved. They turned to the maze. There was a large tunnel leading forward. Roseabelle took the jar and opened it. She took a splotch of Lypith on her fingertip and hurled it forward. The stone didn't break.

They advanced forward. Once through the tunnel, Astro pointed out a fork in the maze. Eleven passages led forward. Roseabelle took a bit more of the Lypith and flung it at a passage on the far right. The stone staggered and then crumbled.

Roseabelle tried the passage next to that. It broke too. Each tried passage crumbled into dust. The last passage was yet to be tried. Roseabelle let the Lypith touch the stone. It stayed. They raced forward.

There were many other drop-offs, and stone breaking echoed throughout the maze. Twice they reached dead ends and had to retrace their steps.

Finally they came to the end: a heavy oak door. When Astro touched the door, it felt ice cold. It surprised him, and he withdrew his hand.

When Jessicana leapt forward, the door was scorching hot.

When Roseabelle touched it, the wood was warning her. It seemed perfectly normal except for the ugly gargoyles on the door, which were staring at her with piercing red eyes. There was a sense of forbiddance in the air. She pushed it open quietly.

Below her was a set of stairs. With each step she took, a faint echo reached her ears.

At the bottom of the steps was a door with metal bars and standing in front of it were—

"Hide!" Roseabelle hissed.

CHAPTER 14

Danette

SHE DRAGGED ASTRO TO THE SIDE, AND JESSICANA HID behind them. Three Darvonians wielding trapitas and Thepgiles were guarding the door.

Now that Roseabelle listened, she could hear a sorrowful humming from inside. Roseabelle's heart took a leap. She knew that tone. Tears began to gather in her eyes. It was her mother. After all that searching, she had finally found her. More than ever she wanted to embrace Danette and hear her mother's gentle soothing words that they were going to be okay.

She touched the stone arrows that she had bought and stroked the hilt of her dagger. She handed her spear to Jessicana.

"You'll need it," she whispered. Jessicana nodded gratefully. Roseabelle readied her crossbow with an arrow and watched as Astro pulled on silk gloves and drew his ray. Jessicana set a determined face and swung her spear for practice.

Roseabelle looked at her friends. "On the count of three," she mouthed. She held up one finger, then two, then three, and they burst into action.

Astro tackled a beefy cloaksman on the right. The cloaksman swung his Trapita at Astro, but the lightning boy threw down his ray and shot an enormous lightning bolt out of his fingers. The guard was distracted because he had clearly thought that Astro would use his ray. The bolt hit the guard's armor and left a hole in the metal.

The Darvonian slumped to the floor. Astro turned to help the girls.

When Jessicana jumped out, she hoped that she could help. She wasn't much of a fighter. Luckily she was taking down a tall, wiry guard who seemed like a bit of a non-warrior too. *Pretty fair,* she thought.

She thrust her spear at him, but it just clanged harmlessly against his armor. With a quick flick of his wrist, the guard sent his Thepgile hurling at Jessicana. The bird girl hesitated, then dropped her weapon and turned into a parrot.

The Thepgile lodged itself in a block of heavy, gray stone. Jessicana flew up, pecking him. It did nothing really, but it was just enough to buy herself some time as Astro picked up and swung his Dragocone Ray at him. The cloaked guard was knocked back and he hit the wall behind him. He was unconscious immediately.

"Nice work!" cried Jessicana to Astro.

Roseabelle sent an arrow at her opponent. It bounced from his armor and flew back at her. She could have sworn that the guard was wearing two layers of metal armor. He was bulky and covered in sweat. Roseabelle watched as the arrow fell to the floor.

She pretended like she was going to shoot another arrow. Roseabelle dropped her crossbow and stared at a rock on the floor. It rose behind the guard's head.

He began to run to her, winding up his Trapita. Roseabelle stared even harder at the stone and it slammed into his helmet. The guard felt it and swatted it. She stared at his helmet. It began to lift higher and then it was levitating above his head.

She fixed her eyes on the stone and it hit the guard's head. He froze and fell down.

Astro and Jessicana rushed over to her. "We got all of them!" Astro cried. "I can't believe it!"

"Let's go get your mom, Roseabelle," Jessicana said.

They rushed to the door. Astro shot a bolt at it, but it bounced back at him. He ducked, and it burned the back wall.

"We need the keys," Roseabelle said urgently. They searched the cloaksmen and found the keys on the belt of the cloaksman Roseabelle had attacked. Roseabelle unlocked it and pushed the door open. Inside was Danette sitting on a hard bed, tapping her foot against the stone.

"Roseabelle!" she cried, her eyes sad and alert. "Go! Get out of here. Get out of the cell. You have to. Listen. Do it. I'll find a way to get out. Just go."

"I d-don't understand," Roseabelle stammered. There was a squeal behind her. Danette's face was pale. "Go, Roseabelle," she said.

Roseabelle took a step backward, confused. What did her mother mean? They had knocked out the Darvonians back there. There was no danger. The faint sound of a click of a lock sounded.

"Well, well. Come to take a little visit at last?" a cold voice asked. Roseabelle turned around slowly.

CHAPTER 15

Sheklyth

When she saw the speaker, Roseabelle could have fainted. How could this be? It was traumatizing, but Roseabelle knew somehow that it was her. This was the horrible truth.

It was Shelby.

"A little surprised to see me, Roseabelle? Yes, of course. I've been waiting for you. Oh yes, waiting for so long to have this little talk."

"B-but you're a Benotripian," Roseabelle stammered, not believing her eyes. Shelby smirked.

"Being an IB is so useful at times. Benotripians can never tell the difference."

"You're an IB," Roseabelle cried. "But I don't get it. You taught me at the academy. How did you get in if you're a Darvonian?"

Shelby laughed. "Easy. I made sure no one could suspect me by giving them no reason to. I didn't bring any weapons. Or Darvonian marks. IB's look perfectly like Benotripians. Too simple."

Roseabelle was still trying to figure out everything. She realized that Astro and Jessicana weren't in the room with her. They were outside the door, fighting a whole army of Darvonians. She had to get out of here with her mother and her friends. Maybe if she kept talking, she could figure a way out to fight the so-called "Benotripian."

"Why did you come to Benotripia?" Roseabelle asked.

"We had planned to capture your mother long before. I was supposed to keep an eye on you, so you would stay out of the way until it was time. See, if we captured your mother, we knew you would come after her. We could get you and your friends. Benotripians would be frantic for their leader and her daughter. They had already lost Magford. We could make a trade: Benotripia for you. Then at last Benotripia would belong to Darvonia. Carefully devised plan, yes?"

Roseabelle tried to conceal her anger. *Keep talking*, she thought as one hand went to her dagger.

"The feather that Jessicana picked up. What was up with that?" Roseabelle asked, stalling.

"I believe your parrot friend was right about the dream world. You see, you could say Asteran is in some sort of league with us. He was simply communicating with us. When you felt the feather, you entered too. You also met my impossible, mad twin, Ugagush," Shelby explained.

Roseabelle remembered Ugagush saying that he was Kinetle's son. Her mouth opened in horror. "Don't tell me you're Kinetle's daughter," she squeaked.

Shelby smiled slyly. "Not only that, but I'm also Darvonia's second-in-command. If something happens to Kinetle, I'm the leader."

Roseabelle was in pure shock. How could she have trusted and learned from the heir of Darvonia? How could someone be so cruel? She remembered the letter. *S* stood for Shelby. The book in the tower room. It had said, "*There is a rumor that one of these children is an IB.*" Roseabelle's stomach lurched.

"The pouch," she said. "Why is it so important?"

Shelby sighed. "Honestly, Roseabelle, you're smarter than that. Think, why is the trutan so important to us?"

Roseabelle's heart sank. Shelby knew what was inside. "So you could build large sea vessels," she suggested.

Shelby shrugged. "Something like that."

"When you were teaching, you wouldn't allow me to feel the emotions of that nasty creature. Why was that?"

"Because," Shelby said, "it was from Darvonia. If you felt its emotions, it would've felt a strong affection toward me. You would probably figure that it was Darvonian, connect two and two, and you know the rest."

"Were you one of the Darvonians that came to get the pouch?" Roseabelle asked, secretly pulling her dagger from inside her robes.

"Nope, that was my sister, Heltonine. She is only seventeen. She's not as brave as perceived. She doesn't always meet expectations. Heltonine has always looked up to her elder sister, Sheklyth."

"Who's that?" Roseabelle wondered aloud.

Shelby shook her head. "You disappoint me, Roseabelle. My real name is not Shelby. Haven't you realized? I am Sheklyth, daughter of Leader Kinetle, second-in-command of Darvonia.

Roseabelle, still trying to piece it all together, was silent.

Sheklyth looked closely at Roseabelle. "Any more questions before I leave you and your friends in this grimy cell with your mother?"

"Yeah, I have one," Roseabelle said coolly. "How come you were so clueless to let us keep our weapons?" She drew her dagger.

Sheklyth's eyes widened. Roseabelle advanced forward.

"Roseabelle, listen. I don't really see what you can accomplish with that. You can't really harm me," Sheklyth said calmly. She brushed aside her sweeping black robes to reveal a sensible fitting suit of armor to prove her point.

Roseabelle stopped and said, "Darvonians are hopeless. Not only are they mean and spiteful, but they have only cruelty and weapons. Nothing else."

Sheklyth's eyes narrowed. "Who said we only have weapons?" she asked.

"You lack the powers that you trained me on. What else do you have?" Roseabelle asked.

Sheklyth looked pleased. "Something you don't have," she said slyly. She took a deep breath, and then Roseabelle felt an overpowering emotion.

It was fear. Fear like Roseabelle had never imagined before, fear that told her she would never get out of this place. It was penetrating. A blue fog shone from Sheklyth's body, and then it stopped. Roseabelle felt normal.

"That's what we have," Sheklyth said proudly. Roseabelle was stunned. There was a moment of silence. Roseabelle took an arrow and loaded it onto her crossbow.

She lifted it and shot. Sheklyth averted the shot. She smiled in a pleased way and made the penetrating emotion happen again. Roseabelle dropped her weapon.

Fear flooded through her body. She looked at the bars on the door. Astro was still struggling with the Darvonians.

Roseabelle caught his eye. She pantomimed him sending a bolt flying through the room. Astro cocked his head, showing that he wanted her to repeat the message. Roseabelle showed him again. This time he nodded, showing that he understood.

If the bolt that Astro shot earlier bounced against the door, it will bounce against the walls, she thought. Sheklyth was howling with laughter. Astro stretched forth his finger, and then a streak of sliver and blue came hurling out.

The mass of crackling silver light bounced against the back wall. Roseabelle dived at Sheklyth and wrestled the keys from her. The Darvonian spit in rage and tried to seize the keys. She quickly stopped her pursuit as Astro's stray lightning bolt barely grazed her face and singed off the bottom of her hair.

Roseabelle rushed to Danette and pulled her up. She took her mother's hand, and Roseabelle unlocked the door.

"Mom, after being locked up, do you think you can still fly?" she shouted over the sound of fighting. Flying was one of Danette's powers. The other was turning invisible. Danette nodded in response to her daughter's question.

Roseabelle and Danette raced out and locked Sheklyth in. Meanwhile, Astro and Jessicana were dealing with the Darvonians.

Only two were unconscious, but twenty-two fierce Darvonian warriors remained in the fight. Roseabelle's heart sank. The battle seemed to be tipping in the Darvonian's favor. Roseabelle turned to her mother. "Fly up on the ceiling. You're too weak to fight."

Hugging her mother one last time, she gripped her cross-bow and loaded it, sneaking from behind a wall of Darvonians and firing. The arrow made its mark and the Darvonian crashed to the dungeon floor. But Roseabelle's victory was short lived, as his two companions whirled around and sent their Thepgiles spinning at her. Roseabelle quickly dodged one, but as the other was aimed at her feet, the blade grazed her shoe, tearing the top part of the leather sandal. Roseabelle wasted no time nocking an arrow on her bow and shooting it at the Darvonians. They deflected it with their Thepgiles, and Roseabelle took off at a run before they could aim again at her.

As Roseabelle secretly crouched between the rows of Darvonians, she realized that Jessicana and Astro were cor-nered. They were still battling the Darvonians and Roseabelle knew that they were about to tire. Reacting quickly, she fired three arrows at a small group of Darvonians, who collapsed as the deadly missiles penetrated their armor. Astro and Jessicana quickly squeezed through the mass of enemies, Jessicana blocking a warrior's sword strikes while Astro used his ray to burn through a Darvonian's helmet. Roseabelle looked up and saw Danette hovering above them, her tired eyes staring sadly down at them. As the Darvonians closed in on them again, Roseabelle shouted, "Astro, drop your weapon!"

Her vague message came across clear to him; he stretched forth a finger and three large jets of electric light bounced across the room. Half the Darvonians were lying on the ground, the lightning having struck them forcefully. The remaining ones were blocking the exit on the far side of the room.

Roseabelle shouted to her mother. "Fly overhead to the exit!" Danette shook her head, and Roseabelle knew what she was trying to say.

"*I won't leave you.*"

Gathering courage, Roseabelle turned back to the fight and was dismayed to find that Jessicana and Astro, though near the exit, were struggling to escape. All that could be seen was the blur of the figures that were Jessicana and Astro and the glow of Astro's Dragocone Ray. They were working furiously to keep their enemies far away from them. The dungeon was filled with the sounds of clashing metal.

Jessicana had a cut on her left cheek, and Astro's leg was bleeding; an arrow had nipped his skin while zooming past.

Trying desperately to turn the Darvonians' focus away from her friends, she drew her dagger and, with both perfect agility and speed, hurled it at the Darvonian closest to Astro. It struck the warrior in the leg, and the impact jerked him backward and onto the cold stone floor.

Multiple Darvonians whirled around, and Roseabelle found herself desperately shooting arrow after arrow at her foes. She was relieved to see that amidst the commotion, Jessicana and Astro had managed to sneak out the doorway. A dozen Darvonians were closing in on her, and Roseabelle knew that she wouldn't be able to hold them off for long. Just as they had formed a tight circle around her, two gentle hands scooped her up into the air, and Roseabelle nearly cried with relief. Danette was flying over the Darvonians, Roseabelle on her back.

Danette shot out of the room and past the Darvonians, eyes firm and focused. The Darvonians, shouting with rage, followed not too far behind the flying mother and daughter. A few feet ahead, Jessicana and Astro were sprinting as fast as they could, covering more ground than they would have in normal circumstances.

"Astro! Jessicana!" Roseabelle shouted. "Follow our lead."

The four Benotripians tore through various passageways, doors, and hallways. Danette and Roseabelle flew; Astro and Jessicana ran. The Darvonians were right at their heels.

Astro suddenly flung open a door and his face filled with hope. "This leads to the courtyard!" he shouted ,and Danette shot through as quick as an eagle. Astro and Jessicana followed behind. Much to their horror, the drawbridge began to rise.

Doubt filled Roseabelle's mind. "*Will we make it*?"

"Astro, get on my back! Jessicana, transform! We're going to have to fly over it!" Danette shouted. Roseabelle wrapped her arms around Danette's neck, and Astro hung on to Roseabelle. Danette lifted into the air.

Roseabelle heard angry shouts of Darvonians and looked back fearfully to the ground. The Darvonians were loading arrows onto bows that had been concealed in their robes. "Mom, they're firing!" Roseabelle screamed.

Danette fought against the harsh wind to fly faster, but just before they soared over the top wooden plank of the drawbridge, the Darvonians pulled back their bowstrings and fired their arrows. A dozen arrows shot toward them at lightning speed. Astro shot a bolt at one but missed. As a bird, Jessicana could dodge the arrows more quickly, but Danette was the most vulnerable target. Ten arrows couldn't withstand the wind and took off in different directions, but two remained strong and battled it. Roseabelle stared in utter horror as the two arrows came zooming at her at top speed.

She had no time to think before the missile headed straight for her arm, where her bow was hanging. The arrow split the bow and Roseabelle sighed in relief but not after seeing the other arrow head right to Danette's shoulder. "Mom!" Roseabelle shouted. A gust of wind blew upward, and the point of the arrow tilted up—cutting through her sleeve. Roseabelle sighed with relief but then grimaced as Danette bit her lip. "Are you all right?" Roseabelle cried out. Danette nodded, and both her daughter and Astro could tell that she was in pain. "It just nipped me," she said, forcing a smile. Roseabelle felt Danette shudder and realized that she was struggling to remain in the air.

Jessicana flew over and tried to support Danette, but it was no use. Although they were gaining momentum in their flight pattern, Danette was starting to fall.

Roseabelle saw the land of Darvonia below whiz past: the market where they had bought supplies and the village that Roseabelle had discovered after arriving in enemy territory. She looked ahead, and her heart skipped a beat. Blackwater Sea was just ahead, and on the shores of the beach were a crowd of two dozen Darvonian warriors, gleaming swords waving in their hands. Danette began to lower herself even more, and Roseabelle whispered to Astro "They haven't spotted us yet. Quick, we need to land without being seen."

He scanned the land below, then pointed to an outcropping of rock. "Under there," he suggested quietly. Danette heard him and aimed for the spot that Astro had indicated. She began to pick up speed and momentum, and soon Roseabelle realized that Danette didn't have enough strength to stop them from crash landing. As the black rock came nearer and nearer, Roseabelle wrapped her arms around her mother's waist. "Hold on," she whispered. Just as the pointed mass of shiny black rock came just a few feet away from Danette's face, Roseabelle pulled her mother up, and they landed on the dry, dirty beach.

Jessicana landed beside them and Astro hissed "Quick, they're looking our way!"

Danette was so weak that Roseabelle had to gently lift her underneath the covering of the rock. Astro also ducked behind it, and Jessicana flattened herself against the rock wall.

"Roseabelle," Astro whispered, "shadow tumble to the cave and bring back the raft. We'll be waiting for you."

She nodded, immersed herself in the shadow of the rock, pictured the cave, and stomped her foot.

Thankfully, no Darvonians were guarding the cave, and Roseabelle quickly snatched the raft. Taking a quick peek of the exterior of the cave, she crept out and saw that the outcropping of rock that her friends were hiding under was directly below her.

As the Darvonians viewed the area, Roseabelle knew what her only option was. She had to jump to her hiding place.

Roseabelle knew it was risky, but, gathering courage, she aimed for her landing and leapt.

When she landed, she saw a hooded face turn her way and she ducked. Roseabelle glanced around the corner of the rock. The Darvonians knew where they were and were slowly and silently advancing. Terror filled Roseabelle. Escape seemed almost impossible.

She crept around to where her friends were crouching and showed them the raft.

"They know," she whispered. Her friends understood the message. Danette looked more pale than ever.

A crazy idea formed in Roseabelle's mind.

"We're going to have to surprise them," she whispered. "If we jump out suddenly, they'll be distracted for a second. It'll give us a head start." She looked to her friends for approval and they nodded. It was a desperate attempt but their situation was frightening.

Roseabelle motioned for Jessicana and Astro to take hold of the raft as well. "I'll help my mother," she whispered to them. Jessicana shook her head.

"No, Roseabelle. It's too risky."

"I'll be fine," she whispered back and put her arms around Danette. "You go first."

Jessicana and Astro darted out of their hiding spot, and Roseabelle heard a shout of rage from the Darvonians. Half carrying, half dragging Danette, Roseabelle emerged and saw that the Darvonians had broken into a full sprint. Roseabelle stared at the beach. It seemed as far away as ever.

Adrenaline rushed through her and she ran, helping Danette across the shore and to her friends and the raft.

The Darvonians were gaining, swords drawn and Roseabelle was losing energy. The sight of her foes gaining on her motivated her to reach Blackwater Sea.

Astro and Jessicana had made it to the water; the oars were in their hands. Their expressions were full of fear and horror. "Roseabelle!" Jessicana screamed as the Darvonians rushed to her.

Using her last bit of energy, Roseabelle tore to the waters and felt the soothing and comforting sensation of water on her ankles. Rushing deeper, she placed Danette on the deck and climbed onto the small watercraft. The Darvonians were now wading in the water. Astro and Jessicana raised their oars and determinedly steered the raft away from the beach and the Darvonians.

Roseabelle and Danette held each other for a long time and didn't let go.

It had been more than two weeks since they had left Darvonia, and the island of Benotripia was nearing. During the journey, Danette told them all about what had happened.

Roseabelle secretly vowed that she would never let this happen to Danette again. There was a pit of anger in her heart. Roseabelle was still upset about the betrayal of Shelby—or Sheklyth.

She still had the folder from Darvonia and entrusted it into Astro's care. He told her that the folder was how he had gotten the information to get inside the castle.

Jessicana started reading Kinetle's autobiography. After the first few pages, she tossed it angrily into the ocean.

"I thought it would reveal secret battle plans," Jessicana said wrinkling her nose, "but all it talked about was how much she dislikes Benotripians. It's such a waste of trutan."

When the small group pulled up on shore, the two mottels were there. Jessicana made her transformation and circled them, squawking cheerfully. Astro went to tell everyone what had happened to Danette. Roseabelle and her mother walked around the beach, chatting with their arms around each other.

There were thousands of Benotripians that came to the beach and celebrated. They all made their way to the closest Benotripian village.

CHAPTER 16
Celebration

Roseabelle, Astro, Jessicana, and Danette spent a night in Lokomonok, a Benotripian city. Danette was a frequent visitor there, so the residents had no problem housing the three friends.

The following day, Jessicana's family and Astro's parents came to Lokomonok. Astro's father said he was only here to interview his son for *The Tropical Times,* but Astro knew better.

Jessicana's siblings praised her. Jessicana was so stunned because she had never heard a word of goodwill from any of her brothers or sisters. The eldest child, Henryl, couldn't stop patting her back.

That night, Astro and his father (who both had the same power) shot brilliant, silver and blue lightning bolts into the sky like fireworks. They went so high into the sky that probably all of Benotripia saw them, even if they were tiny specks in the distance. Danette then traveled to Central Square to make an announcement to the people of Benotripia.

Naturally, not all of them would come, but the news would pass along. Roseabelle, Danette, Jessicana and her family, and Astro and his parents traveled to Central Square. The next day, Danette stood on a high rock facing a large multitude of people.

She told them how she had been drawn into captivity by the Darvonians and how they brought her there. The Benotripians listened intently. Danette stopped in her speech. "But this is not all of the story. May I invite my rescuers up here. Make way for Jessicana Wingling, Astro Jagged-Bolt, and Roseabelle Leading-ton." Jessicana, Astro, and Roseabelle climbed up the stone steps embedded in the rock and joined Danette.

Danette turned to face them. "Would you please tell us the rest of the story?" she requested.

The three nodded. Danette backed away. Jessicana went first, telling them her version of the story. Astro went next. Roseabelle shared her part last, and the audience gasped and screamed more than ever.

When they finished, Danette stepped up. "Thank you," she said solemnly, "for sharing that with us. But before you sit back down I would like to award you."

A Benotripian dressed in green went up to them and handed Danette a wooden box.

She opened it and pulled out a medal made of gold. Engraved on the surface was a parrot feather with a potion bottle. She gestured to Jessicana. The parrot girl blushed and bowed her head so Danette could place it on her neck. "For quick wit and healing talent," Danette said loudly. The Benotripians clapped.

Danette pulled another medal from the box. It was fashioned from silver and had a large lightning bolt on the front. "For profound bravery," Danette announced, resting the medal on Astro's neck.

There was another roar of applauding. Danette pulled one last medal from the box. This one was the most majestic of all. Roseabelle couldn't quite place what it was made of. It was swirling with many colors. Roseabelle could make out a large island with many twists and turns. Beside it was a scepter. "For outstanding leadership," Danette called. She put the medal on Roseabelle.

The clapping went on for at least five minutes. Roseabelle hugged Danette and Jessicana. She grinned at Astro.

"You know, after this," Roseabelle said to them, "I don't think I'll be able to stand going back to my normal schedule."

Astro sighed. "You're right," he said. "It really was a great adventure."

* * * * *

FROM BEHIND THE STAGE, A RED-HAIRED MAN WATCHED the auburn-haired girl who had grown so much since the night he had made a promise to Danette. Only part of that promise had been fulfilled.

Discussion Questions

1. If you were faced with Darvonian opponents, what strategies, powers, and weapons would you use to defeat them?
2. If you were a son or daughter of Danette and you discovered your mom was captured by the Darvonians, what would you do?
3. When Astro fell asleep on watch when the friends were traveling to Darvonia by sea, what were the consequences? What would have happened differently if Astro *had* stayed awake?
4. If you were a Benotripian, what power(s) would you like to have? How would you use your power(s)?
5. What was Jessicana and Astro's friendship like with Roseabelle?
6. If you were faced with the danger of making a choice between two paths, which path would you take? Or would you choose to go back altogether?

If the Stones of Horsh are real, they could destroy the island.

Benotripia

The Stones of Horsh

From the author of *The Rescue*

McKenzie Wagner

Sweetwater Books
An Imprint of Cedar Fort, Inc.
Springville, Utah

Contents

CHAPTER 1
Thoughts

Roseabelle ran her fingers through the soft sand, sifting it between her hands, deep in thought. The rumble of the ocean always helped her to relax and settle into her thoughts of the past. A soft breeze whisked past her, causing her long auburn hair to flutter.

These days, she needed some time alone. Only one year ago, her life had fallen apart. The Darvonians—the ruthless, cunning, cold-hearted people that lived on a small, twisted island far away—had captured her mother, Danette, the ruler of Benotripia. Roseabelle and her best friends, Jessicana and Astro, had set out on an adventure to find and rescue Danette.

Successful in their mission, they brought Danette back to the island. Shortly after her recovery, she was up and ruling Benotripia again. But the worst part of the journey to Darvonia still lingered in Roseabelle's mind.

While rescuing her mother from her prison, her former trainer, Shelby, turned out to be the ruthless Darvonian second-in-line, Sheklyth, who had betrayed her without a second thought. Roseabelle had felt hurt beyond belief, wounded, and torn. Every night since then, she wished that she would wake up from this long dream at any moment and that Shelby would be waiting at the Academy to teach her a new trick.

But deep inside, Roseabelle knew this wasn't a dream.

Jessicana and Astro had tried to get her mind off things, but nothing worked. Nevertheless, she appreciated them for trying. Roseabelle smiled as she thought of her friends. Jessicana was a smart and spunky blonde who had the ability to turn into a parrot, and Astro, an outgoing boy, could shoot lightning bolts from his fingertips.

The best part about her life happened the day before. She graduated from the Academy and now had two months of free time. Yesterday, as the soft manila trutan, a writing material for Benotripians, bearing her graduation certificate was placed in her hands, she couldn't help but feel happy.

Roseabelle stood and brushed sand off her clothes. She tilted her head to listen to one more round of the crashing waves and then walked home.

As Roseabelle climbed the rope ladder to her front porch, she heard the window creak open above her and a cheerful voice ring out: "Roseabelle, where have you been? Dinner's on the table!"

Roseabelle looked up to see her mother hanging out of the window, her long blonde curls gracefully forming around her face. "Be right there, Mom!" she called up and entered through the bronze doorway.

The two of them sat down at the table, silence permeating the room. Roseabelle picked at her bright purple fruit and prodded her bowl of orange broth. She finally sighed and dropped her spoon with a clatter. "I'm sorry, Mom," she said quietly. "I just can't eat tonight." She started to get up when Danette gently clasped her hand.

"Roseabelle, I know this is hard for you. I have an idea that might get your mind off everything that happened. Why don't you invite Jessicana and Astro out on a ride in the dinghy?" Danette suggested.

Roseabelle knew exactly what she was talking about. Danette had enforced that every family in Benotripia be provided with some kind of a boat—a quick getaway if Darvonians invaded. "That's a great idea, Mom," Roseabelle replied, offering her a fake smile. "Thanks."

As Roseabelle walked out the door, Danette called out, "Be back before sundown!"

* * * * *

JESSICANA'S DAY WASN'T GOING GREAT. THE FIRST REASON: school was out. Most kids got excited at this prospect, but with the Wingling family, school-out vacation translated into one result: endless cleaning.

It wasn't that Jessicana didn't like to tidy up. But she also believed in a time for fun and books. She wished that she could go over to Roseabelle's, plop down in the middle of the tower room, pick out a nice thick novel, and read it from start to finish.

Jessicana sighed as she washed the table off for the fifth time that day. "Mom, are you sure the table isn't clean enough?" she asked.

"One can never be too tidy," her mother answered cheerfully, and Jessicana groaned. This was going to be a long day.

A loud rap at the front door made her jump with excitement, and Jessicana ran to answer it. They didn't get many visitors. As she swung the door open, Jessicana sighed in relief. It was Roseabelle, her long auburn hair flowing, and Astro.

"Hi!" Jessicana greeted them enthusiastically.

Roseabelle smiled at her. "Hi, Jessicana. So I was wondering if you wanted to go boating with us. We won't go too far, and we'll get back before sunset."

"Sure!" Jessicana shouted over her shoulder, "Mom! Astro,

Roseabelle, and I are going out boating. We'll be back before sunset."

Mrs. Wingling, a plump woman with mousy brown hair tied up in a bun, appeared in the doorway. "O-oh hello," she stammered. Jessicana crossed her fingers, hoping her mother would say yes.

"Mom, please?" Jessicana fixed her mother with a pleading blue-eyed stare so persistent that Mrs. Wingling bit her lip furiously.

"Well, all right," she said, sighing, and Jessicana quickly sped out the door.

Roseabelle eyed her friend quizzically. "Well, good day, Mrs. Wingling."

Jessicana's mother nodded and shut the door softly.

Astro flashed Jessicana an amused grin. "What was that all about?"

Jessicana blushed. "Mom's a clean freak. Thanks for saving me back there. I think I've swept the place fifty times by now."

Astro rolled his eyes. "Jessicana, your house is a tree. Doesn't your mom realize that it's going to be pretty hard to get the floor perfectly clean with all the plants growing underneath?"

Jessicana shrugged. "She's determined." It was true. Mrs. Wingling was known for her excellent potion making, which Jessicana had inherited, but more important, she was known for her cleanliness and order. It may have been a good thing for customers (Benotripians bought potions from her), but for her children, it was a heavy workload.

Roseabelle led them to the beach. "Come on, you guys!" she said. "Here's the boat."

Roseabelle and Danette's boat was old and weathered but still managed fine. Jessicana had actually been there when they had picked it out. It was carved out of wood and had three seats and three pairs of oars. A small box in the corner was filled to the top with dry snacks, a canteen of water, and rope, to be used for emergencies, although Jessicana remembered that Danette had told Roseabelle she could use the rope any time.

"Climb in!" Roseabelle invited and slung the rope around her waist.

"You're going to turn into a dolphin?" Astro questioned. Transforming into a dolphin was one of Roseabelle's many abilities.

Roseabelle shrugged. "Just enough to get us out in the middle of the water." Jessicana watched in awe as her friend secured the other side of the rope to a seat and dove into the water. Gradually, the boat began to move.

They soon picked up speed, and Jessicana leaned over the side of the boat to brush her fingers against the light spray of cool water. A soft smile spread over her lips as the water made her relax, lulling her into a pleasant dreamlike state. And then, just like that, Jessicana thought back to the day she and Roseabelle had met.

CHAPTER 2
The Black Ship of Shadows

When she was six, Jessicana and her family had gone boating on their watercraft that they had just bought. It had been a great trip, and the whole family had had a fun time.

Soft rays of sunlight shot down from the heavens and bounced across the water, heating the water slightly. Little Jessicana, her hair braided and hanging down her back, gazed at the crystal cool waters with her big blue eyes. It was the most beautiful thing she had ever seen.

As her family sipped on coconut milk and mango smoothies, Jessicana leaned over the side, captivated by the ocean. She felt it drawing her in, and she showed no resistance, bending closer and closer to the water. Jessicana splashed her face with the cool water and dipped her arms in, enjoying the feeling, enticed.

A wave of water crashed over her head, and Jessicana plunged into the sea. She panicked and flailed her arms wildly, fighting to get to the surface, but the water resisted her, pushing her deeper and deeper from the light.

The ocean was no longer beautiful but a trap, and Jessicana struggled to breathe as water filled her mouth and nose. Black spots danced before her eyes, and she could barely feel the sensation of motherly arms pulling her toward the surface.

Strong arms pushed on her chest, and Jessicana's eyes fluttered open. Coughing wildly, Jessicana realized she wasn't on her family's boat and sat up, panicked and scared. A pale hand—much like her own, only larger—touched her shoulder gently, and soon Jessicana was staring into a pair of blue eyes that strongly resembled hers.

A beautiful woman was gazing at her, and Jessicana tilted her head in wonder. What was going on?

"Are you all right?" the woman asked softly. Jessicana then noticed a girl with reddish-brown hair who looked to be about her age standing behind the woman. The woman was biting her lip but had the face of a leader.

"Y-yes," Jessicana stammered, but before she could say anything more, her family's boat pulled up beside the woman's. Her parents embraced her. Jessicana could hear them repeating over and over again, "Leader Danette, how can we thank you?" and "How can we ever repay you?"

It was true. Danette had rescued Jessicana from drowning, and in the process, the blonde little girl had gained a new friend, Roseabelle. The two became close friends despite their differences. Roseabelle was brave, bold, and a deep thinker. Jessicana had a thirst for learning, some spunk, and much loyalty.

JESSICANA BLINKED AS THE MEMORY FADED, AND SHE LOOKED at Astro and the dolphin that was pulling their boat. The craft suddenly stopped, and Roseabelle, dripping wet, pulled herself out of the water into the boat. Astro handed her a towel, and she squeezed her drenched hair, drying it only somewhat.

"It's beautiful out here," Roseabelle said, and Jessicana wondered if her friend remembered the memory she had just relived.

"Yes," Jessicana replied softly.

"Anyone got snacks?" Astro asked, and Roseabelle rolled her eyes, pulling out a mini lunch sack. Jessicana could have sworn she heard Roseabelle mutter, "Boys."

Roseabelle passed a banana to Jessicana and a thermos of hot soup to Astro. Jessicana ate her food slowly, while Astro drained the thermos in a few gulps. There was silence for a few moments as they all enjoyed the view, and then Astro stood up and suddenly gasped.

"Did you see that?" he asked incredulously.

Jessicana's brow crinkled. "See what?" she asked.

Astro pointed wildly out to sea. "There's a huge black ship over there!"

Jessicana squinted, and she could see Roseabelle doing the same. "I don't see anything," she replied.

Astro kept pointing. "Keep looking," he insisted.

A cloud of mist Jessicana hadn't noticed before cleared away, and in its place stood a large black ship that was sailing toward them. Her breath caught. Benotripians didn't have black ships.

"Roseabelle," Jessicana started nervously. "You don't think—"

"I do," Roseabelle answered. "We have to check it out."

"What?" Jessicana yelped. Even Astro looked slightly uneasy.

"But, Roseabelle," Astro protested. "If it's . . . well . . . the—"

"It's got to be the Darvonians," Roseabelle confirmed, squinting even harder. "I can tell. Please, trust me on this one."

"Shouldn't we be turning around then?" Jessicana squeaked. "I mean, if it is them?"

Roseabelle shook her head. "No. We need to sneak up on them, make sure it really is them before we tell everyone that Benotripia is about to be invaded. Maybe the Darvonians are lost in the fog."

Astro snorted. "Yes, I'm sure they set out on a quest to find a friendly sea monster, but before they could, they got lost in some fog and ended up so near to Benotripia, they could be spotted. Yeah, no."

Roseabelle glared at him. "Thank you, Captain Sunshine, for clearing that up. Look, we need to go after that ship." She turned back to the front and then squinted. "Where'd it go?"

Jessicana surveyed the ocean. Where was the ship? Well, at least one thing was clear.

It had disappeared.

* * * * *

As soon as the boat docked, the three friends leaped out and headed their separate ways with plenty to think about. Astro headed north, Jessicana east, and Roseabelle west, each toward their own homes.

The truth was, the ship was the least of Astro's worries. Astro had another problem, something that he feared was much worse. Every time he shot a lightning bolt, something felt wrong. It wasn't the same; it was almost too powerful. One time he was aiming at the sky, and after a few minutes, the bolt came sailing back down and struck him.

Of course Astro had just absorbed the charge, but it still bothered him. Even worse, it now took effort to shoot a lightning bolt. He just didn't know what to do.

Astro had thought of talking to his dad about it and asking if maybe this was a traditional thing that happened to their family, but for some reason he felt compelled to stay quiet. For one thing, Mr. Jagged-Bolt was almost never around, and their father-son relationship had never been too strong. And as for his mother . . . well, as much as Astro loved her dearly, she wasn't the kind to believe his story.

He'd been tempted many times to tell his friends, but how exactly could he? There'd been countless opportunities, yet Astro didn't know why he'd resisted. His thoughts drifted back to the day he had figured out what his power was.

He was only seven years old, about to start school at the Central Power Training Academy. Astro sighed. He still hadn't gained his power and he knew no one who would be attending with him. His parents told him every day that his power was sure to appear any day now.

But it still hadn't come.

Those days, Astro was pretty much a loner. Most mornings, he'd wake up, get dressed, have a quick breakfast, and rush to the forest to try to find his power. He'd tried lifting weights, but he didn't get far, so obviously he wasn't super strong. He'd jumped off a high boulder into a pool of water, scraping his knee in the process. It soon was clear he couldn't fly. Astro had tried practically everything.

As Astro struggled to turn invisible, a dark cloud overshadowed him. Unsettled, he looked up. Large storm clouds were crowding up above, and Astro blinked. A huge storm was brewing, which was unlikely for Benotripia. Sure, they often had light drizzles, but they hadn't had a nasty storm in years.

Thunder rumbled across the sky and, panicked, Astro ran. Sheets of rain came showering down, blinding him, and Astro fought to see through the torrent of water. Where could he run? Which direction was his home? With a sickening jolt, Astro realized he couldn't tell.

He bit his lip and sat down on a large wet rock, underneath the protection of a tall bush, and decided to wait the storm out, even though his parents would be worried sick. Astro had just settled into a stupor when a small cry echoed out in the opening.

Astro immediately sat up, alert with his ears and eyes. The sound was coming closer and closer now. "Help!" a young girl's voice called out.

"Jessicana, I hate to say it, but I don't think anyone can hear us," another girl's voice responded.

"But I can't see anything! I want to go home."

"It'll be all right. We'll just have to wait the storm out."

Astro pushed through some soaked leaves and burst into the wide clearing that revealed two girls huddling under a clump of bushes. One had auburn ringlets cascading down her back, and the other had blonde hair pulled into a ponytail.

"Hello?" he called out, and the two girls spotted him. "Hi, I'm Astro," he said nervously. He'd never really spoken to kids his age. "I'm stuck in the storm too. Do you want to find our way home together?"

The auburn-haired girl stood up, a confident expression on her face. He could tell instantly that she had been the one soothing the other girl, Jessicana. She eyed Astro warily and finally extended her hand. "I'm Roseabelle. My mom is Leader Danette, the ruler of Benotripia."

Astro accepted her hand and shook it. "Wait. Your mom's the ruler of Benotripia?"

Roseabelle nodded like it was no big deal. "Yeah. This is my friend Jessicana." Roseabelle turned to the blonde. "Do you think you could see better if you transformed?"

Jessicana shook her head, watching Astro with piqued interest. "I'm not sure."

Astro's interest suddenly climbed. "Transform into what?"

"Jessicana can turn into a parrot. It's her power."

"What's yours?" Astro pressed, excited to meet someone his age who had powers.

Roseabelle grinned broadly. "My mom suspects that I might be a Meta-Mord, someone who has many different unique abilities. The only power I know how to do right now is to move things with my mind, but I'm not very good at it. What's your power, Astro?"

Astro gulped. "I don't know yet."

Roseabelle shrugged. “That’s okay. You’ll surely find out at the Academy.”

Jessicana stood up. “Let’s find our homes together. Can we try and find mine first? I live in a tree, kind of next to Juniper Jungle.”

Above them, lightning flashed, and Jessicana flinched. It was extremely close.

Astro figured she was getting more scared by the minute, so he gestured forward. “I think I can find that jungle. Come this way.” He set out underneath a large tree, the girls in front of him, when a flash of white and yellow snaked toward him. “Watch out!” he yelled and plowed into Roseabelle and Jessicana, knocking them aside just in time.

The girls screamed as lightning struck Astro, but he didn’t even cry out. There was no pain. He felt as though he was getting stronger. But that was impossible.

And then it dawned on him: he had his father’s power. He could shoot lightning bolts out of his fingertips.

Astro stood and brushed himself off, ready to meet the surprised stares of his newfound friends. He managed a small smile. “I think I know what my power is,” he offered, and they slowly began to grin as well.

ASTRO SHOOK HIMSELF OUT OF THE MEMORY AS HE TRUDGED along in the sand. That day had been truly memorable because that had been the day he’d met his two best friends and gained his power—the very thing Astro had been worried about.

CHAPTER 3

Ribbon of Passageways

Jessicana knocked on Roseabelle's door with her knuckles, hoping that her friend would answer. Her mother had warned that she needed Jessicana to be quick and back before noon—not a minute less—which meant that Jessicana had only an hour to perform her errand.

The bronze door swung open, and Jessicana sighed in relief to see that her auburn-haired friend was standing in the doorway. "Hey, Roseabelle," Jessicana greeted breathlessly. "Is it all right if I go up to the tower room? Mom needs this specific book and she sent me to borrow it."

"Sure, go on up," Roseabelle said. "Do you want to have lunch with me?"

Jessicana shook her head. "That'd be great, but Mom wants me back right away. Sorry to bother you."

Roseabelle laughed. "You're fine, Jessicana. What are friends for?"

Jessicana whispered a "thank you" and then ran up Roseabelle's staircase and into her library. It looked just as it always did—thick books stacked in neat rows on the wall, and scrolls stacked on the bookshelves in the corner. The odor of fresh ink and paper filled the room.

Jessicana always felt light-headed when she entered the tower room because it was filled with what she loved most—books. Some days, Jessicana went to Roseabelle's and spent the entire time devouring book after book, delighting in every moment. But right now Jessicana needed to find *Ten Ways to Clean a Fireplace* for her mother.

The blonde scoured the shelves, frantically searching, but found nothing. Jessicana continued to fight the urges to borrow books for herself. She needed to get out of the tower room fast because Jessicana was guessing she only had a few minutes left until her mother was expecting her back.

A golden twinkle suddenly caught her eye, but Jessicana ignored it and bent down to the lowest shelf. And, of course, there it was. She gently pulled out the book. Just as she was about to leave, the golden twinkle caught her eye again.

It was a book sticking halfway out of its shelf. It had a drab black cover but shiny golden lettering. When Jessicana leaned closer, she could see a handprint against the dusty surface. As she bent closer to examine it, she realized with an unsettling feeling that the handprint was much too large and bulky to have come from Roseabelle or Danette's hand.

It's fine, Jessicana thought. *Someone probably wanted to borrow it or something, just like I'm doing now.* Nevertheless, Jessicana pulled it out and placed it on her knee.

The fancy lettering read *Fables & Myths*. Jessicana cautiously flipped through the pages, skimming some of the words, not really paying attention to any particular headings or chapters.

It seemed to be just a classic fairy-tale storybook. Just as Jessicana was about to shut it and run back to her home, she landed on an extremely colorful page that had a faded black ribbon hanging out of it. Jessicana cautiously raised the ribbon and examined it more closely. It was frayed and torn. She couldn't imagine any Benotripian wanting it as a bookmark. It radiated darkness and cold. Jessicana shivered. It distinctly reminded her of the feather that had taken Roseabelle into the dream world.

Then chills ran up her spine. What if the ribbon didn't belong to a Benotripian? What if Darvonians were here on the island? No, no, it couldn't be. But still it would all make sense—the boat out on the water, the ribbon, and even the handprint. Something important had to be in this book.

Jessicana trained her eyes on the page where she had found the ribbon. "The Lost Stones of Horsh," she read quietly and continued. "Once, a poor young Darvonian named Horsh set off on an adventure. He was completely oblivious to his surroundings and to what sort of culture he was being raised in. Darnash Horsh, as we know him, left his home seeking adventure and eventually found a bright colorful island called Benotripia.

"The young man ventured onto the island and soon realized where he came from and who he was. Horsh listened to the Benotripian stories with sympathy and discovered that he had been born in the wrong territory. He became one of Benotripia's people.

"But Horsh had a secret: he was very powerful and had three magical Stones. One could create, one could destroy, and one could heal. He decided to hide the Stones, fearing that his former kindred would find them, and lived the rest of his days peacefully."

Below the story were large silver letters in a fancy font reading, "The End." Jessicana knitted her brow. She had never heard of this fairy tale before and couldn't help wondering why a Darvonian would want to read it. Absentmindedly, she slipped the ribbon into her pocket.

Of course Darvonians aren't on the island! Jessicana decided that she was just being silly and ran out of the tower room.

* * * * *

ROSEABELLE SAT ON HER PORCH, SLOWLY SIPPING A mango smoothie and staring out at the lush landscape of Benotripia. She couldn't help but think about the large black ship she and her friends had spotted yesterday. Of course it could've been just an illusion, but Roseabelle was so sure she had seen it.

Another option was that it was the Darvonians, ready to invade the island. But that ship would've reached Benotripia by now, and Danette would've been notified if the Darvonians had attacked them.

"The Darvonians aren't here," she told herself. "Stop being silly, Roseabelle." She tried to relax and lie back against her chair but eventually just snapped her eyes open.

"Roseabelle! Roseabelle!" a strangled voice cried out, and Roseabelle bolted up in her seat. Jessicana was running toward her, one hand gripping something. "What is it?" Roseabelle asked.

"Roseabelle," Jessicana panted. "I found this in one of your books. Here, look."

Her blonde friend was displaying a worn black ribbon. "I went home and gave Mom the book I borrowed from you. You see, while I was looking for it, there was this book that was sticking out on its shelf. The ribbon marked a specific chapter. That book had something important in it, Roseabelle. And I'm pretty sure the Darvonians took it, read it, and brought it back so it wouldn't look suspicious."

Roseabelle blinked. "And why are you assuming this?"

"I put the ribbon up in my room," Jessicana said frantically. "And honestly—I don't know—I just felt so angry and tired. I felt like I'd done something terribly wrong. I wanted to curl up into a little ball and hide."

"Jessicana," Roseabelle breathed. "What if this is like the feather? Remember how it took me into the dream world?"

Jessicana turned pale, started to shake as though she was having a seizure, and instantly ripped the ribbon from

Roseabelle's hand. "If it's a passage to the dream world," Jessicana stressed, "we can't keep it!"

Roseabelle put a hand on Jessicana's shoulder. "This is proof that Darvonians might be on the island. I'm going to talk to my mom about this. You stay at home and rest. Thank you for bringing this to me."

Jessicana nodded and hurried off, leaving Roseabelle with the ribbon. The auburn-haired girl rubbed her fingers over it and was surprised to realize she felt none of the emotions Jessicana had described. Puzzled, she deposited the ribbon in her pocket and walked inside. Danette was out and about, signing petitions in Fetherbark City, although she had promised Roseabelle she'd be back before sunset.

And Roseabelle knew she'd keep her promise.

CHAPTER 4
Darvonians!

ASTRO JOGGED ALONG THE SMOOTH SHORES, BREATHING heavily. He wiped the sweat from his brow and continued on, his eyes trained on the path he was taking. Astro felt he needed to get out of the house, breathe some fresh air, and exercise.

It was refreshing to be outside in the cool breeze, and, for a moment, Astro forgot about all the things that were troubling him.

He headed for Juniper Jungle, ready to jog through, when a flash of black caught his eye. Astro jerked his head up, on the alert. Just as he was ready to dismiss the sudden movement as a figment of his imagination, there it was again. Astro leveled his fingers at the trees, ready to strike at any moment.

Suddenly, two branches parted. Before he could react, Astro realized he was staring into the face of a pale-skinned, dark-haired man. The face staring at him mirrored the shock of Astro's own expression. Then the branches were released, and the face disappeared from view.

"Hey!" Astro roared, and he plunged into the jungle, his face red with fury as the truth set in. Who he had just seen was no ordinary person, and he intended to catch him. Without even thinking about it, a jagged silver lightning bolt erupted from his pointer finger and bounced off a series of tree trunks. Astro felt as though he'd just been punched in the stomach, and he grimaced. Whenever he shot a large bolt like that, consequences followed.

Up ahead, Astro could hear the nimble sprinting of feet, and he panted as he struggled to keep up with the man. It wasn't working. The man was too fast. A strangled shout sounded up ahead, and Astro gulped. It wasn't a common Benotripian language, so he couldn't understand.

Astro felt a rush of air above him and looked up just in time to see an open metal cage falling down. He quickly burst ahead, and the trap thudded behind him. He could hear alarmed cries coming from the treetops, and he bit his lip. They knew he was here, and he no longer knew where he was going.

Dark shapes appeared in the trees, and an arrow whistled past his ear. Panicked, Astro randomly shot a bolt at a palm tree with a dark shape balanced behind it, and a scream rang out. Astro winced as pain filled his entire body. What was going on?

Half a dozen arrows came hurtling toward him, their piercing points gleaming. Three, by a miracle, somehow missed him completely, two grazed his knee, and one tore his shirt. Astro clenched his fists. He had to find them. He had to find the camp.

Just as he was about to charge through a clearing, several armed figures in cloaks and battle armor appeared in his path. Without even thinking about it, Astro turned and ran. A few arrows whistled above his head, but none of the men's shots could match his frightening speed.

Why was Astro running? Why didn't he stand and fight? Because the men were Darvonians.

* * * * *

"ROSEABELLE!" DANETTE CALLED SOFTLY. "ROSEABELLE, come down please!"

Roseabelle sat up in bed, disgruntled, her hair frizzy and out of control. Had someone just called her name? She wasn't sure. Roseabelle paused for a moment, waiting for the voice, but nothing came. She got up out of bed and strained her ears. Nothing.

Deciding it had just been from her dreams, Roseabelle was about to climb back into bed when she heard her mother call, "Roseabelle! Please come down."

"So it wasn't just my imagination," Roseabelle whispered. She walked out of her room, curious. Why was Danette calling for her in the middle of the night?

The auburn-haired girl trudged sleepily down the stairs, dressed in pajama pants and a T-shirt. "Yes, Mom?" she asked sleepily.

"Roseabelle, I must leave." Danette sighed quietly.

Roseabelle couldn't believe her ears. "What?" she cried out.

"There's been an attack in Northern Benotripia," Danette explained. "I have to go and help. Many Benotripians have been hurt, and it is my duty to aid them."

Roseabelle buried her face in her hands. "Mother, you can't! Please, no. I think the Darvonians may be on the island." The redhead recounted seeing the large ship on the sea and Jessicana discovering the book in the library. "They have to be here," she said desperately. "We need you, Mom! I need you."

Danette put a hand on her daughter's shoulder. "Roseabelle, I have to go. The people are calling me, and it is my duty to respond. Send a mottel if you find real proof that the Darvonians are here." Mottels were birds that were used to send messages in Benotripia. "But for now, I must go. I'm truly sorry."

Roseabelle was close to tears. "But, Mom—"

Danette stroked her daughter's hair. "Be careful, Roseabelle. We still don't know what caused the attack, but it's a major issue. There are families out there that need my leadership and hope. If I could, I'd investigate what you said about the Darvonians. When I get back, I promise that will be the first thing I'll do."

Roseabelle managed a small smile. "Thanks, Mom."

Her mother planted a kiss on her head and squeezed her tightly. "I should be back in less than a month. If not, I promise you I will be back no later than two months. Thank you for being so understanding, Roseabelle."

With those last words, Danette slipped out the door. "I'm not understanding," Roseabelle muttered. "I need you. Now."

She peeked out the window and watched as a figure rose into the sky, hair tumbling down its back. Roseabelle knew it was her mother. As a late-night snack, she pulled out some orange juice and small nuts in some milk. After she ate the small meal, she slowly walked up to her room and climbed into bed.

Tap, tap, tap. Roseabelle jolted upright and wildly looked around the room. What had made that sound? She slowly lowered herself back down, but then she heard it again. *Tap, tap, tap.* Confused, Roseabelle wrenched open her window, and her jaw went slack. Astro was hanging on to the windowsill, face distraught and pinched.

"Astro!" she shrieked. "What are you doing?"

"Is Danette here?" he demanded. "I need her. Now."

Roseabelle felt a pang in her stomach. "Astro, Danette just left for Northern Benotripia. There was an attack there, and she's gone to help."

Astro looked so startled, he almost dropped from the sill. "What? But, Roseabelle, you don't understand. I saw Darvonians!"

Roseabelle froze. "You can't be serious," she said hoarsely.

"I'm dead serious," Astro assured her.

"Tell Jessicana," Roseabelle ordered. "Then go back to your house and orchestrate a plan."

Astro opened his mouth to protest but then shrugged. "Okay. I will. But I'm coming over in the morning. Early. We need to do something about this." He paused. "Wait, can't we just tell the Benotripians?"

Roseabelle snorted. "How? I may be the daughter of Danette, but there's no way I could reach all those people in time. And besides, some of them might not believe me."

"What? That's ridiculous!"

"But it's true," Roseabelle answered grimly. "I'm not the ruler of the island. They have a right not to listen to me."

"But you saved their leader," Astro argued. "You're going to inherit the island in the future someday, anyway. They should listen to you!"

Roseabelle shrugged. "Without confirmation from Danette, my words are meaningless. Now go get Jessicana and start planning. I need some time alone."

Astro sat on the thick tree branch and nodded to her. "Good luck." Then he dropped to the ground below.

"I'm going to need it," Roseabelle muttered dryly, and then she shut her window softly.

* * * * *

JESSICANA GAVE ASTRO A BLANK STARE. "ARE YOU CRAZY? So the Darvonians are here. You almost got killed. And now you want to go after them without Roseabelle?"

Astro shot her a pleading look. "I just want to verify. Jessicana, this might be our only chance to locate the Darvonian camp. And besides, Roseabelle needs some time alone. She has a lot to think about."

Jessicana crossed her arms in an annoyed sort of way and glared at Astro. "All right," she said. "But if we die out there, I'm going to kill you." And with that, she flounced from her porch, transformed into a parrot, and flew off. Astro ran after her, trying the best he could to be stealthy.

Jessicana flapped her wings and soared over the forest.

"Awk, awk," she squawked. "Stay behind." If the Darvonians saw a parrot flying in the sky, they'd think it would be completely normal because there were countless parrots in Benotripia. But if they saw Astro, they would figure out Jessicana's true identity.

The blonde girl soared over the treetops, scouting for any sign of the Darvonians, but the only sight that met her eyes was the lush vegetation of the jungle. Monkeys swung from tree to tree, and a jaguar lurked inside the murky shadows of the vines.

Plumes of smoke curling into the air finally caught her attention, and Jessicana dove toward it, trying as best as she could to act like a normal parrot, intrigued by the smoke. Astro was now far behind her, and she decided that it might be better that way. He could easily give their hiding spot away without even trying.

The low murmuring of soft voices reached Jessicana's ears, and she dove even faster, then slowed considerably before perching on a tree. The voices suddenly broke off, and Jessicana's eyes lit up. The Darvonians had to be here. Jessicana flapped her wings twice and lifted into the air, gazing below, her sharp eyes searching frantically for her enemies.

An arrow whizzed past her beak, and Jessicana squawked in alarm and took off. Of course, they would shoot at her. She had been mistaken. They had to be suspicious because they already knew of her power, due to Sheklyth's spy report while she had pretended to be Shelby.

Jessicana rose even higher into the sky, hoping that Astro had found a way to prove that the Darvonians were there. Of course, the arrow was almost enough proof. No Benotripian would shoot at a parrot no matter the circumstances, just in case the bird was actually a shape-shifter.

She dropped down onto a thick branch and morphed back into a girl. Then she looked around. Jessicana estimated that she had heard the voices not too far away, so she carefully swung onto a branch, her sweaty palms grasping the thick wood. She grimaced. She could do this. Jessicana remembered how Asteran had trained her to swing from the ropes in case she ever fell from the sky. "If that ever happens," he had told her gravely, "quickly turn back into your human form and grasp on to whatever you can find."

Jessicana felt a pang of sadness as she thought about Asteran. They'd never truly learned where his loyalties had landed. One day, Jessicana had followed him through the forest and found a feather that he had dropped. It had turned out to be an entrance to the Darvonian dream world, so the three friends had never really discovered whose side Asteran had been on.

Jessicana grimaced and swung to the next branch, blisters forming on her bruised hands from gripping the hard wood. *Come on*, she thought. *You can do this, Jessicana.*

A hand suddenly tapped her shoulder while another hand covered her mouth, smothering a scream that came within her throat. Jessicana froze, barely holding on to her branch. A voice whispered in her ear, "It's just me. Astro. Step carefully onto the trunk of the tree."

Jessicana obliged and glared furiously at her friend. "You scared me to death," she hissed.

Astro shrugged. "Sorry. I didn't want you screaming because you thought the Darvonians had found you. Anyway, I think you should see this. Follow me and don't make a sound."

Jessicana gestured to the trees. "I'll travel up here and meet you." Astro nodded and disappeared in a cloud of swirling leaves. Jessicana turned her attention back to the trees and bit her lip. Unbeknownst to Roseabelle and Astro, Asteran had given her a magical object that Jessicana had kept secret from both of them until now. She vowed to herself that as soon as she returned, she would tell them about it.

It was a silver ring with an emerald embedded in the center

of it, and when the jewel was pressed, it turned into some kind of grappling hook. Jessicana reached deep inside her pocket, pulled out the ring, put it on her finger, and pressed the gem. Two large ropes with metal hooks sprouted out of the ring noiselessly, which Jessicana was grateful for. Just as she had suspected, they had a golden aura of power around them. The ring wasn't just a normal grappling hook. One of the ropes was used for actual grappling and could never miss as long as she kept the destination she wanted it to take hold of in her mind. The other hook could fight off enemies or pursuers that were below or above, knocking them out of the air and away from the person who was wearing the ring.

The ring was a Grapplegore, and, for some reason, Jessicana had never used it. Until today. She unwound the first hook and hurled it to a high thick branch. She focused on the picture in her mind intently, imagining the hook digging deep inside the solid wood. Jessicana wasn't surprised to see the hook sink into the tree as though it was made of putty. She made a note for the other hook to knock out any enemies that might be lurking below, and swung off the branch, eyes trained upward.

Jessicana landed on the high branch and continued to swing the Grapplegore, never missing. Chills ran down her spine at her success, and a broad grin stretched over her face. She felt invincible, as if she could accomplish anything. Transforming into a parrot was nothing compared to this.

"Psst," someone hissed from below, and Jessicana glanced down to see Astro staring up at her, an expression of mild surprise frozen on his face. "What is that thing?" he breathed, and Jessicana dropped to the ground silently beside him.

"I'll explain later," she whispered back. "Where are the Darvonians?"

Astro put a finger to his lips and then motioned for her to follow him. They soon crept into a clump of bushes. When Astro silently parted a few branches, Jessicana peered through the vegetation.

Their enemies' camp was so small that Jessicana was surprised they had found it at all. There was one large silver tent with two small black ones. A black boat was anchored to a wooden platform, and three hooded Darvonians crouched over a fireplace full of soot. The smell of burning wood drifted into the air.

"We go after the journal tomorrow," a deep voice commanded.

"Do we even know where it is?" a second voice demanded. Jessicana bit her lip. She could have sworn it was female.

A cold voice that made goose bumps rise on her arms spoke. "Of course we do, Heltonine. The Aku Mountains. Haven't you been attending the meetings?"

"Silence!" the man's voice boomed. "Horsh's Stones are very valuable. We must retrieve them before those twisted little younglings find out as well."

"Yes, we would all hate to have them on our trail," drawled the colder voice. Jessicana wondered why it seemed so familiar. She sensed a trace of sarcasm in the figure's voice.

"Don't underestimate them," the masculine voice corrected. "Each of the brats are powerful in their own way. I thought you would have learned your lesson since the dungeon escapade. That was entirely your fault."

"Agree to disagree," the cold voice answered, and suddenly Jessicana recognized it. It was Sheklyth's. Sheklyth was here. The woman who had thoughtlessly betrayed Roseabelle. Of course.

Jessicana glanced at Astro, who had a shocked expression on his face. Then it hit her. The book. The Stones of Horsh. Their theory that a Darvonian had read that specific chapter. It all made sense. Could the Stones of Horsh be real?

The Darvonians definitely seemed sure about what they were saying. What if the Stones were so powerful that their enemies could use them to take over Benotripia? One look at Astro, and Jessicana knew he was thinking the same thing.

Astro pointed to the jungle and Jessicana nodded. They needed to get out of here. As they inched out of their hiding place, Astro stepped on a dry twig, and Jessicana winced as a loud crack filled the entire jungle.

"What was that?" the cold voice questioned.

The man answered, "Over there. They're over there!"

Jessicana seized Astro's arm, and they burst out of their hiding spot, oblivious to the warning shouts of the Darvonians behind them. "Go!" Astro demanded. "Transform into a parrot. I'll hold them off."

Jessicana shook her head. "No. I'll distract them. Run as quick as you can to Roseabelle's."

"But, Jessicana—"

"Go!" she ordered fiercely, and Astro ran. Jessicana quickly vaulted up onto a thick tree branch and pressed the gem on her ring. She could hear the Darvonians behind her. Aiming for an extremely high spot out of the Darvonian's reach, Jessicana hurled the grappling hook and pictured in her mind where she wanted it to land. The hook obeyed her, and Jessicana jumped, swinging the second grappling hook toward the ground, throwing off her enemies.

Arrows whizzed past her, missing her by inches. Jessicana forced a lump down her throat and tried to concentrate on escaping. Jessicana kept grappling, and behind her she could hear the angry shouts of the dark ones. Her pale arms shook as she swung from tree to tree, her blonde hair flapping in the wind. From up ahead she heard an urgent call from Astro. "Jessicana, hurry!"

Spears were thrown at her, but the hook effortlessly knocked them away. The steel wire that connected the ring to the hook sliced the arrows in half without any strain. Jessicana grimaced. She only had yards to go before she would be clear. She could hear Astro's anxious shouts ahead, which forced her to concentrate more.

Jessicana narrowed her eyes; she was so close. Only a few

more swings. Two more swings. One more swing. She closed her eyes, waiting for the sunshine to enclose her, but instead she was greeted by a severe dose of pain. Jessicana gasped as she fell to the ground, dazed and unmoving.

Then an arm pulled her upright and almost dragged her into the sun. But, try as she might, Jessicana couldn't focus. Stars danced before her eyes, and she tumbled to the ground.

CHAPTER 5

Aku Mountains

Jessicana blinked as water dripped slowly onto her forehead, completely mesmerizing her. She lay still for a second and then couldn't help it anymore. She sat up. She was in Roseabelle's living room. Astro was kneeling beside her, and Roseabelle stood above her, pressing a cool cloth to her forehead. "You're awake," she commented softly.

"What happened?" Jessicana whispered.

"You got shot," Astro replied. "An arrow went straight into your palm. You're going to be all right though." His voice was uneven, and Jessicana got the feeling he was a lot more shaken up than he let on.

"Did you use my potion kit?" Jessicana asked weakly. Roseabelle shook her head. "We didn't want to risk it. For all we knew, we could be force-feeding you poison instead of a healing powder."

Jessicana looked at both of her friends. "So is Astro officially grounded for dragging me out there?"

"Hey!" Astro protested. "It was for a good cause!"

A small smile played across Roseabelle's lips. "Yes, definitely. No more spying on the Darvonians or getting into life-or-death experiences for a week, Astro."

He pretended to pout. "Darn it! I was hoping to outdo Jessicana. Maybe get an arrow in my elbow or something."

Jessicana gritted her teeth as pain surged through her hand. She realized it was wrapped in bandages that were slightly tinted red. "Believe me, you don't want it to get any worse than this."

Roseabelle's fingers brushed Jessicana's uninjured hand where the silver ring rested. "What's that?" her friend asked curiously, and Jessicana quickly laid out the shorter version of how she had gained the ring. Roseabelle nodded thoughtfully. "Interesting," she muttered.

"What?"

Astro's face darkened. "You know what this means, right?"

Jessicana blinked. "Start over again?"

"The Stones of Horsh are real. And the Darvonians are looking for them. They must be powerful to catch their interest."

Roseabelle tilted her head. "So how do we stop them, then?"

Astro tapped his chin thoughtfully. "Easy. Find the Stones first, destroy them before the Darvonians can get them, and then drive the Darvonians off the island. Simple and effective."

Jessicana rolled her eyes. "Thanks for summing that up. But I don't think it's going to be as simple as that. We don't even know where the Stones are."

Astro stood up so suddenly that Roseabelle's hair lifted a few inches. "Wait! Jessicana, didn't the Darvonians mention something about the Aku Mountains?"

Jessicana nodded enthusiastically. "Yeah. And something about a journal."

Astro's face glowed with excitement. "What if that journal used to belong to someone who knows the location of the Stones? And it's hidden in the Aku Mountains! We can find the journal, learn the location of the Stones, find them, and destroy them. You follow me?"

Roseabelle poured some ointment onto Jessicana's wound. "Astro, are you sure the Darvonians weren't just trying to distract us from the real reason why they're here?"

"Positive," Astro responded. "They didn't even know we were listening until we tried to leave."

"You don't know that," Roseabelle warned him. "The Darvonians can be crafty."

Astro rolled his eyes. "Are we just going to ignore this, then? Come on, Roseabelle. First the ribbon in the book. Then we eavesdrop on them, and you say they're just tricking us."

Roseabelle glowered at him. "This is the Darvonians we're talking about. They kidnapped my mother, betrayed me, invaded the island, and now they've driven out of our reach the only person on this island who could help us to Northern Benotripia."

Jessicana frowned. "Can't we reach her by mottel?"

Roseabelle sighed, sounding defeated. "She can't help us now. If she returns, then the Darvonians might attack Northern Benotripia again."

"Wait, so you think the Darvonians attacked Northern Benotripia?" Astro questioned.

Roseabelle snorted. "Who else?"

Jessicana bit her lip. "Roseabelle, I hate to say it, but I think Astro's right. We have to go after those Stones."

Astro frowned. "Excuse me? You hate to say it?"

Roseabelle sighed. "The Aku Mountains, huh?"

Jessicana nodded enthusiastically. "Please, Roseabelle."

Her friend shrugged. "Well, I guess it can't hurt to embark on another dangerous mission. You guys in?"

Astro pumped the air with his fist. "Oh yeah!"

"Let's do this," Jessicana said, and Roseabelle pulled out the magical trutan they had found last year. Roseabelle had inherited the trutan, which possessed magical qualities, from Danette. Whatever you drew on it came to life.

"All right. Astro, scout for animals we can ride and make

sure that the Darvonians don't go anywhere. Jessicana, go with him. I'll draw what we need."

Jessicana nodded. "C'mon, Astro!" she urged, standing up, wincing only slightly at the pain coming from her bandaged hand.

* * * * *

WITH HER POINTED PEN DIPPED IN CHERRY-RED INK, Roseabelle slowly drew three large backpacks on the trutan, careful to include lots of details. She added deep pockets in the front of the pack, bags of food and water, sleeping bags, and solar hand warmers. "We're going to need something to defend ourselves with," she muttered and climbed the stairs to her mother's study.

This year, Danette had come up with two different and completely original weapons. One was a web of steel wires. At the head of each wire, a spearhead was attached, tilting to the right. All one had to do was twirl the contraption and all the spearheads would detach and fly straight at the enemy. Danette had called it a Spidegar, due to all the wires twirling in complicated patterns. A few minutes after, new spearheads would grow in.

The second weapon was a long-range device. It was a black cylinder shaped like a cannon, but much smaller. It spat out masses of iron, fire, earth, and electricity. One shot in the face with that could easily dispatch an enemy. It was commonly known as the Flame-hurler.

Roseabelle stepped inside her mother's study and instantly spotted a Spidegar hanging on the wall, its polished wires gleaming brightly in the sunlight. Roseabelle gritted her teeth, stood on Danette's desk, and wrenched the weapon to the ground. Now where would she find a Flame-hurler?

Roseabelle searched and searched but found nothing. A small cupboard finally caught her eye, and she quickly knelt down next to it and pulled the long, ornate golden handle open. But the thing wouldn't budge. Roseabelle pulled harder and harder but then let go and sat back. It was locked.

Where could the key be? If Danette had it, then there was no way she could open it, but maybe if her mother had left the key sitting around here somewhere . . .

Roseabelle checked the desk drawers, frantically groping for a key, a hammer, or something that could smash the cupboard and let her in.

At last, her bare fingers closed over a cool piece of metal, and Roseabelle lifted it up triumphantly. It was a large silver key, the edges jagged and fitting the exact shape of the keyhole in the cupboard.

Roseabelle stood and walked over to the cupboard, then thrust the key inside. She heard a small clicking noise, and the door swung open. Just as she had thought, two Flame-hurlers rested inside. She heaved them out along with a whole package of ammo: medium-sized, ash-colored spheres that could fit easily inside.

She walked downstairs with the weapons in her arms and crouched down next to the backpacks. They were fully formed, and Roseabelle tossed them aside as she carefully copied the models of the weapons on the trutan, making multiple drawings.

The three friends were going to be fully armed, no doubt about that.

Jessicana and Astro returned late in the evening, their faces flushed from sprinting back to the house. "The Darvonians didn't leave their spot," Astro panted. "But we're pretty sure they plan to leave tomorrow."

Roseabelle held up the three backpacks, the Flame-hurlers and Spidegars, and the other assortment of swords, shields, spears, daggers, bows and arrows, javelins, Thepgiles, Trapitas, and Dragocone Rays she had found underneath a hidden floorboard in her mother's study. Danette was definitely prepared.

They all distributed the weapons. Astro took a broadsword along with a Spidegar, a shield, a spear, and a Flame-hurler. Jessicana stuffed a javelin, a couple of throwing knives, and a Thepgile inside her pack, and Roseabelle grabbed a Flame-hurler, a bow and a couple of quivers of arrows, a shield, a sword, a Trapita, and a Dragocone Ray. They pushed the rest of the weapons against the door and faced each other, their faces grim and determined.

"Are we walking, then?" Jessicana asked uncertainly.

"Yes," Roseabelle confirmed. "If we hurry, we can be to the mountains before dawn. Jessicana, you'll fly behind us to make sure the Darvonians don't sneak up on us. I will go in front. Astro will be in the middle."

"Wait a second," Astro interrupted. "Why don't you draw some kind of land animal on the trutan so we can ride to the mountains instead of walk? The Aku Mountain Range is far from Royalton City."

Roseabelle nodded. "Good idea. I drew some food and water inside our packs, but stocking up a bit more won't hurt. Would you two do that for me?"

"Sure," they agreed. Roseabelle then ascended the stairway where the trutan was waiting.

* * * * *

ASTRO STOOD ON ROSEABELLE'S FRONT PORCH, GAZING AT the stars. Here they were, ready to go on another dangerous adventure while their parents stayed behind, worried sick. Of course they wouldn't know they were gone for a while. As usual, his father wasn't home and his mother had just gone for a four-day trip to Northern Benotripia so she could help out with all the wounded people. He knew that Jessicana's parents and older siblings had done the same, so it would be four days before anyone realized they were gone.

But who knew how long this would take?

Roseabelle walked around from her backyard with a broad

grin on her face. She waved her arm in a flourish to a dark shape behind her. "So, what do you think?"

The creatures stepped into the light, and Astro nodded in instant approval. Their gleaming coats were speckled in gold and brown and their heads were a peculiar shape. The animals had four legs, feathery wings, with glittering golden and purple scales on their lower parts.

Basically the creatures were flying, underwater-breathing horses. Besides their legs being scaly, their heads were a bit too pointed, and their necks were about the length of a giraffe's. "What are those?" Astro asked.

Roseabelle shrugged. "Well, I meant for them to be horses, but then I added wings and gills, and I'm not exactly the best artist ever. I call them Persopians!"

She patted the shorter one. "This is the female. Astro, you can ride her. Jessicana and I will take the males."

Jessicana appeared out of the darkness. "Are we going to fly, then?"

Roseabelle shook her head. "I think we should save that for climbing the mountains. These things are wicked fast on land, fairly swift in the air, and pretty slow underwater, but, hey, they can still do it all. Everyone get your packs. We're leaving right now."

Astro reached for his pack, slung it over his shoulder, and hopped onto the speckled Persopian. He waited for his friends to mount and then shouted, "Let's go!" The Persopians cantered off into the night.

The ride was exhilarating. The wind whistled through Astro's hair, and he gripped the animal's mane tightly, willing that he wouldn't fall off.

This was going to be a long ride.

DAWN CAME, AND ASTRO BLINKED AS THE SUN'S RAYS CREPT through his eyelids. He rubbed his eyes and sat up in his saddle. They had been riding for hours, and Astro had eventually fallen asleep. He looked up, and his smile widened as the jagged Aku Mountains came into view. "Roseabelle! Jessicana!" he shouted. Their Persopians pulled up beside him, and he saw his friends' limp forms hanging over the sides of their animals.

They instantly sat up, rubbing their eyes. "W-what's going on?" Roseabelle muttered.

"We're here!" Astro told them. "The Aku Mountains."

Jessicana's eyes lit up as well. "Hurry! Let's go!"

The three Persopians galloped to the foothills below the range, and Astro hopped off his steed, jumped onto a rocky ridge, and opened his backpack. "Come on," he urged, and Jessicana and Roseabelle soon joined him. He then furrowed his brows as the Persopians cantered away.

"Where are they going?" Astro asked.

"I talked to them," Jessicana told him in a normal tone. "They said they'd come back."

"Uh, how?" Astro asked.

Jessicana rolled her eyes. "Winged creatures can communicate with one another, genius."

It took a moment for Astro to figure it out. He blinked and then dug out his spear and shield from his backpack. "Arm yourselves," he announced. "We're going to need our weapons."

A cold voice laughed icily and sent chills down Astro's arms. "Oh, yes, you will."

The three friends whipped their heads around to see Sheklyth, her dark hair spilling out of her cloak, perched in a tree.

Roseabelle snarled and stepped forward, brandishing her sword and shield. "What do you want, traitor?" she demanded.

Sheklyth nimbly dropped from a branch as Roseabelle lunged for her. The Darvonian swiftly drew a knife from beneath the folds of her cloak and blocked Roseabelle's strikes, finally flinging the young Benotripian against the rocky ridge.

"Roseabelle!" Jessicana shouted and rushed over to her

friend while Astro kept his eyes fixed on the Darvonian.

"What do *you* want?" Astro snarled, tempted to throw his spear at her, but he knew it wouldn't do any good. Sheklyth was well trained with her knife and he had a feeling that that wasn't the only thing she was hiding under her cloak.

Sheklyth smirked at him. "Why, I was sent to deliver a message, of course. We won't bother you on this mountain."

"Why do I find that hard to believe?" Astro shot back.

Sheklyth smiled, her expression cold and heartless. "Well, it's true. Of course, you might be fighting for your lives on this mountain. But we won't be the ones you'll be fighting."

"What are you talking about?" Astro hissed. He was getting nervous, and agitation was gnawing at him furiously. "Stop speaking in riddles."

Sheklyth gave a mock sigh. "Very well then." She clicked her tongue, and a dark shadow began to spread over Astro. A rhythmic pounding shook the ground, and Astro stumbled back a bit. He could see Jessicana and Roseabelle shakily standing up, Jessicana's eyes filling with utter terror and Roseabelle's with grim determination.

Sheklyth gave a hearty "Ta-ta!" and zipped away into the foothills.

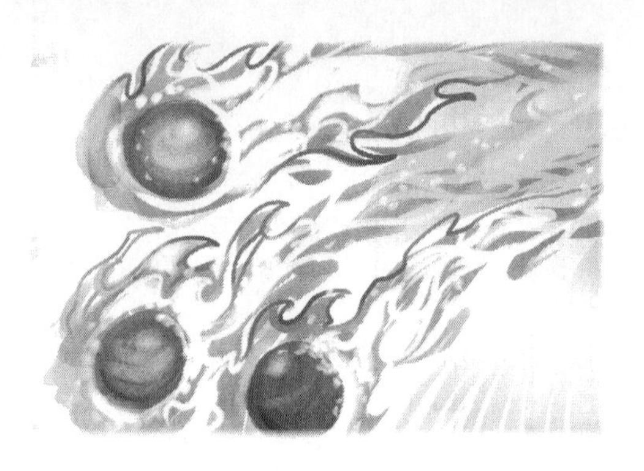

CHAPTER 6
Garaganta

A MONSTROUS SHAPE EMERGED FROM THE SHADOWS, and Astro's heart skipped a beat. When he looked straight forward, he could see green scaly legs with multiple large zits and knots. When Astro tilted his head back, he could see the legs connected to a giant furry body with an ugly green head and horns. Astro had never seen anything like it. "They must have brought it from Darvonia," he whispered.

Jessicana screamed, and Roseabelle tripped over her backpack. Astro was left alone, his fear growing by the minute. His spear was a toothpick compared to the monster. "Hey, Bigfoot!" Roseabelle suddenly yelled. Both the monster and Astro turned their heads to see Roseabelle aiming a Flamehurler at the beast. She cranked the lever, and three iron balls came flying out, hurtling toward it.

Jessicana, now standing, shouted to Astro, "It's a Garaganta!" Astro turned back to the monster as it batted away two of the spheres from its chest, but the third zoomed in between the Garaganta's claws and hit the monster squarely in the chest.

"Hit the deck!" Roseabelle screamed. Astro dived underneath a pile of rocks as an explosion of red and black erupted above them. Smoke entered Astro's nostrils, and he starting coughing. "Roseabelle? Jessicana?" he shouted. *Is the Garaganta dead?*

A loud bellow answered his question, and Astro stood, his eyes watering because of the smoke. The gray fog cleared, and Astro winced as the Garaganta staggered forward. He could see Jessicana, slumped against a large boulder, and Roseabelle trying to revive her.

The Garaganta turned toward him, and Astro immediately extended a finger and shot a silver-blue lightning bolt at the beast. It struck the Garaganta in the thigh. Bellowing with rage, it advanced toward the boy. Astro gulped. Now he'd only made the situation worse. He opened his pack and pulled out the Flame-hurler, trained it at the beast, and reached for ammo, only to realize he didn't have any. Roseabelle had all the iron spheres tucked away in her pack.

Astro quickly pulled out his sword and shield, gritted his teeth, and charged, knowing that this was one battle he couldn't win. The monster stared down at him, mesmerized for a second, as though he was surprised that such a puny little thing thought it could oppose him. Then he jumped, making the ground shake. Astro stumbled but managed to stay on his feet. Behind him he could hear Roseabelle shouting "Astro, no!" but he kept going anyway.

As Astro reached the monster's foot, he plunged his sword into the soft part between the Garaganta's claw and the bone. His foe yowled in pain and kicked him off, sending Astro flying into the air. Astro landed hard on the ground, which knocked the breath out of him. His head ached, as if it were being shaken, and he felt tempted to fall asleep. He could hear Roseabelle's faint screams and forced himself back to consciousness.

As his eyes fluttered open, Astro realized that his "headache" was actually the Garaganta running toward him. He could see Roseabelle behind the monster, whacking it with her sword and trying to distract it from Astro, but it wasn't working. The beast's black eyes, dark as tunnels, were intently fixed on the lightning boy. Astro's sword was lying three feet away, so he was armed with only his shield. Astro scoured the landscape, looking for something he could use as a weapon, but nothing looked promising. All he had was his lightning, which didn't seem to affect the monster.

A black object came sailing toward him, and Astro caught it. It was his backpack. He quickly opened it and realized that Roseabelle had placed some ammo inside and then tossed it to him. Astro grabbed the Flame-hurler, loaded the iron sphere into it, and braced for impact. But just before he fired, a small slip of paper on the sphere made him stop.

He quickly read out loud, "Maximum force." Suddenly Astro understood. Most ammo was enough to get rid of a person. But earlier, Roseabelle had shot a "Maximum force" sphere at the monster, and that was why it caused such an explosion. He silently thanked Roseabelle for labeling it, or else he wouldn't have known to take cover.

"Astro, hurry!" came Roseabelle's voice. When Astro looked up, he saw the Garaganta getting closer and closer. Its shadow soon hovered over him, and Astro looked away and fired at the monster's chest.

Astro clenched the Flame-hurler tightly, and when he opened his eyes, he could see the sphere about to plunge into the Garaganta's chest. He spotted an alcove, jumped into the rocky cave, and covered his ears, waiting for the explosion.

Instead, a rumble shook his cavern, and Astro trembled as his hiding spot crumbled into several different pieces. One piece bit into his back, and he cried out in pain. A sharp claw lifted him into the air, the sunlight blinding him. He soon found himself facing the dark eyes of the Garaganta. Astro struggled to breathe as the monster tightened its grip.

"Hey, you big bully!" someone shouted. But it wasn't Roseabelle. It wasn't even Jessicana. Astro painfully turned his head to see a red-haired man holding a large catapult, loaded with large boulders. He had a black cloak on and Astro tensed. Could he be a Darvonian? But something inside told him that a Darvonian wouldn't come to rescue his enemies.

Roseabelle was next to him, wielding a large, thick wooden club that the man had obviously given to her. Jessicana still lay slumped against the boulder, and Astro wished that she was a safer place. It was the second time this week she had been unconscious.

"Take cover!" Roseabelle yelled as the man pulled back on his catapult. A large boulder sailed into the air. Astro ducked right when the rock soared over his head. He could feel the monster's claw tightening against his body. Astro struggled to draw in another breath.

The monster loosened its grip at the impact. Astro tumbled to the earth below, flailing wildly, and then everything went black. He was unconscious before he hit the ground.

CHAPTER 7
Dastrock

Roseabelle stood over Astro and faced the red-haired man that had just saved her friend's life. "All right," she demanded. "You owe us an explanation. Who are you?"

The red-haired man smiled gently. "I imagine you aren't going to believe me straightaway, Roseabelle. But, please, hear me out."

Roseabelle thumped her foot against the barren ground. "I'm waiting."

The man sighed and stated plainly, "I'm your uncle."

Roseabelle blinked. Her uncle? Danette didn't have a brother! Was this guy actually expecting her to believe him? She burst out laughing, her hearty bellow echoing throughout the mountains.

"I'm serious," the man said. "My name is Dastrock."

"I think my mother would have told me if she had a brother," Roseabelle reasoned.

"Who said I was your mother's brother?" Dastrock asked, folding his arms across his chest.

"Y-you're claiming to be my father's brother?" Roseabelle asked incredulously.

"That's right," Dastrock confirmed.

"How do I know you aren't a Darvonian?" Roseabelle questioned suspiciously.

"Would a Darvonian save him?" Dastrock pointed to Astro, and Roseabelle sighed. The man did have a point.

"Well, even if you aren't a Darvonian, that doesn't mean you're my uncle," Roseabelle told him. "You could be some crazy Benotripian who lives in a hut on the mountain peak."

Dastrock shrugged. "True. But what kind of crazy hermit knows Danette's daughter's name?"

Roseabelle blinked. He was right. Dastrock had known her name without asking. "All right," she admitted. "Let's say that you are my uncle. What are you doing here dressed up as a Darvonian?"

Dastrock sighed and glanced over his shoulder. "I suppose by talking to you I've already blown my cover, so I might as well tell you the rest of it. I'm a spy for the Benotripians and have been posing as a Darvonian for eleven years, since your father disappeared. I've worked my way up through the system and finally got into the position of a Missonair, a scout who could embark on top-secret missions along with the royal family. I never, not once, got in touch with Benotripia, which helped my cover."

"What's the point of being a spy if you don't gain any information?" Roseabelle asked.

"If you don't *share* information," Dastrock corrected her. "I learned many things."

"All right then," Roseabelle reasoned. "For all I know you could be an IB, an Imitation Benotripian. So show me your power."

Dastrock blinked. "What?"

"If you are a Benotripian, then you are born with a power," Roseabelle supplied.

"Oh. Right." Dastrock spread his arms and closed his eyes, softly humming. Roseabelle raised her eyebrows, trying to figure out what he was doing, when goose bumps crept onto her arms and she shivered. Why was it so cold all of a sudden? Of course, it was Dastrock causing the temperature shift. He could obviously drop or raise temperatures. How terrifying. The hairs on the back of her hand stood up.

"All right," she said loudly, "you've made your point. You're a Benotripian. You're possibly my uncle. And you saved Astro. Thank you."

"Well, finally I get some credit," Dastrock said. "And I think your friend right there is waking up."

Roseabelle whirled around to see Jessicana standing up sluggishly, muttering to herself. When she swooned, Roseabelle ran over to catch her, one hand on her friend's shoulder, the other on her back. "You okay, Jessicana?" she asked softly.

Jessicana blinked. "W-What happened? There was a monster—and Sheklyth . . . a-a-a—"

"It's all right, Jessicana," Roseabelle soothed. "You're going to be fine. Astro fought the monster, and my uncle here, Dastrock, killed it."

"U-uncle?" Jessicana stammered. "Dastrock? Who?"

"Just rest," Roseabelle comforted. "We're going to fly up the mountain in an hour, so you can sleep for now." Jessicana nodded, muttered something Roseabelle couldn't make out, and slumped against the boulder again.

Dastrock cleared his throat. "So . . . ?"

"What?" Roseabelle snapped. She didn't mean to be irritated with Dastrock, but she wanted to care for her friends, fly up the mountain, find the journal, and get the Stones of Horsh before the Darvonians could. They were wasting precious time.

Dastrock put a hand on her shoulder and looked into her eyes. "Roseabelle, please. I must warn you. The Darvonians must know by now that you've defeated the monster, something they were not planning on. They'll block you, ambush you, and do whatever it takes to get to the journal first. Your friends need rest, and so do you."

"What if they get the journal and then run off?" Roseabelle protested.

"They won't," Dastrock promised. "They know you'll just follow them.

"I can't believe I'm trusting you," Roseabelle grumbled as she lay down on a large smooth stone for some rest.

Dastrock gave her a small smile. "Neither can I."

ROSEABELLE JOSTLED JESSICANA AND ASTRO AWAKE, HER OWN eyes weary from sleep. "Guys, wake up," she whispered urgently.

Both of them sat up, and Roseabelle pointed to the large carcass of the Garaganta. "Dastrock's gone. He probably betrayed us and is now telling the Darvonians our location. I was a fool to believe him," she fumed.

Astro raised an eyebrow. "Who's Dastrock?"

Jessicana rubbed her eyes. "Her grandfather, I think."

"Uncle," corrected a masculine voice. "And no, I haven't betrayed you, Roseabelle. I didn't know it was a crime to doze off where you couldn't see me."

The three of them turned to see Dastrock stretching. Roseabelle glared at him. "Very witty. Come on, we need to go. Dastrock, thanks for the help." She picked up the backpacks and whistled for the Persopians.

"Hey, wait a second!" Dastrock protested. "I can help you."

Roseabelle sighed sadly. "I'm really sorry, whoever you are. It doesn't matter if you're a good guy or a bad guy. Because no matter what, I'll never really know where your loyalties lie. I'm sorry, Dastrock. It's true you could be my uncle, but what if you've been biding your time, waiting to strike. What if you're the one who made my father disappear?"

Dastrock looked taken aback. "I would never," he stated solemnly.

"Yeah, well, either you're telling the truth or you're a good liar," Roseabelle spat. Her voice softened. "Listen, I'm sorry, Dastrock, but I can't."

He sighed. "I understand. But please let me at least distract the Darvonians from you."

Roseabelle shrugged. "All right. But we're not telling you where we're going."

"Fair enough. Get your friends ready. You'll need all the time you can get."

Something about the man's tone made Roseabelle shiver.

CHAPTER 8
The Journal

JESSICANA HOISTED HERSELF ATOP HER MOUNT, RUBBED her eyes, and bit her lip. How could she have done this to her friends? Just when they could have used her help, she'd fainted, becoming utterly useless. She felt terrible.

"Ready to go?" called Roseabelle. She had laid out the plan just a few minutes ago. They would fly to the peak of the mountain, find where the journal was buried, and fly off with it. Roseabelle had gone back to her tower room to read more about the fairy tale "The Stones of Horsh" before they had left for the Aku Mountains. She had learned three things:

1. The journal would be under a silver statuette.
2. It was indeed hidden in the Aku Mountains.
3. Many traps were laid out to keep intruders from stealing the journal.

Jessicana could only hope that these were actual facts and not just made-up details to the fairy tale. "Fly!" Roseabelle shouted, and Jessicana dug her heel into the flank of the Persopian. His feathery wings rose up around her, and Jessicana let out a shriek of delight as the animal bolted into the air at high speed. "Left!" Roseabelle shouted. Jessicana tugged on the animal's mane, and they veered to the left. Jessicana kept a sharp ear out as Roseabelle shouted out commands.

Dastrock had told Roseabelle where the Darvonians were planning to ambush them, so they decided it would be safest to avoid those areas, even when they were in the air. As they rose in altitude, Jessicana's ears popped, and she bit her lip furiously. In her human form, this was extremely uncomfortable. But when she was a parrot, she could soar wherever she wanted.

Jessicana felt tempted to transform, but that would probably lose the Persopian, and she didn't want to fly all the way to where the Stones were hidden! She fought the urge and concentrated on their destination.

"Stop!" Roseabelle shouted, and she landed roughly on a small peak of the mountain. Astro followed her, while Jessicana chose a more precise spot to land.

Astro gulped as he stared over the edge of the peak. "That's high," he whispered. "Really, really high."

Jessicana rolled her eyes. "Come on, Astro. It's not so bad."

He shrugged. "It's easy to say when you can just fly on down."

"Guys, we don't have time for arguing! Search for the statuette. It has to be here somewhere," Roseabelle scolded. The three friends instantly knelt down, pawing in the dirt, hands groping for something metal.

After a long search, Jessicana sat up, breathing heavily. "It's not here. There are too many mountain peaks, Roseabelle."

"I found it!" Astro exclaimed. "It's here."

Jessicana blinked. "Let me just say, that was pure luck." The girls rushed to Astro's side, and he held up the small silver statuette of a man holding a thick book. "Dig!" Jessicana urged. They all scooped handfuls of dirt, flinging it off the mountain, desperately prying through the soil. Their hands suddenly hit rock, and they sat back in disappointment, staring at all the dirt they had excavated.

"Where is it?" Astro asked hollowly.

Jessicana ran her hands over the smooth stone, questioning each detail. Her eyes then lit up. "I think I know what to do," she announced, and she put all her weight on the left side of the stone, pushing as hard as she could. "Help me!" she groaned. Astro and Roseabelle placed their hands on the stone too, putting so much weight on the stone that their cheeks were pressed against the ground.

The right side of the stone suddenly came up, and Jessicana quickly pulled Roseabelle and Astro out of the way as the slab of rock nearly hit their faces. Astro stared at it in amazement. "Jessicana, you're a genius!" he shouted. "I think I see the journal!"

"There's no need to announce it to the whole island," Roseabelle hissed.

Astro blushed. "Sorry. Look, here it is."

He held up the right side of the slab to reveal a worn book clasped together with an iron buckle. Astro reached for it, but Jessicana quickly pulled his hand back, glared at him, and moved out of the way so sunlight could shine inside the hole.

A number of tripwires were strung, and Astro could now see hidden weapons stuck inside the hole. He gulped. If he had brushed even one of them, a knife would've sunk into his hand. "Thanks, Jessicana," he said, gasping.

Jessicana nodded. "Horsh may have turned out to be a good guy, but he sure learned how to make traps like a Darvonian."

"No kidding," Astro said. "I almost got skewered."

Roseabelle smiled grimly. "This reminds me of the maze we had to go through last year. Remember that?" she asked them.

Astro laughed softly. "Yeah, I do. I'm the one who saved Roseabelle from falling down an endless abyss. Guess I wasn't so careful this time."

Jessicana patted him on the back. "It's all right."

Roseabelle gestured to the journal. "So how do we get it?"

Jessicana held out a hand to Astro. "Silk gloves and Dragocone Ray, please."

Astro handed the items to her, and Jessicana slid the gloves on, then handled the Ray. She took a deep breath, held the Ray away from her as if it were poison, and dipped the edge of it into the hole. There was a loud crack, and Jessicana withdrew the weapon. A pile of blackened burnt knives lay at the edge of the hole. As Astro reached for them, Jessicana warned, "Don't. They may be cursed." Both of her friends looked at her questioningly, but Jessicana didn't notice.

"Roseabelle, can you use telekinesis to get the journal out?" Jessicana asked.

Roseabelle nodded. "Sure." She faced the hole, all of the tripwires sprung and broken, and concentrated hard on the journal. It slowly lifted, shuddering as it came from its four-hundred-year-old resting place.

The book finally came to a rest in Roseabelle's hands. "We have it!" she cried. She opened it, scouring through the pages. "Here it is," she exclaimed, pointing.

Jessicana leaned over to read:

> *The Stones of Horsh, named after me, are hidden underneath Whipla Falls. I can only hope that they do not fall into the wrong hands.*

Astro shook his head, reading the message silently as well. "I can't believe it," he stated in a hushed voice. "We've got it."

CHAPTER 9
Shadow Horses

Roseabelle heard a *swoosh* through the air. Within seconds an arrowhead impaled the book, a cord attached to it. She realized what was happening too late. "No!" she yelled and lunged for the journal.

But it was Jessicana who beat her to it. A multi-colored bird swept down from above, bit the cord with her beak, and pushed it toward Roseabelle, who quickly caught it in her hands. Roseabelle turned around to see Heltonine, Sheklyth's sister, crouching in a tree and holding a bow and a quiver of arrows.

The Darvonian reached for her fingers to whistle for help, but Roseabelle quickly snatched up the arrow and flung it at their adversary. As Heltonine reached to bat it away, Astro was already on his feet, blasting lightning bolts at her. The Darvonian shrieked in pain, tumbled out of the tree, and fell to the ground. Roseabelle hopped onto the Persopian and shouted, "Hurry! Get on!"

Jessicana, who had shape-shifted back into a girl, and Astro stumbled onto their animals and lifted into the air. Roseabelle turned her head to see a mob of Darvonians appear on the peak, and she felt a rush of worry. They had been watching and listening the entire time. Had they learned the location of the Stones? They hadn't said it out loud. She exhaled in relief until she saw a small brown rectangle lying on the stone.

Her heart skipped a beat. They had left the journal.

Arrows and javelins streaked after them, and Roseabelle yelled, "The battle isn't over yet!" She saw Astro slump over his Persopian, looking exhausted. A javelin almost embedded itself in Roseabelle's hand, but she managed to lean away as it flew toward her.

Soon they flew out of range, and Roseabelle clutched the Persopian's mane, feeling like a failure. They had left the journal. But at least they knew where to go.

But the Darvonians would know too.

Roseabelle motioned for her friends to gather closer. "I left the journal," she told them glumly. She braced herself, waiting for her friends to get mad at her.

"It's all right," Jessicana stated soothingly.

"No one expected the Darvonians to come busting down our doors," Astro added, which made Roseabelle smile. "So where is Whipla Falls?" he asked, trying to change the subject.

"I've heard of it!" Jessicana piped up.

"Of course you have," Astro grumbled.

Jessicana rolled her eyes and continued, "It's on the outskirts of Eastern Benotripia. It's a beautiful waterfall. I've never been there, but I've always wanted to."

"How long will it take us to get there?" Roseabelle questioned.

Jessicana bit her lip. "In the air? I'm guessing it'll be a two-day trip."

Astro sighed. "Oh, boy."

Roseabelle's eyebrows creased. "Wait a second. The Darvonians didn't leave till this morning. How did they get to the mountains so fast?"

Astro and Jessicana shared a look. "Roseabelle, the Darvonians obviously brought the Garaganta to Benotripia because there are no monsters on the island. Who knows what else they've brought? Maybe they have an amazingly fast mount or something," Jessicana explained.

Roseabelle's voice was hollow. "Which means that they can probably get to the Falls before we can."

There was silence, save the wind and the snorting of the Persopians. Jessicana broke the silence with a falsely cheerful tone. "It'll be all right. How about this? I fly beneath the Persopians so I can scout and find out how the Darvonians are traveling so fast. I'll sleep during the day and scout at night."

Roseabelle asked uncertainly, "Are you sure you can change your sleeping pattern like that? What if you get caught?"

Jessicana smiled genuinely. "Believe me. I won't get caught."

* * * * *

ASTRO WAS IN MORE AGONY NOW THAN EVER. EVER SINCE he had blasted Heltonine, an incredible surge of pain had filled him. He'd done his best to hide it, but he feared that his condition would only get worse. Now, as he lay on the Persopian's saddle, he wondered what his condition was.

Astro felt terrible not telling his friends about his lightning, but what could he do? Of course, Jessicana might have some smart-aleck answer—you never knew with her—but they had a more important mission to complete. He sighed and slipped into a deep sleep.

ASTRO DREAMED THAT HE WAS RIDING ON A SHADOWY HORSE, its red eyes glowing and its body almost wisps of smoke. Where was he? Part of him didn't really want to know. He knew this was only a dream, but, all the same, he felt extremely apprehensive.

When Astro chanced a glance behind him, he gulped. There were other shadowy horses all with riders with black cloaks. Darvonians.

Astro looked around at the scenery and saw everything else becoming a blur. Was this how the Darvonians were going so fast? Horses made of shadow? That didn't even make any sense. Astro heard a deep voice coming from within him: "Keep riding! Faster!"

The dream then evaporated in a cloud of silver mist.

ASTRO WOKE UP ON THE BACK OF THE PERSOPIAN. JESSICANA'S ride was tied to Roseabelle's, and Astro figured she had flown off to scout for them. Roseabelle was slumped on the back of her mount, fast asleep. Astro laid his head against his animal's but couldn't fall asleep again.

"Awk, Astro!" a voice squawked loudly, which made him almost jump out of his skin. Soon Jessicana was seated on the tail end of his Persopian transformed back into her human form. "Hey," she greeted him.

Astro raised an eyebrow at her. "What are you doing up here? I thought you were supposed to be down there scouting."

"Yeah, well, Roseabelle's asleep, and I want to talk to someone," Jessicana blurted out. Astro looked at her strangely. His friend was definitely acting strange. Jessicana opened her pack and rummaged through it, then pulled out a loaf of bread. "You want some?" she asked but with a look that said, "Say no. Say no. Say no."

Astro shook his head. "No, thanks. I'm good."

Jessicana rolled her eyes and reached over behind Astro. "Oh, so you'll only eat food from your pack? Fine. I'll get some from it." She leaned forward, grasped the pack, and whispered hurriedly in Astro's ear: "Darvonians are just ahead of us. They're listening in. I saw a group up ahead too. They're riding these transparent horses that make them go extremely fast."

She pulled away, fished out a loaf of bread from his pack, and tossed it lightly to him. "Eat up," she commented, smiling. "I'm going to get some shut-eye."

Her demeanor was calm, but as she transformed and flew

back to her Persopian, Astro knew from her gaze that they were in trouble.

* * * * *

JESSICANA WAS NERVOUS. LAST NIGHT, WHEN SHE HAD flown in below, she had witnessed the most horrific and majestic creature she had ever laid eyes on. A shadow horse. They weren't solid, but somehow the Darvonians were able to ride them. They moved quicker than any animal should be able to. Jessicana had seen a group of Darvonians moving so fast that by now they must be at least halfway to the waterfall.

Darvonians had been perched in high trees, holding large stone cone-shaped devices that Jessicana somehow knew they were using to eavesdrop on Jessicana, Roseabelle, and Astro's conversations. It was true she had managed to warn Astro, but now she had to figure out a way to alert Roseabelle.

Her auburn-haired friend was now in front of them, leading the way toward the Falls. There was still hope. The Darvonians hadn't reached the Falls yet. In actuality the three friends were making pretty good progress. They had to be at least halfway there.

"Roseabelle, stop!" Astro suddenly yelled, and all of the three friends came to a stop in midair.

"Astro, what . . ." Jessicana started but then trailed off.

They were entering a dark forest. Discreetly hidden beneath a tall tree was a thick iron pole with a pointed edge at the top. Jessicana could make out tiny holes in the metal that looked like arrow slits. Jessicana's blood froze. She was almost positive that they didn't have giant Sephlotine spikes in Benotripia. Were they hallucinating?

Somehow, she knew that they weren't.

Jessicana transformed into a parrot and slowly approached the spike. "Be careful, Jessicana," Roseabelle whispered from atop her Persopian. Jessicana gently brushed the tip of her wing against the spike and then flew up quickly, just in time to avoid a sharp piece of metal that extracted and shot straight at the spot where Jessicana had been.

Jessicana reached her Persopian and changed back into a girl. "That was crazy," she gasped. "If you even touch a spike, you get impaled. It's extremely up-to-date technology. The Darvonians must have planted it."

"Are there more?" Astro asked.

Jessicana sighed, transformed into her bird form, and flew over the forest, scanning the area for more black spikes. An iron arrow suddenly hurtled toward her, and she barely dodged the missile. Jessicana could see more ammo flying at her. Her heart sank, and she flew back to the Persopian, turning back into a human.

"So?" Roseabelle prompted.

"There's several more," Jessicana affirmed grimly. "And worse too. The spikes shoot out arrows above them."

* * * * *

ROSEABELLE WASN'T EXACTLY PLEASED WITH THE NEWS. She gritted her teeth and sighed. "Is there a way around the forest?" she asked.

Astro nodded. "Right over there." He pointed to a pebble-lined path to the right of the forest.

Jessicana rolled her eyes. "Why didn't you say so? Let's take that direction, then." Roseabelle put a hand to her forehead. Why did she feel as though that wasn't a good idea?

"Wait!" she cried. "We need to go through there."

"Why?" Astro asked.

"I think it's a shortcut," Roseabelle stated. "The Darvonians know we'll never make it unless we take the shortcut so they planted these spikes so we'd choose the other way. It makes perfect sense."

Jessicana bit her lip. "I guess you're right."

"The only way to go is forward," Astro agreed.

CHAPTER 10
Sephlotine Spikes

ROSEABELLE HAD SENT JESSICANA'S ANIMAL THE LONG way so it wouldn't get hurt. Jessicana would venture on as a parrot. The other two Persopians would be mounts for Roseabelle and Astro. On the ground, the spikes were so tightly compressed together, there was no way they would make it out alive.

"You ready?" Astro asked nervously.

"No," Roseabelle answered. "Let's go!"

Their animals darted forward. Roseabelle looked over her left side. If the arrows were triggered, they would strike the underbelly of the Persopian, so both Astro and she had strapped their shields to the bellies of their animals.

The Persopian shuddered, and Roseabelle instantly knew that a few arrows had thudded into the shield. "C'mon, boy," she spoke soothingly. "We can do this." The two friends soared over the landscape. Soon they noticed the spikes were pointed lopsided so that they could come in from either side of them. "Oh no," Roseabelle muttered as an arrow approached her from the right and missed her arm by centimeters.

"Astro, watch out!" she yelled. An arrow was coming at

him from the left while he was staring down at the right. Her friend moved just in time, but Roseabelle wasn't so lucky.

An arrow had zoomed toward her without her notice, and a searing pain filled Roseabelle's arm as she realized she had been struck. She grimaced. The end of the forest of spikes was almost up. She could do this. Roseabelle wrenched the arrow out of her arm and fixed her gaze on the end of the forest.

She could see Jessicana up ahead, morphing back into a girl and dropping to the ground. To her left, Astro was staring at her in horror. Roseabelle tried to shout, "I'm all right!" but the words died in her throat. Blood was oozing from her wound, and she fought to stay conscious.

The last arrow came sailing toward her, and she ducked just in time, but the world spun, and Roseabelle dropped to the ground like a stone.

CHAPTER 11
Broxlorthian

ASTRO STARED AT THE UNCONSCIOUS FORM OF Roseabelle as Jessicana slowly wrapped bandages around her arm. Luckily the injury wasn't deep, and their friend would be okay, although it was a lot worse than Jessicana's incident. Her hand was in great shape now.

The auburn-haired girl's eyes fluttered open. "Hey, Roseabelle," Astro greeted her. "We need to stop taking turns fainting."

A smile lit up her face. "I think I agree." Her two friends pulled her up, and Roseabelle winced when she saw her injury. "Ouch. That doesn't look great."

"You'll be all right," Jessicana assured her. "We have to move. I'll share a Persopian with you so I can tend more to your wound. Astro will be on the other, and we'll leave the other here."

Roseabelle hobbled to her Persopian, and Jessicana climbed on next to her, strapping down their backpacks to their saddles. "You ready?" Jessicana asked.

Roseabelle could only groan in response. Astro watched as his two friends lifted into the sky. He steered his own mount skyward but hung back a little as Jessicana treated her friend properly. Astro's lightning was getting worse. He could feel it inside him, boiling, wanting to burst and come out of its shell.

He knew that the stormy horses had something to do with his lightning. In his dream, they had almost looked like storm clouds, crackling and rumbling with thunder, yet smooth and swift at the same time. He promised himself as soon as they got to Whipla Falls, he would tell the girls what had been going on. Because whatever it was, it was getting worse.

He took out his backpack and twirled his broadsword in the air. Most likely the Darvonians were already at the Falls with their steeds that could run like the wind. But there was still time to stop them. In the book of fairy tales, it said only someone worthy could obtain the Stones. The Darvonians were assuredly not worthy.

Astro wondered what kind of power the Stones held. Could they command water and fire? Were they used to raise mountains and valleys? What did they look like? He tried to imagine if he had to use the Stones what he would use them for.

"Bring Magford back," Astro whispered. But that was impossible. The Stones probably couldn't save Roseabelle's father. It was a nice thought, though.

As Astro surveyed the sunny skies of Benotripia, he wondered if they should get help from villagers, then almost instantly decided against it. Some of them may have been trained with the sword and the bow, but most around this area weren't. The Falls were somewhat of a scenic place to live. Aged Benotripians were the main occupants, and they would do more harm than help.

"Astro!" Jessicana exclaimed in awe. "We're here." Astro cocked his head to one side.

"Are you sure?" he responded.

"Yes!" Jessicana shouted over the sound of rushing water. They emerged into a plentiful clearing. Crystal-blue water descended from the mouth of a cave, tumbling over a collection of wet boulders and down a sharp cliff, then into a clear sparkling pool.

"It's beautiful," Astro said, and he hopped off his Persopian, drew his sword, and looked around. "Come down!" he shouted. "There aren't any Darvonians."

"You sure?" Jessicana's muffled voice came from above.

"Pretty sure," was Astro's response. The two girls dropped from above next to him. Roseabelle was holding her Dragocone Ray, Jessicana her throwing knives. Astro looked around apprehensively. No flashes of black or thunderclouds or psycho Darvonians leaping out at them. "I think the coast is clear—JESSICANA, WATCH OUT!"

A green tentacle sprang from the Falls and wrapped around Jessicana's stomach, enfolding her in a slimy green weed and plunging her into the water. Were they being attacked by some sort of creature? Another green tentacle shot out to grab Astro, but he quickly jumped out of its reach and swung his sword at it, cutting off the very end. "Jessicana!" Roseabelle shouted, and she ran toward the water, just as something rose from the depths.

It wasn't a sea monster. It wasn't even a Garaganta. It was a plant.

It was poisonous green and had a long stem and a rounded head that looked oddly humanoid. Shiny green lips barely hid the rows of extremely sharp teeth, and many earthen tendrils were attached to the stem. And one of those tendrils had a struggling Jessicana within its grip.

* * * * *

JESSICANA HAD NEVER SEEN ANYTHING LIKE THE CREATURE that was squeezing the breath out of her. Well, it wasn't exactly a creature, she realized. It was a plant with wickedly sharp teeth that Jessicana really didn't want to come across.

She struggled to breathe as the plant flung her around like a noodle. *I'm not going to faint,* Jessicana thought. *Jessicana, you are not fainting on me.*

Black spots danced before her eyes, but Jessicana managed to stay conscious even though the plant was strangling her. On the shore, Roseabelle was loading up a Flame-hurler, but as Jessicana watched, the plant took a breath and exhaled. A cloud of acid erupted from its mouth. She shouted, "Roseabelle! Astro!" just as the cloud descended over them.

Roseabelle and Astro came coughing out of the cloud, and Jessicana fought to escape, squirming. Then she realized she had a throwing knife in her hand. Somehow she hadn't dropped it when the plant had whisked her up. She twisted her body so the knife was pointed at the tentacle and leaned on the hilt.

The plant let out an earsplitting screech as the knife plunged into it. A light green substance oozed from the wound. Jessicana's years as a potion maker told her that it was poisonous and she needed to get out of there fast. She stabbed the plant's meaty tentacle again, and it screeched once more, loosening its grip on Jessicana. Just as the green poison was about to reach her, she squirmed out of the plant's hold and free-fell to the Falls below.

Jessicana quickly pulled herself to shore and saw Roseabelle and Astro fighting to keep clear of the acid clouds that were constantly spilling from the carnivorous mouth of the plant. Jessicana scrambled along the beach, trying to find a weapon of some sort. Her backpack had fallen into the Falls, and they weren't likely to find it anytime soon. She transformed into a parrot and swooped down to her friends, who were rolling and feinting to avoid the large acid clouds.

"Jessicana!" Astro yelled. "Are you all right?"

"I need a Fire-hurler," she shouted back. "You guys keep dodging and distract it. I'll fire at it and take it by surprise."

"Roseabelle's backpack is over by the boulders!" Astro responded. "Hurry!"

Jessicana quickly flew off, snatched her friend's backpack, and flew to a large boulder where the monstrous plant couldn't see her. She shape-shifted into a human, dragged the heavy iron Flame-hurler out of the pack, pointed it at the foul green head, loaded it with three iron balls, looked away, and pulled the lever.

There was a loud pop as the ammo was released into the sky. Jessicana had pulled it with such force that she had to make an effort not to tumble down the side of the rocky boulder. That wasn't exactly on her to-do list. Jessicana transformed into a parrot to use its sharp vision and watched as the tiny ammo balls came closer and closer to the plant.

One of its tentacles lashed out, knocking an iron ball inside its mouth. It then opened its mouth and swallowed the other too.

Jessicana gulped. It would take at least a few minutes for the balls to take effect. And they didn't have that much time! The Darvonians could get here any minute. Jessicana dug through Roseabelle's pack, and the Dragocone Ray caught her eye. A crazy plan hatched in her mind, and she grimaced. This was probably the only way to kill the creature.

Jessicana slipped on Roseabelle's silk gloves, seized the Dragocone Ray, and charged toward the plant, trying to run as quietly as possible. She kept the glow of the ray behind her.

As she reached the Falls, Jessicana made sure the ray was concealed underwater and slowly crept around the massive plant. She took a deep breath, made sure the plant wasn't facing her, and dove underwater. As she had suspected, the plant had earthen tendrils that were anchored to the bottom of the Falls. The Darvonians had to have planted it just like they had with the spikes. A chill ran up Jessicana's spine. Did that mean the Darvonians were here? Now that she thought about it, it seemed like a sure possibility.

Jessicana crept up to the tendrils, a stream of bubbles issuing from her mouth, and swung her Dragocone Ray at the vegetation. The vines instantly separated from each other, and Jessicana grinned. That should have killed it. But as she surfaced from the water she saw that the plant was shifting, moving, rising . . .

And that's when Jessicana realized she had just made it worse. A lot worse. The plant was standing. It could now move.

* * * * *

ROSEABELLE WATCHED IN HORROR AS STICKY EARTHEN tendrils planted themselves in the solid ground, the head and body of the plant bobbing along with it. She knew that this was a rare species called the "Broxlorthian," and there were only supposed to be three of them in Darvonia. Apparently the Darvonians had brought another nice surprise with them.

The Broxlorthian breathed out a cloud of acid but then coughed as though something was preventing it from breathing anymore. Roseabelle knew that Jessicana had shot iron ammo into the creature's throat, which was due to explode any second. That would surely kill it.

But how long until they exploded? She and Astro were weary from dodging the blows, and Roseabelle knew they couldn't hold up much longer. And how could the Broxlorthian suddenly walk?

Roseabelle looked up to see Jessicana drop out of the sky. "I'm sorry, Roseabelle," she said. "I thought cutting its roots would kill it."

"It's all right," Roseabelle assured her. "It's going to explode soon."

Roseabelle could see Astro shooting rapid lightning bolts, his face twisted with pain. "Are you all right?" she yelled to him, and he nodded, his face flushed.

Roseabelle looked furiously at the Broxlorthian. "I think I have an idea," she suggested.

"What is it?" Jessicana asked.

"Just before I graduated from the Academy, I got taught one last new power. I can Cloud Ride."

Jessicana cocked her head to the left. "Cloud Ride?"

"I can ride on clouds," Roseabelle explained. "Wait a second." Cloud Riding was simple. All Roseabelle had to do was face a cloud, spread her arms out, and close her eyes, thinking all the while about the sky. This would cause the tips of her fingers to transform into a soft, almost transparent material that could hook onto a cloud. Then she imagined herself flying like a bird, and she would fly up and catch a cloud. She could take at least two passengers, but it took a lot of effort to do so.

Jessicana backed away as Roseabelle spread her arms out with fingertips extended and closed her eyes. "The sky," she muttered. "It's all about the sky."

A cool feeling settled on her fingertips, and Roseabelle felt a wind swirl around her. "Jessicana, hold on to me," she ordered, and she felt her friend's fingers close around her arm. Suddenly, Roseabelle felt weightless and heard Jessicana gasp next to her. "Roseabelle, look," she urged, but Roseabelle knew it wasn't safe to open her eyes yet. If she did it too early, they could drop from the sky like a stone.

"I'm as light as a bird," she muttered, and she felt something catch on to her fingertips. When she opened her eyes, she was hanging from the underside of a cloud. "Get on top," she told Jessicana. "It's time to teach this plant a lesson."

Roseabelle could see the Broxlorthian advancing on Astro, who was still shooting bolts. Each one punctured a hole in the monster's tentacle, and it began to slow down considerably, but Astro's bolts weren't enough to kill it. "Jessicana, do you have my pack?" she yelled over the carnivorous plant's growling.

"Yes!"

"When we get close enough to the plant, I want you stab it in the head. Then I'll reach for you and you grab on to me. Got it?"

"Sure," came Jessicana's nervous reply.

Roseabelle tilted the cloud downward. As it dipped toward the Broxlorthian, she could see Jessicana adjusting her silk gloves tightly. Roseabelle took a deep breath. "Everything's going to work out," she whispered to herself. The cloud wobbled, and Roseabelle straightened it so it soared over the Broxlorthian. "Now, Jessicana!" she shouted. Her blonde friend dropped onto the slimy green head below.

Roseabelle watched as Jessicana plunged the Dragocone Ray into the monster's head. The loudest screech of pain Roseabelle had heard yet echoed throughout the forest. She quickly extended her uninjured hand to Jessicana as the creature started to shake.

"Hurry, Jessicana!" Roseabelle yelled. To her relief, just as the Broxlorthian began to topple over, her friend's shaking pale hand appeared in hers. She quickly pulled her up onto the cloud and then dipped it down even further, sailing to Astro.

"Grab on, Astro!" Jessicana yelled, and she pulled him up, pack and all. Roseabelle pushed the cloud upward. They all watched as the ammo finally exploded inside the giant beast, scattering its remains all over the lush and plentiful fields.

THE THREE FRIENDS DESCENDED FROM THE CLOUD AND dropped to the ground. Roseabelle's arm hurt badly, and she landed on her knees, letting out a cry of pain. "Roseabelle!" Jessicana exclaimed. "Are you all right?"

She grimaced. "I'm fine. We need to get the Stones."

"Where's the entrance?"

They began to search behind boulders, alcoves, and tight spaces for trapdoors. "Wait!" Jessicana exclaimed. "What if the entrance is behind the waterfall? There might be a door embedded in the rock there."

"Good idea," Roseabelle said. "I'll go check." She waded across the water, avoiding the disgusting remains of the Broxlorthian, until she was standing beside the rushing fall of water. "Here goes," she muttered. She took a deep breath and ducked through the water.

The water pressure was so great that Roseabelle felt as if she were being pelted by sledgehammers. Water enclosed around her, and Roseabelle finally found herself in a cave that smelled of sulfur. As she turned around, she realized that the water held an odd greenish glow. It quickly disappeared, though, and Roseabelle leaned against the dry cave wall to rest. Then she yelled, "Jessicana! Astro! In here!"

She waited for her two friends to reach her and walk through the pool. Roseabelle gazed intently as they walked through the waterfall but saw no greenish glow. "We can't get in!" came Jessicana's voice. Roseabelle, puzzled, stepped out of the cave. Sunlight reached her eyes, and she found herself behind Jessicana and Astro, whose backs were visible as they tromped underneath the waterfall.

"Guys! I'm over here!" she exclaimed, and her two friends walked to her.

"Where did you go?" Astro asked.

"For some reason I can get through and you can't." Roseabelle frowned. Then she grasped both of their hands. "Let's try it together."

They walked underneath the center of the waterfall and once again Roseabelle winced at the pressure of the liquid. For a moment her vision became a bright green glow, but then it vanished, and she was in the dry cave again with her two friends.

"Amazing," Jessicana said. "It's some kind of a portal."

Astro frowned. "How come only Roseabelle could get in here?"

Jessicana's eyes suddenly lit up. "I know. Toss me your pack, Roseabelle!" Roseabelle did, not following her friend at all. Jessicana pulled out a dingy black ribbon. "The ribbon we found in the book. I see now. The Darvonians must have left it there accidentally or—" Jessicana's face practically glowed as she exclaimed, "What if it was Dastrock who snuck the ribbon inside the book? He knew it was a portal to Horsh's Stones. Roseabelle, are you sure we can't trust him?"

Roseabelle sighed. She really did want to believe Dastrock.

But at the same time memories of Sheklyth (aka Shelby) came rushing back to her. She had trained Roseabelle for three years, helping her grow and develop her powers. Roseabelle didn't want to be betrayed again. She sighed. "Can we move on? We have to find an actual door to Horsh's room."

"Already done," Astro stated, and he pointed to a depiction of a man holding three jewels: one in his left hand, one in his right, and one on his head.

Jessicana put her finger on one of the Stones, and it glowed brightly. Astro did the same with the Stone on the right. Roseabelle took a deep breath and placed her thumb on the Stone on Horsh's head. All of the Stones glowed brightly, Roseabelle heard a sharp click, and a slab of stone thudded to the ground, almost crushing Jessicana's foot.

"Let's go," Astro said, and they entered the dark tunnel. Roseabelle found some stairs, and she went next. Jessicana went last and made one fatal mistake.

She forgot to close the door.

CHAPTER 12
Caverns of Horsh

ASTRO HAD NEVER FELT DARKNESS LIKE THIS BEFORE. He felt as if spiders were crawling up his arms, or as if black fog was encircling him, or as if he were falling into a bottomless pit. "It's just an illusion," he whispered, but that didn't offer up much comfort.

They continued down the winding staircase. Astro once knelt down to study the steps carefully. They were carved of stone with many cracks in the surface. A thin layer of dust covered the staircase, and as proof Astro wiped his finger on one of them. "Astro, come on," Roseabelle commanded. He was about to stand up, when he shouted, "Wait! Stop!"

The two peered curiously at him. "Do you have a light?" he asked.

Both of them shook their heads, but then Roseabelle paused. "Of course!" She got out her Dragocone Ray and shone it on the spot where Astro was pointing.

A collection of hieroglyphs ran down the steps. Astro started at the top of the stairs and slowly went down, pressing each picture. "What are you doing?" Jessicana asked.

Astro shrugged. "I don't get why Horsh would spend all

this time decorating a stone stairway unless it's a vital part of finding the Stones."

"Maybe he was into décor," Jessicana suggested, and Astro rolled his eyes.

"I doubt it." As Astro pushed on the last hieroglyph that the girls could see, they heard a small click. Seven cannons suddenly burst out of the wall, illuminated by Roseabelle's Dragocone Ray.

"Well done, Astro," Jessicana commented dryly. "Well done." Then her eyes lit up. "Wait a second!" She ran to the cannons. "I don't think these are cannons."

Astro looked at her curiously. "What do you mean? What else could they be?"

"They're entrances! And only one of them leads to the Stones of Horsh." At her words, the room lit up and a piece of parchment fell from the ceiling. Jessicana snatched it up. Roseabelle gave her an appraising look.

"Nice job, Jessicana," she commented.

Her friend scanned the paper and then gestured for Astro and Roseabelle to have a look. "Come here," she urged. "Look." Astro read:

Seven doorways, a single choice
Which one shall you take?

One holds a monster under a lake,
One has a griffin with a major toothache.
The next three hold a fiery nightmare,
Another contains a child's worst fear

But only one keeps what you seek
And here are the clues of what you speak:

The second doorway is hot with an ugly face inside
The doorway to the left of the last holds a many lick of flame
The three that hold the very same thing are neighbors in space

The first is not the best but better than the fourth
And darkness be resting in the last.

Jessicana paced the room muttering to herself. "It's a puzzle. The ugly face . . . that has to be the monster under the lake . . . maybe it's a lake of lava . . . The doorway to the left of the one that's last is the sixth . . . That has to be a fiery nightmare . . . the fourth, fifth, and sixth are fiery nightmares . . . Darkness has to be a child's worst fear. . ." Jessicana turned to her friends. "It's the third. I'm positive."

As Astro stared at the cannons, he gulped. "You sure, Jessicana?"

The blonde nodded and said in a clear voice, "We choose the third." The other cannons slid back into the wall and Astro stepped into the third. "I'm going to regret this," he muttered as he began to crawl through the darkness with Roseabelle right behind him.

* * * * *

ROSEABELLE WAS GLAD THAT JESSICANA WAS RIGHT. THE dank tunnel opened up to a bright empty room with nothing but a silver cage in the corner. As soon as the three friends stepped out, the tunnel closed behind them. There was no turning back now.

"What do we do?" Astro whispered nervously.

Roseabelle gestured to the cage and winced. Climbing through the tunnel hadn't been kind to her arm. She'd been functioning fairly well, but the pain was becoming more unbearable. And Roseabelle had a feeling that things weren't going to get much better.

They walked slowly over to the cage. "There's nothing in it." Roseabelle sighed, peering inside.

"How are we supposed to get out of this room then?" Astro asked.

Roseabelle walked over to the cage and ran her hands over

it. "It's connected to something," she said in surprise. She ran her hands up the small transparent twist of thread. "It hangs from the ceiling."

Jessicana stepped up to the cage. "It's made of vegetation," she stated. "And birdseed." She leaned forward and ripped a piece from the cage triumphantly only to see it grow back.

Roseabelle shook her head. "I really don't get this . . ." She paused. "Wait a second. Jessicana, can you please turn into a bird and try to eat the cage?"

Jessicana shrugged. "All right." She transformed and ripped off a piece from the cage. They all held their breath, but nothing grew back. Jessicana began to devour the mixture of leaves and seeds, and if parrots could have smiled, she would have. Then the "smile" disappeared and Jessicana choked. A flash of silver fell on the ground, and she turned back into a girl. "There was a piece of metal in there!" she exclaimed, and Roseabelle saw she was right. A piece of silver was on the ground. She bent down to pick it up and saw that the cage had risen and that something else was coming down—a door.

Astro saw it too. "Wait," he reasoned. "The metal weighs down the cage so when a part of the cage is eaten, a piece of metal is gone. It's like a scale. I bet that's the door up there. If Jessicana eats the whole cage then we can go through the door."

"Impossible," Jessicana muttered.

Roseabelle nodded. "There has to be magic influencing this."

Astro shrugged. "We don't exactly have time to argue about the laws of physics, so can Jessicana just start eating?"

Jessicana rolled her eyes. "Fine." She transformed and flew over to the cage, then snapped a long piece entwined with seeds and vegetation. As she ate, metal clattered to the floor and the door continued to lower. Roseabelle continued to urge on Jessicana while Astro stared at the door.

Something about this place made Roseabelle uneasy. And

it wasn't her painfully throbbing arm. Roseabelle had the feeling that something lingered here. Some kind of presence. Part of her didn't want to know what it was.

As the last piece of metal dropped to the ground, the three friends let out a cheer and rushed to the black wooden door. Astro opened it, and without warning, a brisk wind whisked them inside and the door shut behind them. The wind continued to wrap around them. Roseabelle struggled to breathe, gasping for air. "I-is this the next challenge?" she choked. In response, the wind stopped, and the three friends were dumped on the floor.

Roseabelle groaned when she realized she had landed on her arm. A flash of pain shot up her elbow, and she moaned and clutched it tightly.

"Are you all right, Roseabelle?" Astro asked with concern.

"Never been better," she answered sarcastically, gritting her teeth. Astro pulled her up as black spots danced before her eyes.

"Roseabelle, we need you to stay conscious," Astro demanded. "The three of us are a team, and we can't do this without you." Astro said the words with such force that Roseabelle made her eyes open. Her vision cleared, and she saw that three of them were trapped in a sparse stone room. Roseabelle stood up and spun in a circle, dizzy at the prospect.

Jessicana stood and brushed herself off, looking perfectly fine. For some reason fighting monsters and completing challenges didn't change her appearance in the slightest. How did she do that? Astro's messy black hair was even messier, his shirt was torn, his flip-flops looked as though they'd been dragged through a metal grinder, and his tan skin was even tanner than usual. Roseabelle imagined she didn't look much better.

Roseabelle looked around at the bare room the size of a large field. "How do we get out of here?" she wondered. Astro tapped his chin thoughtfully and then pointed to a small metal box on the other side of the room. "Over there!"

The three friends walked carefully over to the box when Jessicana groaned. "Another cage? I'm full!"

Roseabelle realized it was another cage. And inside it was the cutest little animal she had ever seen.

CHAPTER 13
Silver Eyes

ASTRO HAD TO ADMIT THAT THE CREATURE WAS CUTE. It had black and purple spots, white fur, and big brown eyes. A pink tongue stuck out of its mouth, and its eyebrows wiggled.

"Oh, how cute!" Jessicana cried.

"It's adorable!" Roseabelle agreed. Astro blinked. Were his friend's voices . . . robotic? He jumped in front of them.

"Guys, what—"

Astro trailed off to see that the girls' eyes were silver, their expressions utterly blank. He waved his hands in front of their faces. He realized the little animal must be pulling them into a trance. Astro jumped in front of the girls' faces and shouted, "Roseabelle! Jessicana! Wake up!" He turned back to the animal. "Why are you doing this?" he demanded. Then Astro stopped. Why was he yelling at this cute little creature? It hadn't done anything wrong. He walked forward to pet it. Maybe it would forgive him if he did.

Roseabelle turned to face him, her expression becoming painful. "Ouch," she muttered.

He looked at her. Her eyes were silver. Why were they silver? Weren't Roseabelle's eyes amber?

Astro snapped out of it, blinking, and realized that the creature was luring them in. To what? He shot a lightning bolt at it, a perfect shot in between two bars, but the bolt simply bounced off of the creature's head. Jessicana was close to it. She squatted down about to poke her hand through the cage bars.

"No!" Astro yelled and dove for his friend, tackling her to the hard stone floor. Jessicana blinked, and the silver drained from her eyes.

"W-what?" she whispered, and Astro pushed her down.

"Stay here," he ordered, and he turned toward Roseabelle, who was getting closer and closer to the creature. Astro studied the creature. What was making it so mesmerizing? Then he saw a small collar around the neck of the creature. It was pink and sparkly, and Astro knew instantly that it was dangerous.

He stretched forth a finger and a blue-silver lightning bolt came shooting out of it. Just as Roseabelle had bent down and was about to stretch her arm through the bars, the lightning hit the collar, and the creature's appearance began to change. What was once soft fur changed into slimy green scales. Soon Astro was staring at a scowling, slimy, green creature that looked like an angry baby with tufts of red hair, white eyes with a purple pupil, and extremely pointy teeth.

Astro immediately pulled Roseabelle back from the cage. She blinked and, just like Jessicana, the silver drained out of her eyes. "W-what?" she mumbled. "W-what happened?"

Astro steered her to the back of the wall as the creature growled at them. "It's all right. That creature right there put you and Jessicana under a spell. Its appearance was an illusion."

Roseabelle stared at the creature. "I-I think I know what that is. A Siren."

Astro scrunched up his nose. "Aren't Sirens part of a fairy tale?"

"Isn't this whole place supposed to be a fairy tale?" Roseabelle retorted.

Astro looked around for an entrance out of the room. "Where in the world is the door?"

Roseabelle looked all around the room, from the wall to the ceiling and then to the floor. She walked over to the wall and ran her hands over it. Astro watched her, confused. Finally she looked satisfied, and she waved Astro over. "Bring Jessicana. Here it is."

"The door isn't visible?" Astro asked.

Roseabelle nodded. "Not at all. It's another precaution."

Astro helped Jessicana up as she muttered something he couldn't make out. "You all right?" he asked her, and she nodded.

"I'm fine," she commented breathlessly, and she shakily walked over to where Roseabelle was standing. She appeared to twist open a doorknob. Astro groped for something until he felt the polished wood of a door. He shook his head.

"Incredible."

"We need to get going," Roseabelle urged. "The Darvonians have got to be in the caverns by now."

"Maybe they took the wrong cannon and ended up lost in darkness forever," Astro added cheerily.

"That'd be nice," Roseabelle admitted. "But I'm pretty sure the Darvonians are smarter than that, Astro."

"Or maybe they got trapped in a lake of lava with a monster inside," Astro suggested jovially.

"Astro . . ." Jessicana growled.

"Or maybe they never figured it out and kept going down the staircase and then fell into a bottomless pit," Astro continued enthusiastically.

"Astro, quit it! We need to go on!"

"Or maybe they—"

"Astro!" both girls yelled in exasperation. He smiled at them sheepishly.

"Just trying to be positive here."

Jessicana rolled her eyes, stepped through the door, then

disappeared in a cloud of mist. "Jessicana?" Roseabelle called out nervously.

There was no answer.

Astro gestured forward. "Ladies first?" he suggested hopefully. Roseabelle glared at him until he stepped forward.

"Fine." He sighed huffily and disappeared also. Roseabelle took a deep breath and disappeared into a fog of darkness.

CHAPTER 14

Maze of Ropes

JESSICANA LANDED ON A SMALL WOODEN PLATFORM IN A brightly lit room. The first thing she recognized were ropes strung in every direction. They connected together like spiderwebs, and some were rigged with spikes and clubs. Jessicana could make out a hard-packed dirt floor beneath all the webs. The ground was far away, but she could see it had various jagged rocks, their points facing skyward.

Below the webbing, Jessicana could also see a brilliantly shining door, like a beacon. Suddenly Jessicana realized that her friends wouldn't be able to stand on the small platform with her, and she quickly transformed into a parrot just in time to avoid a dark cloud depositing Astro onto the platform.

"Awk!" she squawked, and he looked up at her.

"What is it?" he asked.

"Awk! Make room for Roseabelle, awk! Both of you can't fit, awk, on the, awk, platform!" Understanding dawned on Astro's face, and he quickly jumped to the nearest rope, wrapping his hands around it. Only seconds later, Roseabelle appeared on the platform, dazed and dizzy from the ride.

"Roseabelle!" Astro shouted from below. "It's a maze of

ropes. We have to climb down to the door. And no matter what, make sure you don't fall."

Roseabelle gulped. "I got this!" she shouted back. Roseabelle would've preferred Cloud Riding, but there weren't any clouds. Jessicana suddenly swooped by her, and a silver object fell into her palm. Roseabelle peered closely at it. With a gasp, she realized it was the ring Jessicana used to escape from the Darvonians. Would it work with ropes too?

Roseabelle pushed the emerald, and rope came sailing out of it. She pictured for it to go to a rope that was almost halfway between the ground and the platform. Amazingly, the grapple attached to it, and Roseabelle felt herself slicing through air, going at a speed she wouldn't have thought possible.

She dropped and swung easily to the rope below and caught it. Roseabelle could easily see the ground now. Jessicana was below on the ground, having flown to the bottom, and was shouting encouraging squawks to her friends.

Roseabelle knew she had it easy compared to Astro, and she felt slightly bad for him when she heard a yell from up above. She turned her head to see Astro dangling from a high rope with one hand. "Help!" he shouted. Roseabelle froze, unsure of what to do.

And then Astro fell, his voice carrying throughout the entire maze of ropes.

JESSICANA INSTANTLY FLEW TOWARD HIM AT LIGHTNING SPEED (how ironic) and reached Astro quickly. She turned into a girl in midair and yelled, "Hold on to me!" As Astro reached for her, one of the traps on the ropes activated and a knife came sailing at them. Jessicana was forced to transform and fly away to avoid being hit.

She could hear Roseabelle below, pressing the emerald and pointing it toward Astro. Jessicana held her breath as the grappling hook shot out from the ring toward Astro. To Jessicana's dismay, it missed him by inches. Roseabelle yelled, "No!" and shot out another grappling hook, determined to catch him.

Jessicana felt as if she was watching it in slow motion. The hook shot toward Astro, twirling in midair, and snagged the collar of his shirt just before he crashed head-on with a large pointy boulder.

Roseabelle swung the grappling hook left and dropped Astro a couple feet to the barren ground. He gazed up at her as she grappled her way down. "Thank you," he said, breathing hard, and they all turned to the multicolored door.

"This has to be it," Jessicana whispered quietly.

"Get the ribbon out. You probably need that to open it," Astro suggested to Roseabelle. Astro and Jessicana watched as Roseabelle took the ribbon out of her pack and held it to the door. She pressed it next to the keyhole, and they all watched in amazement as it transformed into a black key. Roseabelle turned to them. "Who wants to open it?"

Jessicana rolled her eyes. "You, of course. You saved us. And now you're saving Benotripia. Go ahead, Roseabelle."

"But Astro saved me from the Siren!" Roseabelle protested. "And you gave me the ring that I used to save Astro."

Astro gestured toward the door. "This is your party, Roseabelle. Go ahead."

Jessicana watched with bated breath as her friend twisted the key in the lock. The three friends then stepped carefully into a dimly lit chamber, entranced by the swirling colors on the walls.

CHAPTER 15
Ambushed

When Roseabelle saw the colored stones placed on separate, spotless-white, frayed cushions, she knew they had finally found the Stones. "I can't believe it," she muttered. The three Stones looked extremely different in size, shape, and color. The one on the left was a deep Caribbean blue, the one on the right was a bloodred ruby, and the one placed higher above the others was a pure-white diamond.

"They're beautiful," Jessicana whispered, and she walked over to the one on the left side. Astro moved toward the red, while Roseabelle stared at the white gem. It beckoned to her, and somehow Roseabelle knew this was meant to be hers.

She strode to the jewel and picked it up. Roseabelle pushed it onto her arm and gasped as the pain melted away. Trembling, Roseabelle took away the bandages and was amazed to see her arm looked normal. There was no dried blood, no scabs, not even a scar. "It can heal," she whispered.

Jessicana was using her Stone to conjure up another copy of her ring, and Astro was using his Stone to cut his hair, because it had the ability to destroy or make something vanish. When his hair finally looked short and spiky again, he turned to Roseabelle. “Roseabelle, these could help us win the war against the Darvonians. They could change our future.”

“Yes, indeed,” came the cold voice that Roseabelle knew so well. She turned around and, sure enough, there was Sheklyth and a group of Darvonians, swords in hand. Jessicana quickly conjured up three swords and tossed one to each of her friends. Roseabelle caught it in the air without looking and faced Sheklyth.

“We have the Stones,” she hissed. “You’ve lost.”

Sheklyth smiled cruelly. “You don’t know how to use them.”

“Actually I think we have a pretty good idea,” Roseabelle reasoned.

To her surprise, Astro stepped forward. “Do your stormy horses have something to do with my lightning?”

Sheklyth let out a high mirthless laugh. “Why, of course. You’ve felt it, haven’t you? The horses are practically made of electricity and were spreading it across Benotripia. Your bolts were extremely strong because some of the electricity reached you, and you felt pain because you were so overloaded. “

“Astro, what is she talking about?” Jessicana asked.

“My lightning has been too strong, and every time I shoot it, I have overwhelming pains.”

“Why didn’t you tell us?” Roseabelle asked. She and Jessicana could have helped him more. She thought of all the times Astro had shot lightning to protect them. The thought made her sick.

Astro glared at Sheklyth. “Where are the horses?”

“Outside,” she replied vaguely. Roseabelle stepped forward and brandished her Stone.

“Leave, Sheklyth,” Roseabelle snarled. “We have the Stones. You’re no match for us. Astro could make you all disappear in a blink of an eye. If you hurt any of us, I can heal them. And Jessicana could create a whole army to defend us.

Don't mess with us." Although Roseabelle said the words confidently, inside she felt apprehensive.

Sheklyth raised her sword. "How about this, Roseabelle? You and I duel together, and if you win, we'll leave in peace. If I win, you have to hand over the Stones."

Roseabelle studied her enemy's face. Sheklyth seemed positive she would win. She had to be hiding something.

"I refuse," Roseabelle told her flatly, and Sheklyth blinked.

"Wise of you," Sheklyth commented. She held up an arrow dipped in green ooze. "I would've fought you with these. It contains the blood of the plant you just killed, actually. Your parrot friend knows it's poisonous, don't you?"

"You planted the Sephlotine Spikes. The Garaganta. The Broxlorthian. How did you import all those over here?"

"Simple. The Garaganta and the Broxlorthian have the shortest life spans in all of Benotripia. By the time a month has passed from the moment they were born, they are full size. They live for two more months and then die. We brought them here semi-grown, and by the time we planted them or let them loose, they were full sized. It would have been more simple to retrieve the Stones, but you had the ribbon this entire time. Besides, Horsh rigged the entrance so that Darvonians couldn't use the ribbon to enter. We placed obstacles in your path so you would lose supplies and not be as prepared for the Chambers of Horsh." Roseabelle blinked, then motioned for Astro to come forward.

"Unless you want to be destroyed," Astro growled. "Move back."

Sheklyth just smiled as if she knew a secret. "Go ahead. See what happens to you."

Roseabelle and Astro glanced at each other, and they knew they were thinking the same thing: *Is she lying just to stop us from vanquishing them?* When they looked back at their nemesis, they realized they had just made a big mistake. Sheklyth had taken the opportunity to strike.

A poisonous arrow was shooting toward them, with more

behind it. Astro pulled Roseabelle out of the way just in time. Jessicana quickly conjured herself a bow and a quiver of arrows dripping with a white liquid that Roseabelle couldn't tell if it was poisonous. Roseabelle hid the Stone in her pocket and stepped forward, swinging her sword and blocking the arrows, even sending some flying back at Sheklyth.

The Darvonians behind their leader began shooting arrows too, some of them hurling axes or javelins. Roseabelle let out a cry of pain as a javelin pierced her leg, but she quickly pressed the white diamond to the spot where she had been hit and the cut closed almost instantly.

To her surprise, a flash of red caught Roseabelle's eye. While blocking the arrows with her sword, she managed to see that behind Sheklyth was Dastrock at the very back of the group, in full armor but not shooting at them. He was pointing behind them and mouthing something. Roseabelle couldn't make out what he was saying until he started pantomiming.

"Door," he mouthed. "Door."

Roseabelle jumped behind Astro and whispered in his ear, "Cover me." She searched the walls looking for a button or an awkward panel of stone, anything signaling there was a way out. She began to feel her hands along the smooth stone of the wall. Finally her pointer finger hit a small bump. Roseabelle peered at the spot and, sure enough, saw a miniscule silver button. She grinned and jumped over to Jessicana. "There's a door," she whispered. "Come over here."

Sheklyth's smile began to fade as the friends clumped together, still battling the Darvonians. Roseabelle saw that the battle was finally taking a toll on Jessicana. Her blonde hair was covered in soot, there was a hole in her shoe, and her clothes were covered in dirt. "Ready, now," Roseabelle whispered. She backed up against the button and hit it with her elbow. She could see a wide smile spread across Dastrock's face.

As sunlight crept into the room, Sheklyth jumped forward.

"No!" she shrieked, pulling a sharp sword from her belt.

Roseabelle quickly pulled out her own and barely blocked a vicious strike from her former trainer. Metal clashed against metal as Sheklyth and Roseabelle circled around, the Darvonian on the offense, the Benotripian on the defense.

Roseabelle didn't know how much longer she could battle her former friend. Sheklyth's strikes were hard, and Roseabelle was surprised how well she was holding up on her own.

Astro and Jessicana had already stepped out the door. Roseabelle shouted, "Astro, make her vanish!" Astro held up the bloodred Stone and closed his eyes, but before he could do anything more, Sheklyth lunged for the diamond that was tucked in Roseabelle's pocket.

Just as her fingers were an inch away from the Stone, a red cloud of mist swirled around Sheklyth and carried her away, screaming defiantly. Roseabelle, breathing hard, looked up at the Darvonians, who were staring at her, shocked.

"It'd be good if you could make them vanish too," she whispered to Astro as some of them prepared to fight. A javelin whizzed past her abdomen and Roseabelle flinched.

Astro groaned. "I have to wait a little while longer. Making a person disappear is a hard feat, Roseabelle, and I'm exhausted." The three friends stepped outside. Both Jessicana and Roseabelle put a hand on Astro's Stone and pushed all their energy into it. They jumped to avoid oncoming arrows. The Stone glowed brighter and brighter until everyone in the room had to shield their eyes.

Astro held up the glowing Stone, closed his eyes, and, in the blink of an eye, every Darvonian flickered and disappeared. Only one was left standing in the room. He was dressed in a large black cloak, ash-colored armor, and a heavy helmet. Dastrock smiled broadly at them. "That was very impressive," he commented.

"We couldn't have done it without your helpful hint," Roseabelle remarked.

Dastrock shrugged. "I try. So, now do you believe me?"

"Yes."

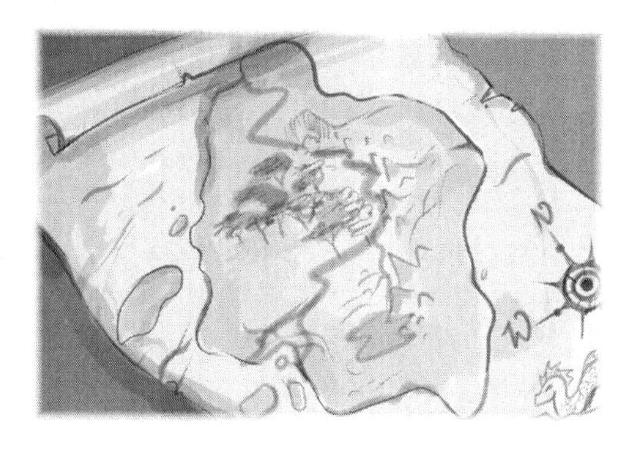

CHAPTER 16
The Lost Island

ASTRO WAS MORE RELIEVED THAN EVER WHEN THEY stepped out into the bright sunshine. To their surprise, they had come out the same way they had come in, and Astro could hear the doorway crumbling behind them. "I can't believe we did it," he said.

Jessicana and Roseabelle stepped out alongside him with Dastrock tailing behind. Astro turned back to them, then stretched and yawned. "I think it's time we got back home." He chuckled and the two friends nodded enthusiastically.

Roseabelle took a deep breath and whistled for the Persopians. Large shadowy shapes flitted across the sky. Astro turned to the large Broxlorthian carcass that was drifting in the lake. He turned to Jessicana. "I think I'll get rid of that ugly thing," he said, and with a wave of his Stone, the body of the large plant flickered, glowed, then evaporated in millions of small red particles.

As their Persopians landed on the opposite side of the lake, Jessicana grinned at Astro. "I'll race you there," she said, laughing with a gleam in her eye. Then she took off running.

"Hey!" Astro shouted, easily catching up with her.

Before they knew it, they were headed home with Dastrock riding on a Persopian that Jessicana had created. The journey took a few days, but eventually they reached their destination. When Roseabelle's home came into view, they landed swiftly and hurried to the porch where their parents were waiting.

Astro's mother and father were on the front steps of Roseabelle's home. Astro bit his lip. Would they be angry? Disappointed? However, when he came closer, his mother hugged him tightly and his father looked at him with proud eyes.

"Don't you ever do that to us again," Mrs. Jagged-Bolt ordered. "We were scared out of our minds when we got back and you weren't there."

Astro didn't even need to speak as he watched Jessicana reunite with her family and Roseabelle hug her mother. They were all together again.

"Mom," Roseabelle began. "There's someone I want you to meet." She gestured at the armor-clad figure. Mrs. Wingling shrieked when she saw him.

Dastrock removed his helmet and spoke in a loud clear voice. "No, I'm not a Darvonian." Danette gasped as he mounted the steps and moved up the porch.

"Dastrock?"

"I'm back."

Danette embraced him. "I haven't spoken to you since the night Magford disappeared."

"It has been a while," Dastrock agreed. "But, Danette, I was thinking . . . Roseabelle needs to know." Astro's brow went up. What could Dastrock be talking about?

"Her friends can know too. They've certainly earned it."

Danette turned to Astro and motioned him to the door. Jessicana saw the gesture and walked inside also, Roseabelle following from behind. Danette and Dastrock shared a look and then walked into the kitchen.

* * * * *

Roseabelle sat at the table with Jessicana and Astro and watched as Danette gracefully took her seat at the head of the table with Dastrock right next to her.

Danette gave Dastrock a meaningful look, and he sighed as he looked into Roseabelle's eyes. "So, Roseabelle. You know you are a Meta-Mord correct?"

Roseabelle nodded. She'd known ever since she'd gone to the Academy.

"Well, this may come as a shock to you, but Meta-Mords aren't exactly Benotripians."

"What?" Roseabelle asked incredulously. "That's not possible."

"Oh, but it is," Dastrock said with a tired look. "It surely is."

"We're not Darvonians," Roseabelle said defensively.

"Right," Dastrock agreed. "I'm a Meta-Mord too. So was your father." Roseabelle blinked. She had never known that.

"Well, then what are we?" Roseabelle asked.

Dastrock pulled out a scroll of parchment and unraveled it, showing it to Roseabelle. It was a map. "This is where you were born." Roseabelle scanned the paper, confused. What did Dastrock mean? She could see waterfalls, rolling hills, forests, and many other beautiful landmarks. This didn't help her confusion.

"This isn't Benotripia," Roseabelle decided.

"Correct."

"But it's not Darvonia."

"Also correct."

Roseabelle gasped. It had suddenly clicked. "There's a third island," she stated. "That's where I was born? Is that where all Meta-Mords are born?"

Dastrock nodded. "Currently it's under the control of the Darvonians." He gulped. "It used to be an ally of Benotripia, but we had to bring you here, so you would be safe."

An idea so ludicrous sprouted in Roseabelle's mind, and she wondered if she dare say it out loud. "And the third island is also where—" She broke off her sentence, unable to finish it.

"Yes, indeed. The third island is where your father, Magford, is being held."

Discussion Questions

1. If someone was disloyal to you like Sheklyth, would you be cautious or would you trust freely? Why?
2. Which stone would you prefer to have the most—the stone that can create, destroy, or heal?
3. What would you do with the stone?
4. If you had to go up against a monster, which one would you go up against—Garaganta, a Siren, or the Broxlorthian? Why?
5. Who is your favorite character?
6. What things do you like about that character that you would like to see in yourself?

ONLY THE FINAL BATTLE REMAINS...

BENOTRIPIA

KEYS TO THE DREAM WORLD

From the author of *The Rescue* and *The Stones of Horsh*

MCKENZIE WAGNER

For Ty,
the most creative Benotripian of them all

Contents

CHAPTER 1
Astro

WHEN ASTRO WOKE UP THAT MORNING, HE HAD planned on doing a lot of things, but falling from the sky was not one of them.

Stretching and yawning, he rolled out of bed, already dressed in rumpled jeans and a black T-shirt. He then crossed over to the window and threw aside the heavy midnight-black drapes so sunlight could pour into the room. He slid open the heavy glass pane and welcomed the fresh air that drifted inside. Slinging his leg over the windowsill, Astro boosted himself onto the ledge.

There. That was better. A lot better. Astro lived inside a gray stone tower that dated back to who knows when. His father had inherited it from his father, who inherited from his father, and so on. It had belonged to the Jagged-Bolt family for generations. They had never moved, probably because (aside from the arsenal in the very top room) there wasn't a smidge of metal to be found in the tower. They'd discovered that the neighbors didn't appreciate a lot of bright flashing, which was what usually resulted when any of them touched metal, because most Jagged-Bolt family members, including Astro, were born with the power to shoot lightning bolts from their fingertips.

He gazed at the beach in the far distance—one benefit of living in a tower was the fantastic view. Astro spotted many Benotripians already gathering to resume building the defenses. Ever since the Darvonians—their heartless enemies who lived on another island—had snuck onto Benotripia in hopes of stealing the Stones of Horsh, Danette (the leader of Benotripia) had decided they needed more security. She had put together a plan for the Benotripians to build watchtowers. If the Darvonians attacked, they would be ready. Danette had personally marked certain places on the beach's outer edges where the ground was hard enough to build a foundation. The defense towers looked pretty good to Astro; they were towering structures with endless barracks of magical tools and weapons stocked inside.

You would think that after obtaining the most powerful artifacts in history, people would pay attention to you, maybe let you in on what they were planning. Dastrock (Roseabelle's uncle) and Danette often had secret meetings—and it drove Astro crazy just thinking about it. Did they know something about the Darvonians' plans? Roseabelle, Danette's daughter and Astro's best friend, had told him she didn't know anything either. Six weeks previous, Astro had gone to her house, but Dastrock and Danette had shooed him away, purposely avoiding his questions and telling him to go find Roseabelle outside.

Shortly thereafter, Dastrock and Danette left Benotripia on a sea vessel, and Astro hadn't seen them for five weeks. They had traveled to the outer edges of Darvonia to monitor their enemy. Astro reckoned Danette just wanted to be extra cautious.

His fingertips crackled with electricity, and Astro sighed with relief. After his Stone had made the Darvonians and their mysterious shadow horses disappear using its own ability, his hands no longer shook with pain when he used his power. When the Darvonians brought the shadow horses to the island, they radiated so much electricity, it had overloaded

Astro and caused immense pain. But that didn't mean the shadow horses weren't out there—he still needed to be cautious. Speaking of the Stones of Horsh . . . Astro reached into his pocket to run his fingers over the smooth, hard texture of the red Stone. Horsh, a Darvonian who had joined forces with the Benotripians, had created the Stones and applied magical abilities to them. Astro still didn't understand why he had created them—that was another mystery still to solve.

Astro had assumed that Dastrock would know a way to destroy the Stones, but Roseabelle's uncle had just shaken his head. "I wish I could," he had said. "They are a true danger to the Benotripians. But they are protected by various enchantments and can't be destroyed by steel, fire, Dragocone Rays, not even the other Stones. For now, you will have to keep them safe and hidden away. Never reveal them." Dastrock wanted to destroy the Stones, because although they had extraordinary powers, if the Darvonians got ahold of them, all would be lost. It was better they didn't exist at all, for the safety of Benotripia. Astro also wondered why in the world Dastrock would trust him, Roseabelle, and Jessicana with the Stones. "If the Darvonians do attack, the first place they'll choose to search for the Stones would be the leaders of the Benotripia. Believe me, they'll be safer in your hands."

It was tempting to show off the Stone to others, but Astro obeyed Dastrock anyway.

Swinging his legs over the windowsill, Astro curled his fingers into a tight fist. It was strange how much Benotripia had changed since the Darvonians had invaded the island. The schools were temporarily closed because most adults needed to help construct the defenses and every child needed to be practicing their powers.

Astro thought back to the last time he'd spoken with Roseabelle and Jessicana, just a few days ago. "I'm a little worried," Roseabelle had said. *Of course she's worried,* Astro thought. *The Darvonians will stop at nothing to conquer Benotripia.*

"Worried about what?" he'd asked her.

"Sheklyth," was her reply. Astro grimaced at the name of Roseabelle's former trainer. Sheklyth had betrayed them all, revealing to Roseabelle when they had gone to rescue Danette that Sheklyth wasn't just a Darvonian, but the heir to the Darvonian throne.

"Why? We all saw Astro's Stone make her vanish," Jessicana said.

"I know, but . . . I can't shake the feeling that she's not gone."

Maybe it was crazy, maybe it was absurd, but Astro had a strange feeling that Roseabelle was right. For some reason, Astro sensed that Sheklyth was alive. He didn't know how or why, but he just did. Astro's gaze locked onto something in the corner of his room, tucked behind a shelf. The files they had retrieved from Darvonia, the ones that had gotten them into the castle, still lay there. He, Jessicana, and Roseabelle had figured out the files had been talking about Metamordia—that was the secret thing the Darvonians had been discussing. What would Metamordia be like anyway? Tropical, like Benotripia? Rocky, like Darvonia?

As he gazed out on the landscape of the tropical island, immersed in his thoughts, Astro suddenly saw a silver projectile hurtling toward him out of the corner of his eye. It happened so fast that Astro barely had time to duck forward. It was a weapon!

Although he avoided it, the act of ducking caused Astro to lose his balance. Before he knew what was happening, he dropped like a stone, the air ripping past his face, his arms flailing wildly. In his panic, silver lightning shot from his fingertips, peppering the ground below.

The wind whistled obnoxiously in his ears, and Astro tried to grasp anything he could. At one point, he grazed the rough-hewn stone of the tower, but he was hurtling toward the earth so fast, it was impossible to hold on.

The only thing he could think of as the ground rushed up to meet him was: "AHHHHHHH!"

Desperately, he shot a large lightning bolt at the ground to boost him up and slow his fall, but it merely created a smoking black hole in the dirt instead. Just as he was about to smash against the ground, something jerked him to a stop, suspending his body horizontally two inches above the earth.

"Wha-what?" he said shakily. Suddenly the hold on his body gave way, and he plopped down on the ground.

"Astro!" said a familiar voice, and he turned to see a wide-eyed and terrified Jessicana running toward him, blonde hair flowing around her shoulders. As Astro moved to get up, he noticed a rope around his waist, tied to a metal hook. Jessicana wore the Grapplegore, a bulky ring on her finger with a glistening green gem. Her trainer, Asteran, had given the ring to her. Every time Jessicana pressed on the green gem, two ropes swung out, one to latch on to something and another to attack any intruders from below. Normally, Jessicana used it for swinging from vine to vine. "Are you all right?" she asked, helping Astro to his feet.

"Yeah," he said, rubbing off the shock of plummeting eighty feet. "What happened?"

"I-I was walking to go to Roseabelle's house, when I decided to come here to invite you, and I sort of saw you falling from the sky," she stammered.

The realization struck him. "You saved me," he said.

"I'm glad you're all right. Um, by the way, why were you falling from the sky?" Jessicana's eyebrows crinkled a bit.

"I saw something coming toward me," Astro explained. "Looked like a weapon ready to slice off my head! And since I was sitting on the windowsill, I tumbled out."

"A weapon?" Jessicana asked, her voice shaking a bit. "Are you sure you weren't imagining things?"

"I'm sure!" Astro said. But it had all happened so fast, he wondered if he really was just daydreaming. Maybe the silver projectile flying toward him hadn't been a weapon—maybe it was just a bird. But he could've sworn it wasn't normal.

Jessicana gestured to the smoking black hole in the ground. "Goodness, your lightning sure got out of hand!"

Astro walked over to the hole. "There goes Mom's garden." As he peered over the edge, a flash of color caught his eye. What was that? All sorts of surprises today! Kneeling down he heard Jessicana walk up beside him. Was that . . . some sort of musty white contrasting against the black dirt?

Reaching his hand into the pit, his fingers grasped a rough trutan, a type of parchment in Benotripia, and he yanked it out, clearing away the dust and shaking off the layers of dirt. "Where'd you find that?" Jessicana asked as Astro held it up against the light.

"Just right here," he said. *What is this? Some sort of outdated scroll?* he thought.

Jessicana pointed to a spot on it in the top left corner. Astro realized it was the symbol of Horsh—three Stones balanced on a person, one in the left hand, one in the right, and one balanced on the head.

"We should show this to Roseabelle," Jessicana said excitedly. She blew away some of the dust. "I can't make out most of the words but the three of us together just might." She and Astro stood together, and he shook his head, almost in amusement.

It was funny how he could discover things completely by accident.

As the two walked away, a pair of large golden eyes peered out from underneath a bush, intensely focused on the young Benotripians. In a moment, they sunk back into the shadows.

Jessicana and Astro hadn't noticed anyone watching them.

CHAPTER 2
Dream World Scroll

As soon as Astro slipped the dusty parchment inside his pocket, Jessicana suggested they head over to Roseabelle's house. It'd been a while since she'd seen her friends, and it would be nice to talk with them.

As they trudged through the sand, Jessicana saw a cluster of bizarre animals race past them—probably a shapeshifting Benotripian family. Danette and Dastrock had left orders to build defenses and be prepared, and the Benotripians had definitely taken them seriously. In the distance, Jessicana could see Benotripians hard at work, structuring the large stone towers that would be used to fight the Darvonians. But personally, Jessicana didn't believe the Darvonians would suddenly storm the island. They were much more clever than that.

She and Astro finally arrived at Roseabelle's home, and Jessicana's heart leaped to see her friend already sitting on the porch, feet dangling in front of the rope ladder. Roseabelle's house was positioned in a large tree. On Roseabelle's arm was a lightly speckled brown-and-white mottel, a special type of bird that could send messages. It kept repeating the same message in Danette's voice. "Roseabelle, check the defenses and make sure the Benotripians are doing their jobs. Dastrock and I are well, and we are keeping constant watch on the Darvonians, making sure they aren't sending any war fleets to attack the island. Be safe. I love you."

"Roseabelle!" Astro called from the ground, and they saw their friend beam at them.

"Hey!" Roseabelle greeted them. "Danette just sent me a message."

"Isn't that the first one in five weeks?" Jessicana asked.

Roseabelle nodded. "Yes, but it's a long way for a mottel to travel." She signaled the mottel to remain on the porch while Jessicana ascended the rope ladder. Astro quickly followed.

"My mother wants to me to check the defenses on the beach. You want to come along?" Roseabelle asked.

"Sure," Astro said. He peered into the distance. "It looks like they're doing their jobs, that's for sure." Jessicana had to agree. The stone towers grew higher every day.

Roseabelle laughed. "I know, but I should probably check them up close anyway. Besides, it's a good excuse to talk with you two." The three friends descended the rope ladder, the mottel balanced on Roseabelle's bare arm.

They trekked to the beach, sand coating their sandals. Jessicana took in the breathtaking view of the crystal blue waters washing up on the golden shores. And then she saw the defense towers before them.

Benotripians were racing to and fro from the massive stone structures, carrying supplies and weapons. The structures seemed to tower over the tiny figures of the three friends. Jessicana could see spiraling staircases when she peered closer. Many Benotripians were using their powers to improve the construction.

"Looks like they're doing what they're supposed to," Roseabelle said, nodding her approval. She gave a report to the mottel and it flew away, darting over the deep ocean, soaring high among the clouds. "I gave him a few hours to rest because he had a long journey. So what's going on with your lives?"

"I nearly died today," Astro said cheerfully.

Roseabelle's eyes nearly bugged out of her head. "What?"

"Long story," Jessicana intervened. "But look what we found." Astro dug out the wadded up piece of dusty trutan from his pocket, and Roseabelle unraveled it, scouring it quickly.

"It has Horsh's symbol on it!" she exclaimed. "Where did you find this?"

"I—" Astro was about to continue but halted in mid-speech. Jessicana felt chills run up her spine. Was it just her or did she feel eyes boring into the back of her head?

Suddenly, her face turned ashen as a silver blur flew toward her friends. "Get down!" she yelled as she plowed into Roseabelle and Astro. She knocked them over and looked up just as a Thepgile Disc soared over their heads. A noisy clatter echoed behind them as the circular weapon with the cord attached dropped to the ground.

"Who threw that?" Astro said, glancing over his shoulder.

"No time to talk! Let's get back to your house!" Jessicana insisted. Something really odd was going on. First, Astro was shot at and now all three of them were being targeted! Her breath caught in her throat. Was it possible? . . . No, she didn't want to think about that now.

Without another word, the three of them raced back to Roseabelle's home, not bothering to search for the weapon someone had hurled at them. They needed to hide now! Jessicana's pulse raced and she searched the sky behind them as they ran, but she spotted no one—and, thankfully, nothing else flying toward them. The Benotripians working on the towers had been so focused on their tasks, it was unlikely that they noticed the attack. And with so many people milling about, Jessicana hadn't noticed any Darvonian dark cloaks. She shivered. Maybe someone had been hiding.

They ran up the rope ladder and threw themselves into

Roseabelle's home, panting for breath. "Well, I guess someone really wants us dead," Astro said, wheezing.

"Close the windows," Roseabelle ordered. "Lock the door. What's going on? What's on that parchment?"

"We don't know," Jessicana said, scrambling to clasp the lock on Roseabelle's front door as Astro pulled out the trutan. "We can't decipher it. It's too faded."

Roseabelle and Jessicana both peered at the document, scrutinizing the faded writing. Suddenly, Roseabelle's eyes lit up. "I have an idea!"

Roseabelle raced upstairs and Astro and Jessicana quickly followed. They burst into Danette's study. "My mother uses a tool for these sort of things," Roseabelle said excitedly. Digging in Danette's two desk drawers, she soon brought out a tiny silver instrument.

It had a small head with a glassy surface and small teeth ruts. The sheen of the metal was distorted and coated with a thin layer of dust. Roseabelle pressed it down on the trutan, the ruts clearing away some of the deep dust, revealing words positioned on the trutan. "This is an Embele," Roseabelle said. "My mother created them because when people sent her documents and letters, sometimes they got dirty. Probably a prank or something." She proudly held the Embele in front of the trutan. "There."

Astro whistled. All of the grime had been scratched off and Jessicana could now decipher the words. Roseabelle handed it to her. "You want to read it aloud?"

Jessicana shrugged. "Sure." She narrowed her eyes a little bit, trying to understand the miniscule writing. She gasped. "It talks about the Dream World!"

Astro raised his eyebrows. "What does it say?"

Jessicana turned back to the paper and began to read. " 'The Dream World is a real, physical place,' " she began. " 'In my studies, I have learned that the ancient Benotripians used their powers to create the Dream World—an invisible passageway between the three islands of Benotripia, Metamordia, and Darvonia. With their powers, the Benotripians turned the Dream World invisible and levitated it, sustaining it to remain in the air. They also gave it the gift of sonic speed, so that anyone inside it can travel at the speed of wind. For centuries, the inhabitants of the islands used the Dream World to travel between the islands, both physically and with their minds. There was, for a time, peace among the nations.

" 'However, years later, the Darvonians betrayed our trust. They attempted to take over the Dream World. Doing so would have allowed them to travel to Benotripia and Metamordia instantaneously with numerous armies and creatures. They failed only because I locked the doorway with the Stones before they could gain access. I must now hide the Stones, before they find the doorway again. The doorway is—' " Jessicana stopped and frowned deeply. "The ink is smudged over the rest of it." She found her friends gaping at her as they comprehended the message.

She remembered how Roseabelle had entered the Dream World with her mind when she had touched the feather Jessicana's trainer Asteran had dropped—it was crazy to think that the Dream World was an actual place. "This document might be phony," Astro said. "It could've been planted by the Darvonians."

Jessicana shook her head. "No, I don't think so. Look." She pointed to the worn writing and the symbol of Horsh. "This lettering is too ancient to be made from the Darvonians just recently. And look at the emblem of Horsh—it's exactly the same as the one behind the waterfall."

Her friends nodded. "It seems as though Horsh really did write this," Roseabelle muttered to herself. "But we can't be sure. It could still be a trick."

"The Stones of Horsh were a myth and they turned out to be real," Astro pointed out.

"Yes, but this is a little too coincidental," Roseabelle said.

Jessicana had to agree. How did a page of Horsh's diary get so near Astro's home?

"Still, it's all we have. We might as well rely on it," Jessicana said, then glanced out the window. "I need to get home."

"Same," Astro said. Roseabelle tucked the trutan in her pocket.

"We'll figure it out," she promised as Jessicana and Astro went to the door.

"We better race home before anything else falls from the sky and tries to kill us," Astro said, assuming a runner's stance. Jessicana nearly laughed at the ridiculous sight.

"Yeah, that'd probably be best." Then they flung open Roseabelle's front door and charged toward their homes, feet flying and hearts racing.

CHAPTER 3
Walk in the Night

Hours later, Roseabelle sat up in her bedroom, reclining on her bed. Liquid moonlight streamed through her window, illuminating the room. She recalled that Danette had made her promise to not leave Benotripia unless there was a dire emergency.

But she wanted to help Danette! And even though Danette and Dastrock had gone to monitor the Darvonians, Roseabelle was sure danger was lurking around in Benotripia. The only problem was she didn't know what. All she could come up with was that it had something to do with the enemy island.

"Only leave Benotripia if there is an emergency," Roseabelle whispered, wondering what counted as an emergency. Probably a known ambush from the Darvonians or black ships in the distance. Definitely not because Astro fell from his tower—Jessicana had finally told her the story.

The trutan lay on her dresser, blending in so that she couldn't even see it from her angle. Would she need to use it sometime soon? Part of her almost hoped so.

She decided to go on a quick walk to clear her head. There was no way she would get back to sleep with all these thoughts plaguing her mind. Roseabelle quietly unlatched the window and slid onto her mango tree, grasping the thick branches and leaping down onto the soft, grainy sand. Striding along a path, she breathed in the cool, fresh air. A light breeze slipped past her face, making her red hair flutter.

Cottages, tree houses, schools, libraries, and other buildings dotted the landscape around her, and she weaved between them and eventually spotted Jessicana's tree home. Crickets chirped and diverse flowers and plants bobbed on their stems from the flower beds.

The looming shapes of the defense towers caught her eye and Roseabelle's interest sprung. She had never been up close to the defenses; she had just watched the Benotripian workers from afar except for her quick visit earlier that day. Roseabelle made her way down to the beach and put her hand against the smooth, polished stone, amazed that the Benotripians could build a structure as large and complicated as this.

Danette had never set any rules about touching or going inside the defenses, she reasoned—though the Benotripian people wouldn't appreciate a mere child investigating one. Still, Roseabelle was incredibly curious. What exactly was inside? She knew there was an enormous stock of weapons and supplies, but were there any plans, any clues? Deciding to be quick, Roseabelle searched for an entrance and eventually found a stone handle.

She pulled with all of her weight, but the handle wouldn't budge. *Oh, well.* When Danette returned, Roseabelle would ask to explore the towers. She plopped down on the white sand and gazed out into the ocean. She could see a tiny dot in the distance, but maybe it was just her imagination. After all, it was dark. She squinted to see the getaway boats docked at the side of the beach, carrying supplies.

A deep low growl broke the silence of the moment and Roseabelle whirled around, eyes scanning the area frantically. What was that?

It couldn't be a wild animal—those creatures preferred

the Benotripian jungles, not the beaches! Besides, the beach was empty except for mounds of sand, some bushes lining the far sides, and, of course, the three defense towers within her reach. Beyond those, open paths stretched back to the city of Royalton.

No animals appeared.

"Hello?" Roseabelle called softly, rubbing her head. Maybe she was hallucinating. After all, it was pitch black, almost midnight. She should head back home.

But as she headed toward a path, the growl once again resounded in her ears, and Roseabelle flinched, quickly pivoting in the direction the sound had come from. The bushes rustled quietly and Roseabelle backed up, groping for anything that she could use as a weapon or at least something to protect herself with. What could it be, some sort of Darvonian animal? Or was it a person?

Roseabelle took a couple of steps back, her eyes wide. A smooth shape glided out of the bushes and a pair of golden eyes stared and then narrowed at her.

In the darkness, Roseabelle couldn't make out the creature and, as another low growl emitted from the figure, she backed up a few more steps. She kept her eyes trained on the creature, waiting for the beast to follow her, but the golden eyes didn't move. "What are you?" she whispered, thinking about her power for sensing animal's emotions. If only she could get close enough to touch it. But what if it was a Darvonian animal that would rip her to shreds? She had never heard of a golden-eyed Benotripian beast before.

The darkness completely immersed the creature. Even in the moonlight, Roseabelle could only make out its faint figure. The eyes stared back at her without the slightest hint of aggression. Tentatively, she took a step forward. "Easy," she whispered as the low growl came again.

Roseabelle froze, afraid it was going to pounce. Instead, the creature moved slowly. Roseabelle watched in awe as the majestic creature suddenly came into her view. She awkwardly stumbled back a few paces, mouth gaping open at the sight before her.

The large creature had mottled black-and-red fur, a slim body, and four paws the size of dinner plates, covered in white feathers. Its head was roundish with a horned snout and a streak of white feathers on its smooth forehead. Roseabelle noted that its body structure reminded her of a wild cat's.

Those enormous golden eyes still stared at her as the creature slowly approached.

Roseabelle didn't know whether to run or to stay put. She had never seen this animal before—it wasn't Benotripian! But she had never heard of animals like these on Darvonia either. It growled again, and she caught a glimpse of its brilliant array of white teeth.

She sensed something else in its eyes, however, that contrasted with the growl—a hint of peace. Its muscles, rippling deep under its fur, were loose, and its expression was almost playful.

Roseabelle inhaled a deep breath and outstretched her trembling fingers to the side of the animal's head, wondering why she was trusting it so much not to attack her. Maybe she was crazy, but she had a feeling that, inside, this wasn't just an ordinary animal.

As soon as her fingers touched the sleek fur, Roseabelle concentrated and slowly closed her eyes. Instantly she felt a rush of overwhelming surprise that she'd found something—found what? Then, as Roseabelle dug deep into the layers of emotions, she began to feel like she was floating in air. The creature was perfectly at peace and full of tranquility. She sensed no hostility or harmful feelings inside, not even gnawing hunger. Honestly, it was weird. There was also a burst of intelligence, and she had the feeling that the creature knew everything that was going on around him.

But the strangest thing was when Roseabelle realized that the energy of these feelings were focused on her.

Roseabelle snapped open her eyes to find the pleading golden orbs staring right back at her.

But what if this was a trap? Despite the peace she'd felt from the animal, Roseabelle couldn't shake her nagging worry. She chanced a quick look over her shoulder. Everyone in the nearby houses was still asleep.

Jessicana. Jessicana would know! She loved animals and she had read probably thousands of books on them. Roseabelle looked in the direction of Jessicana's home. Her friend would know where this animal had come from. But it was still very early, and Mrs. Wing-ling probably wouldn't appreciate her daughter's best friend and a strange animal coming to their house in the middle of the night to talk. Roseabelle turned back to the strange creature.

"I'll come back for you in the morning," she said, kneeling on the ground and rubbing its head. Roseabelle stayed extremely still as the animal whimpered.

"I'm sorry, but you have to stay out here for the night," Roseabelle whispered. "I'll come right back here in the morning, all right?"

The creature just stared at her, but as she stroked the side of his head, he purred softly. As Roseabelle straightened up, the creature, swift as the shadows, darted away into the night. There was a distinct rustle of bushes and then Roseabelle was alone.

CHAPTER 4

Moonstar

ASTRO SPRINTED ALONG THE PATH TO ROSEABELLE'S house, anxious to talk to his friends again. At the crack of dawn he'd been awake, and after meandering around the tower for a little while, he'd decided to get dressed and head over to see Jessicana and Roseabelle again. As he ran, the red Stone thumped in his pocket, reminding him that it was still there.

Around him people were walking, flying, and even burrowing into the earth, traveling around the island. He accidentally bumped into a group of women near a cluster of trees who were practicing using their powers by transforming into various animals. Astro muttered an apology and weaved through the trees, wishing he, like Jessicana, could turn into a parrot and fly for once. As a pair of bird-shaped Benotripians almost collided over his head, however, he decided that maybe it was okay just running.

Surprisingly, when he got to Roseabelle's house, both she and Jessicana were already on the front porch. "We have to show you something," Jessicana said as he rushed up to them.

"What is it?" Astro asked, the wheels in his head already turning. But a breathless Roseabelle just motioned for him to follow them.

"I went walking last night," she said. "And found something crazy."

Astro had seen a lot of crazy things in his life—probably more than he needed to. But what was Roseabelle talking about? They sprinted across the paths to the beach, keeping away from the Benotripian workers. The girls led him to a more secluded spot, where the sand met the cerulean waves and the outer edges of the leafy jungle. "What is it?" he asked.

"Um, please just don't freak out," Jessicana said. "He's friendly."

"Who's friendly?" Astro asked, but the answer came straightaway when a deep, chilling growl rattled his spine. He whirled around to see a large cat with black and red fur pacing toward him. He jumped slightly at the sight of it. "Guys, I'm not really interested in becoming lunch right now." He backed away slowly, staring in wonder at the animal's golden orbs.

"It's fine," Roseabelle said. "I've read his emotions, and he won't attack you."

Astro accepted her words but didn't break eye contact with the creature. "Wait, so he just came up to you?"

Jessicana answered the question. "I think he's been looking for her all along. They must have formed a special animal bond. I've read about those. Anyway, he's not from Darvonia or Benotripia."

"He has to be from Metamordia then," Astro said. There was no way this creature had just appeared from thin air.

"That's what I was thinking," Roseabelle said and knelt next to the creature. Astro flinched but the animal only purred in response.

"Why's he so feathery?"

"No idea," Jessicana said. "But what's even more curious is how he got here."

"Maybe a stowaway of some kind," Astro suggested, and Roseabelle's eyes went wide.

"That could be it," she mused. "But a stowaway on whose boat?"

Astro thought about the weapons flying at him. Was it even possible? Had Darvonians really traveled to the island again? But no sightings had been reported. What about Metamordians? But there had been no contact with that island for years. Why would they suddenly show up? He had the urge to say something but resisted. Right now they had a mystery at hand to solve. "So why did we meet him here?" Astro asked gesturing to the animal. "Someone might see us. Should we go to your yard, Jessicana?"

"He led us here," Jessicana said, and to prove her point, the animal nudged his head on the soft sand. She walked over to Roseabelle, who had been casually folding and unfolding the parchment in her hand. Both of them stared at the parchment. "I wonder if this really is authentic . . ."

But Astro's eyes had veered from the girls and he now stared, transfixed, at the creature. Was it just his imagination or was the animal jerking his head toward something? The large cat purred and pawed through the sand, and Astro's eyes shot up. Getting down on his knees, he dug through the wet sand, getting his elbows deep in the grungy mess. "Something down here, boy?" he asked, feeling a little silly. Talking to a weird creature that was from a different island? Yep, he was going crazy.

But as he dug, Astro felt his arms abruptly enter a hollow space. Looking down at the sand, he realized he had unearthed a small pocket of air in the beach. "Roseabelle, Jessicana!" he yelped. The creature stared at him, its golden eyes almost holding a playful smirk. He could almost imagine it saying, "I told you so."

The girls scuttled over to them and Jessicana grinned. She knelt beside Astro and yanked out something from the dirt, a silvery object. Roseabelle immediately handed her the Embele and Jessicana furiously scraped at it, revealing a spyglass.

"Where did this come from?" Roseabelle asked. Astro gazed at the object, his curious nature perking up. Almost in response, the creature dug into the pit. When he raised his head, something silver hung from his mouth and he dropped it on the beach. Astro lifted it to his face, realizing it was a tag of some sort fashioned out of grimy silver. The worn letters displayed "Moonstar."

Astro glanced at the creature. "Moonstar," he whispered. "So that's your name." Moonstar rubbed up against his leg, purring quietly.

Jessicana suddenly stumbled back, holding the spyglass to her eyes. "No way," she murmured.

"What is it?" Astro asked. He felt as though an extravagant mystery was being unfolded before them, and his fingers tingled with excitement. He had to remind himself to keep his power under control as silver lightning flashed. He quickly stuffed his hands into his pockets.

Jessicana held out the spyglass to Roseabelle, who accepted it. She peered into it and her jaw went slack. "You're not going to believe this, Astro," she said, handing it to him.

He raised the instrument to one eye and stepped back in disbelief. Astro had expected to see only a short distance, but instead he saw a close-up view of Darvonia. The rocky dark landscape brought back bad memories and Astro yanked it away from his face. "No ordinary spyglass, for sure," he said.

"It's not even extended!" Roseabelle exclaimed.

"Must be a magical relic," Jessicana mused.

Astro once again raised the spyglass to his eyes, extending the silver attachments and increasing the view. He tilted it skyward—and saw something floating midair: a shimmery, airborne tube, clear as though it were made of glass. Astro couldn't see inside it, though. He pulled out the other increments in the spyglass, getting an even better view. The tube stretched as wide as the sky. "What is that?" he asked.

"What's what?" Jessicana asked.

"There's some sort of tube," Astro said. He retracted the increments, staring at the sandy Benotripian beach, but the glass floating structure was still there.

He handed it to Roseabelle, and she twisted it around. Astro noticed that when he was staring at the air above the ocean with just his eyes, he saw nothing. But with the spyglass, something was definitely there. "I think this spyglass can see through enchantments," Roseabelle said, concentrating hard on where Astro was pointing. "Wait a second," she said. "Astro, hand me Horsh's papers."

He picked up the trutan from the ground and handed it over to Roseabelle.

"I think this really is genuine!" she exclaimed. "You're not going to believe me but Horsh says the Dream World is a real place, but invisible, right? Well, I think I might be staring right at it."

"No way," Astro whispered. Could that glassy tube actually be the Dream World?

Roseabelle handed the spyglass to Jessicana. "Think about it. What else could the spyglass be? It lets you see faraway distances. Why couldn't it see magical properties of things as well?"

Astro noted that Roseabelle was getting excited, the prospect of discovering something new gleaming in her eyes.

Jessicana set down the spyglass. "Um, guys, I think there's something else you should see."

"What is it?" Roseabelle asked, and Jessicana let her peer into the miniature telescope.

"I think your family might be in trouble, Roseabelle," Jessicana said, her usual perky bounce gone.

When Roseabelle pulled away from the spyglass, Astro saw that she looked troubled. "Let me see!" he said and peeked through the spyglass.

He skimmed across the dark waters, catching a glimpse of the clear glass tube. Astro could now see the outer edges of the dark island and his interest piqued when he saw a fleet of black ships moving. His pulse raced—they were Darvonian ships. Weren't Danette and Dastrock supposed to be monitoring them?

He swiveled the spyglass to see the distinct forms of the Benotripian ships not too far away. But they were sailing right toward the Darvonians, as though they hadn't even seen the dark ships.

Each of the friends peeked through the spyglass once again. "I don't get it," Roseabelle said, pacing back and forth, running a hand through her bright red hair. "Don't they see them coming?"

"Maybe not," Jessicana said. "It's possible the Darvonians have some protective fog around them."

"So Danette and Dastrock think they have the upper hand," Astro said, piecing it together.

"But in actuality," Jessicana said, exchanging a look with Astro, "they're the ones being trapped."

"I think you're right, Roseabelle," Astro said. "The Darvonians might be using an enchanted fog to conceal themselves and we can see it because of the spyglass."

It happened as quick as a flash and Astro didn't even have time to react. A black arrow, appearing from nowhere, sailed toward his midsection. He cringed, waiting for the blow.

But it never happened. Glancing down, he saw the arrow embedded in his pocket—it had struck the glistening red Stone inside. Roseabelle and Jessicana looked at the trees in horror, and Moonstar perked up, alert.

And then time seemed to slow down for Astro as the dark figures of Darvonians appeared in the trees—their black soulless eyes staring straight at him.

This time Astro knew exactly what they wanted.

The trutan had to be genuine—they had seen the actual Dream World with the spyglass and now Darvonians were after the Stones, the Keys to the Dream World.

CHAPTER 5

Setting Sail

FOR A FEW SECONDS, THERE WAS ONLY SILENCE. IT SEEMED as if the Darvonians were scrutinizing them, wondering why the three friends hadn't moved yet. They were still frozen, immersed in shock.

"Run!" Astro shouted, and the trio tore out of the beach, kicking up sand in their wake. Jessicana nearly slipped and Roseabelle quickly steadied her. Running right along the water, Astro felt his fingertips already crackling in alarm, his heart pounding like a bass drum. How had the Darvonians snuck up on them like that?

"Where are we going? There has to be somewhere we can hide!" Jessicana yelled.

In the lead, Roseabelle shook her head, panting. "I have a better idea."

They raced in front of the Benotripian defense towers. Glancing up, Astro saw the citizens looking torn—they could obviously see the Darvonians right there, but there were also three Benotripian kids that they couldn't risk hitting with Flame-hurler Missiles.

Astro chanced a look behind him. The Darvonians were chasing after them like a hungry mob, and Astro saw them release a cloud of black arrows. Knowing that he and his friends couldn't survive such an attack, he quickly grabbed Roseabelle and Jessicana. The three of them instinctively ducked, sprawling on the sand as the arrows flew right past them.

Rising to her feet, Jessicana shouted, "Go, go, go!" They resumed sprinting across the beach. Moonstar bounded behind them, seemingly comprehending the danger they were in.

The Darvonians were right on their tail, and Astro wondered where Roseabelle was headed. But then he saw it—she was racing right for the emergency getaway boats!

"You're not really—" he started but his worst fears were confirmed just seconds later.

"Yes, I am!" Roseabelle shouted back and tore toward the docks. Astro's legs were getting tired but he urged himself to go on. He turned in time to see the Darvonians firing arrows again. He stretched his fingers out, an array of silver lightning shooting rapidly at the Darvonians, peppering them with deadly energy.

Some of his bolts exploded as they collided with a storm of arrows; others knocked the Darvonians off their feet. But to Astro's surprise, the rest of the Darvonians kept coming.

"Get away from here!" Roseabelle shouted at Astro and Jessicana. "I'm Shadow Tumbling back to the house to get the trutan and some weapons. The Darvonians will follow you. Above all else, keep the Stones safe." Shadow Tumbling was one of Roseabelle's many powers—it allowed her to travel through shadows. Astro opened his mouth to argue, but Jessicana beat him to it.

"What about the people?" Jessicana asked.

"I'll make sure they follow us and leave the Benotripians alone. Hurry, they're gaining on us! I'll be right back." Roseabelle dove into the shadow of a large tree, then closed her eyes and disappeared, spinning into the depths of darkness.

The other two reached the docks, and Jessicana hurriedly untethered a particular boat, her hands working at the knots at an unbelievable pace. Astro leaped into the spacious wooden boat, and Moonstar quickly followed after him.

The Darvonians came closer. Out of the corner of his eye, he saw a couple of the Darvonians turning to face the Benotripian people, weapons in their hands. Quick as a flash, Astro leaned out the side of the boat and aimed. An eruption of silver bolts sprang from his fingertips, slicing through the air. The lightning hit the attacking Darvonians and they fell to the ground, unconscious. The lightning attack delayed the other Darvonians who were attempting to revive their fallen comrades.

Jessicana finished separating the boat from the dock and stepped inside the boat, casting a nervous glance at the Darvonians closing in on them.

"I'll paddle, you shoot!" Jessicana instructed, her hands shaking. As the Darvonians raced up the dock, Astro shot a firm wall of lightning at them, his arms trembling. The force was almost too much for him, and he was tiring quickly.

With the Darvonians only slightly delayed, Jessicana and Astro steered the boat away from the docks, paddling furiously. But before they knew it, the Darvonians had cut the main rope and compressed themselves in the boats, eyes glinting, power hungry for the Stones. Roseabelle had been right. They were so driven to retrieve the Stones, they were leaving the island just to follow Jessicana and Astro.

Jessicana paddled furiously, and Astro quickly drove his oar deep into the water—but they were moving too slowly. The Darvonians were speeding toward them now. At the front of the boat, five archers drew back their thick bows, deadly black arrows nocked in place. If those arrows were loosed, Astro knew he and Jessicana wouldn't have a hope—the Darvonians were well known for their deadly aim.

Acting on an impulse, Astro compressed his hands together and formed a crackling ball of electricity, which glinted silver and blue on the waves. Jessicana's eyes widened, but she continued paddling as Astro gritted his teeth, forcing all of his energy into his hands, and raised the charge above his head.

Then, with a mighty yell, he hurled the crackling ball of light at the enemy. Both he and Jessicana ducked for cover. A bright flash followed by a sizzling crack illuminated the water. Cautiously, Astro quickly peered over the rim of the boat. Half of the boats were in splinters, and the Darvonians that had previously occupied them were swimming frantically to the other watercrafts, boosting themselves into them. Astro had created a gaping hole in one of the boats. He grinned—only a couple boats remained perfectly untouched. And the boats that had shattered had lost all their weapons and supplies.

"Nice job," Jessicana said, grinning. "That was like a thunderstorm next to the ground!"

"Maybe that's because it was," Astro said teasingly, and Jessicana rolled her eyes.

"Whatever." They high-fived. Suddenly Roseabelle appeared beside them in the shadow of the stern, red-faced and sweaty, the trutan tucked under one arm and a bulging sack clasped in her hand.

"You nearly gave me a heart attack!" Jessicana breathed.

Astro tried to calm his racing pulse. He hoped that the sack was full of food and weapons.

Roseabelle blushed. "Sorry. I got everything we need."

"Roseabelle, where are we going?" Astro asked. Moonstar purred in agreement, and all three of them jumped. They'd completely forgotten he was there.

"To find my father, Magford," Roseabelle said. "With the Darvonian attack, I'm absolutely sure that Horsh really did write this and that the Dream World is a real place. We've got no one. Danette and Dastrock are too far away to reach. The least we can do for them is send them a mottel. Magford can tell us where the Dream World is."

As the boat pulled away from Benotripia, Jessicana asked,

"But what if this is a trap from the Darvonians? They could be misleading us."

"Right now, I suspect the Darvonians just want the Stones. They aren't focused on tricking us. Because they know, once they have the Keys, it doesn't matter anymore. If they can travel to Benotripia within seconds, they could surprise attack us with armies, creatures of every kind . . . they can take over the island without even trying. We can't let them open the Dream World and take control." Roseabelle spoke firmly, and Astro had a feeling she was right.

The Darvonians didn't care about tricking them anymore. Or did they? Well, whatever they were thinking, Roseabelle had a good point. Astro smiled at Roseabelle's confidence, although he didn't feel confident, if his racing pulse was any indication. "Then Metamordia, here we come!"

CHAPTER 6
Sea Ambush

Leaning against the side of the boat, Jessicana whistled sharply, and the splitting noise echoed across the waves, reverberating all the way to the beach. She was signaling one of her mottels. Jessicana then joined her friends at the stern. She took a bit of time to study the boat they were in.

It was a large boat, fashioned of thick wood and outlined with metal. As Jessicana peered over the side, she could see cerulean waves brushing against the hull. Complete with a billowing white sail, the boat had control levers to steer it, and a sturdy masthead and a trapdoor leading into a cabin belowdecks. Jessicana decided that this was the best way to travel to Metamordia.

Astro was currently steering the boat, and Roseabelle was in back, watching the Darvonians with the spyglass. "They're quick on our tail," she reported. "Not within weapon range, though. We need to keep out of their reach, because they're not afraid to destroy our ship. Remember, they just want the Stones."

Tingles ran down Jessicana's arms. "Roseabelle, what weapons did you bring?" she asked, and Roseabelle motioned to the trapdoor.

"Astro, can you handle the upper deck for a bit?" Roseabelle asked. "I'm going to grab our supplies."

"Sure," he responded. "But hurry."

Jessicana followed Roseabelle as they descended the rope ladder. Moonstar was in the corner, sprawled out on the wood, fast asleep. Roseabelle led Jessicana to the sack and yanked out their old backpacks. She tossed one to Jessicana.

Jessicana unzipped it to find a javelin, a bow and quiver of arrows, a coil of rope, a collection of snacks, and two water bottles. When she dug in farther, she also discovered a Spidegar and her mini potion kit. The Spidegar had multiple threads attached to tiny blades. When someone held onto one end and threw the other part of it, all of the threads lashed out at once to create a deadly weapon.

"Wow, you grabbed all that in a few seconds," Jessicana said in admiration. "How did you do it?"

Roseabelle shook her head. "I've had these packs in my bedroom for months. Danette had me store them there in case of an emergency." She picked up the other two packs and started up the rope ladder.

Jessicana followed her. Once she reached the top deck, she spotted one of her mother's mottels perched on top of the stern. Astro was looking questionably at it. "Uh, Jessicana, you're the bird expert. Do something about this thing," he said

She rolled her eyes and stepped forward. "I summoned it here. It's to carry a message to Danette and Dastrock." She clucked her tongue, and the mottel instantly leaped onto her forearm, its floppy toes curling around it. Its deep brown eyes stared into hers.

Roseabelle shot her a grateful smile, then bent low next to the mottel. "Mom, this is Roseabelle. Darvonians are surrounding you and Dastrock; we're going after Dad. It's a long story. Just get off that ship at all costs. I love you." Roseabelle paused, and Jessicana figured she was finished. She nodded at the mottel and it flapped its wings and flew away into the sky.

She watched as it rose among the clouds and then soared away from sight.

As her face split into a grin, Jessicana turned to Roseabelle. "Well, that worked out!" But her friend just stared into space. "You all right, Roseabelle?"

She nodded. "I'm fine."

Astro rolled his eyes. "You're such a bad liar, Roseabelle."

Roseabelle seemed to snap back to reality and offered him a lopsided grin. "Uh-huh. Keep steering the boat or we'll crash into Blackwater Sea. And that's not recommended."

"Are we sure that Metamordia is only accessible across Blackwater Sea?" Jessicana pointed out. They didn't have a map and that worried her a bit.

"No, I'm not sure, but all we can do is hope for the best. I'll look for any detours." Roseabelle then scooped up the spyglass to her face, pressing her eye against it once more. Jessicana peered back, but she couldn't see the Darvonians anywhere. With luck, they would stay that way.

Astro seemed to know what he was doing, but Jessicana felt inclined to do something on the ship. "I'll steer if you want," she offered.

He shook his head. "Nah, I'm good. But we do need a good scout."

"Of course you do," Jessicana said teasingly, then began transforming into a parrot. A tingle shot up her spine as vivid feathers grew on her arms, sprouting into various bright colors. Her aqua blue eyes started moving from the front of her face to the sides. A folding sensation raced through her as she shrunk and developed a more squat, roundish shape. Whenever she performed her power, Jessicana felt like her transformation took a while, but it actually passed in a matter of seconds.

Squawking, she rose into the air, and the boat shrunk into a tiny dot. Jessicana swooped back to survey the miniscule fleet of Darvonian boats. All they were doing was collecting supplies and weapons. Her friends were in the clear, at least for now.

She settled into the rhythmic wave of gliding through the air.

FIVE DAYS SHOT BY, AND ROSEABELLE HONESTLY DIDN'T remember most of it.

She and Astro took alternate turns manning the controls and keeping a lookout for the Darvonian boats overtaking them. So far, so good. Jessicana patrolled the skies and always alerted them if their enemies were drawing long-range weapons, in which case they sped ahead.

As Roseabelle stood on the deck, veering the boat left and taking a swig of water from her canteen, Jessicana suddenly crumpled on the deck beside her. "Jessicana!" she exclaimed and knelt down to her friend. "You all right?"

She quickly sat straight up. "Sorry, I crashed. Was flying too fast." Roseabelle's friend spoke in hurried gulps of air. "The Darvonians—they're too close. They've developed a . . . new form . . . of the Dragocone Ray. Looks like a harpoon. Going to . . . reel us in."

Roseabelle's eyes shot wide open, and she glanced up at the sky. It was evening, and the sun reflected bright pinks and yellows across the glinting water as it slowly sunk behind the horizon. Astro was asleep belowdecks. "Wake Astro up," she whispered. "We might have a fight on our hands."

Jessicana nodded swiftly and disappeared, darting down the trapdoor. Roseabelle knelt down and unzipped her pack in a flurried frenzy. *This isn't good*, she thought. She patted her tunic pocket, feeling the heavy white Stone inside. They had to keep the artifacts safe.

Just then, Astro appeared through the trapdoor, grumbling. "What is it?" he muttered. Jessicana emerged right behind him.

"The Darvonians are about to attack!" Jessicana said. "And the winds are fast enough to give us an extra burst of speed." That really woke Astro up. Roseabelle turned away from her friends and rummaged through her pack, finding silk gloves, a Dragocone Ray, a sword, a couple of throwing daggers, and a Flame-hurler, complete with six packages of ammo.

"Astro, you steer! Use your lightning against anyone who appears in front of the boat. Jessicana, you stand on the boat with your bow. I'll go in the water."

Astro did a double take. "What? You can't breathe that long underwater!"

Roseabelle and Jessicana both stared at him.

"Dolphin girl, remember?" Roseabelle resisted a grin. She was lucky her friends could lighten the mood in situations like these. She knew that if the Darvonians overtook their ship, they could drown and the Stones would be easy for their taking.

"You're going to attack their ship, right up close?" Jessicana asked as Roseabelle kicked off her shoes. "But you can't carry weapons as a dolphin!"

Roseabelle's idea seemed to fade right before her eyes. Jessicana was right. How could she have forgotten that? Suddenly, she lit up. "You have rope in your pack! Maybe I could tie my sword around my waist with it. Make sure to give some slack too. I'm a lot thicker as a dolphin." Jessicana nodded and quickly obliged, digging in her pack. Astro seized the spyglass and raised it to his eyes.

"Jessicana was right. They do have some sort of harpoon. They're lining it up against the boat," he reported. Roseabelle's blood ran ice cold. They couldn't let the Darvonians get the Stones.

Roseabelle grabbed her sword and sheathed it, then accepted the rope from Jessicana. This had to work. If she attacked the Darvonians from behind, maybe they wouldn't get the chance to harpoon their boat. Even now, without the spyglass, she could see their group of boats speeding toward them.

"Hurry!" Astro urged.

Jessicana placed the sword against Roseabelle's back, then began to wrap the rope around her waist. Roseabelle held the sword in place as it was tethered around her. When the sword was finally bound in place with quite a bit of slack rope around her midsection, Roseabelle flashed a quick smile in her friends' direction.

"Shoot your bow toward the Darvonians," she told Jessicana. "And, Astro, you know what to do." Then before either of them could speak up, Roseabelle turned and dived into the water, picturing herself blending in with the smooth cerulean waves and her legs morphing into a tail.

Just as the cool water touched her face, Roseabelle felt her skin become more leathery and her feet bind together. She could suddenly breathe in the water and felt the sword's heavy weight on her back. Sound became distinctively muted, and, sure enough, she knew she had turned into a dolphin.

Diving deep, Roseabelle flicked her tail, heading toward the enemy's boats. She headed straight toward them, slightly held back by the weapon she was carrying. She allowed the slack to take place and let the sword carry its own weight in the water, drifting above her, held by the ropes around her midsection.

Bubbles swished up from her mouth. Speeding up by flicking her tail faster, Roseabelle was suddenly aware of the wildlife around her. A few bright green fish swam right past her, but she focused on pushing ahead. Above, she could distantly hear an array of frantic shouts, and she hoped desperately that her friends were all right.

Tilting her head, she could see several dark shapes on the surface and immediately recognized them as the Darvonian boats. Propelling herself even quicker, Roseabelle veered around them and came up from behind, momentarily surfacing. She closed her eyes and imagined her legs dividing and her lungs once again breathing in oxygen.

Her wish was granted as the feeling returned to her legs, and when Roseabelle surfaced, her drenched red hair hung around her shoulders and the sword hung from her slim figure.

And she was right behind the cloaked figures of the Darvonians.

CHAPTER 7

Spires of Rock

Breathing in cool fresh air and treading water as silently as she could, Roseabelle counted five boats in all, packed with cloaked Darvonians. She pushed through the water and swam right beside the closest one. The boats were slowing down so the Darvonians could solidify their aim. Placing her hands on the side of the boat, she boosted herself up. Luckily, the Darvonians in the boats were at the stern, focused on the fight ahead, and not in the back where she was.

Jessicana had been right—there were glowing objects that looked like Dragocone Rays, but they were shaped like harpoons instead. Wearing silk gloves, one of the cloaked figures suddenly turned around to grab one. Roseabelle ducked, hanging on to the side of the boat.

Counting silently in her head, she figured it was safe to come up.

"Ready?" said a gruff voice.

Roseabelle poked her head above the boat and reached behind to untie the sword from her body. Her fingers slowly worked on the knots, and she willed them to move faster. One Darvonian stood and suddenly shouted, "NOW!" A dozen brilliantly glowing harpoons flew across the skies, straight toward Jessicana and Astro.

Roseabelle saw most of them erupt in a cloud of crackling silver lightning before they could reach her friends, and she resisted letting out a cheer. But then she spotted a spreading hole in the hull of their boat. One of the harpoons had struck it.

The Darvonians began to throw another array of harpoons, but Roseabelle still hadn't freed her sword yet! She gritted her teeth. *Just a few more knots,* she thought.

As the Darvonians prepared to attack Jessicana and Astro again, Roseabelle spotted a barrel of water right behind them. Clenching her teeth, she focused on it, and her telekinesis took over. The wooden container rose in the air, liquid sloshing over the lid and spilling onto the deck.

At the sudden noise, the Darvonians whirled around, but before they could reach her, Roseabelle quickly tilted her head and the heavy barrel plowed into them. The Darvonians were knocked over and doused with gallons and gallons of water.

Her sword suddenly became free, and Roseabelle quickly unsheathed it. One of the Darvonians in another boat leveled an arrow at her, and she twitched, focused. As he released the arrow, Roseabelle caused it to fly backward, knocking him overboard.

More Darvonians lunged for her. She thrust the hilt of the sword against the helmet of the man closest to her, and he quickly toppled overboard. One enemy seized her ankle, and Roseabelle tripped. The Darvonians rushed to seize her.

Thinking quickly, Roseabelle leaned to the side of the boat with the most Darvonians. The weight of so many people capsized the boat, flipping it over—and the Darvonians' harpoons with it.

A wave of water washed over Roseabelle's head, and she fought to hold her breath. In the chaos, she slipped out from underneath the overturned boat, escaping the Darvonians' clutches. She cast her eyes toward the dark underside of the boat carrying her friends. She could see the glimmering shapes of the Dragocone Ray harpoons that had missed, sinking to the bottom of the ocean.

The Darvonians were still distracted—Roseabelle noticed their waterlogged cloaks were weighing them down. Seizing her opportunity, Roseabelle managed to kick upward, her head breaking through the surface. A shout rang in her ears: "There she is!"

In shock, Roseabelle noticed a new group of Darvonians leaning over the side of their boats, all eyes focused on her. The other boats hurled more harpoons at Jessicana and Astro. Roseabelle realized her sword was gone and she only had her powers to rely on.

One of the cloaked figures found a Dragocone harpoon and quickly aimed it at Roseabelle. Quick as a flash, she closed her eyes and transformed into a dolphin. She dived just as the deadly weapon sank into the waves after her.

Underwater, Roseabelle flicked her tail and came up underneath the boats, ramming into the hull. She rammed it again and again. The boat jostled violently, and sure enough, as she gave it one last try, the boat capsized, spilling a dozen Darvonians and their weapons into the sea.

Roseabelle knew there were three more boats to go. She realized that if she got rid of their weapons instead of the boats, she and her friends would be safe. For now, anyway. Morphing back into a human, Roseabelle resurfaced from behind the Darvonians and saw the cloaked figures searching everywhere for her.

"There!" one yelled. Roseabelle lunged for the boat, spotting the Dragocone Rays inside. A humming filled Roseabelle's ears and using all of her remaining strength, she levitated the deathly weapons. Before the Darvonians could grab them, Roseabelle jerked her head to the left and they dropped into the watery abyss.

But when she looked up, she saw that one Darvonian still had a Ray harpoon. The enemy's eyes narrowed and drawing back, he hurled the weapon straight at Roseabelle. Her eyes grew wide and she sank into the water, the missile singeing the top of her red hair.

Treading water, Roseabelle rose to the surface, but instead of hearing frantic shouts directed toward her, the sound of pouring water reached her ears. She glanced to the left and saw that the harpoon the Darvonian had thrown had impaled the other boat beside it. Water was gushing inside it, and the Darvonians were hurriedly finding a way to escape. Some jumped out and swam to the other boats. She stifled a laugh—the Darvonians had just sunk one of their own crafts!

Diving, Roseabelle closed her eyes and made the transformation once again into a graceful dolphin. It was time to go back to her own boat—she hoped it was still floating.

* * * * *

JESSICANA WORKED FURIOUSLY TO FIX THE GAPING HOLE IN the boat. Moonstar was still miraculously asleep, and Jessicana was plugging the gap with a large piece of thin slated stone that had been stored along with crates and emergency food and water.

She sealed the stone in place with some old chewy wraptook, a kind of bread that stuck like glue. Adding some wadded up cloth to plug in the holes, Jessicana managed to fix the hole, and the water stopped leaking in. Glancing around in dismay, she realized at least four inches of water had seeped in. Still, it was better than the entire boat sinking—and it certainly didn't seem to be bothering the slumbering Moonstar.

Astro poked his head down through the trapdoor. "Roseabelle's back!" he called. Jessicana scurried up the rope ladder to see Roseabelle, drenched, boosting herself back into the boat. Her friend was weak and her limbs were shaking. Astro had to pull her the rest of the way into the boat.

"I saw what happened," he said, grinning despite his exhausted state. "You took down three boats! And all of the harpoons! Nice work, Roseabelle."

"Thanks," she said. "Did you patch up the hole?"

Jessicana wiped the beads of sweat off her forehead. "Yeah. That hole sure was stubborn." In truth, she was just glad to see Roseabelle alive. "We had better steer ahead to get away from those Darvonians. Astro, you should've shot a few Flame-hurlers at them."

"I know," he said. "But Roseabelle had it covered." Astro reached inside his pocket. "It might be a little helpful to use the St—" He stopped abruptly and lifted the Stone to eye-level; Jessicana's eyes widened in surprise. She could see that the once-brilliant light that gleamed in the Stone was gone. The dull red jewel seemed to be lifeless.

Roseabelle noticed as well, and she and Jessicana withdrew their Stones from their pockets. The shimmer, the light glowing from within, had vanished.

"Do they still work?" Jessicana asked, her voice penetrating the shocked silence. She waved her Stone toward Roseabelle, picturing a flower appearing in her red hair. But nothing happened.

Astro tried his as well. "The power's been sucked out of them," he said. "At least, that's what it looks like."

Roseabelle surveyed the Stones while Jessicana studied her own. Had she done something wrong? Maybe the Darvonians had enchanted it. No, that wasn't right. The Stones were extremely powerful artifacts; no one could just tamper with them like that.

"They were glowing when we left," Roseabelle said. "So we can't despair. My father will know what's going on. We just have to focus on protecting them." Jessicana glanced up at the sky, realizing how dark it was. The sparkling stars contrasted deeply against the pitch black of the night.

"Can I go back to sleep now?" Astro grumbled, and Jessicana and Roseabelle both grinned at each other.

"Knock yourself out," Jessicana responded. Astro flung open the trapdoor, then scrambled down the ladder. "Speaking of sleeping, what's wrong with Moonstar?" It was strange—Moonstar had been asleep the entire voyage! Even though Jessicana didn't know anything about this species, she really was worried about him sleeping for so long.

Roseabelle scowled. "He hasn't eaten or drunk anything, has he?"

Jessicana shook her head. "It's odd for an animal. Usually all they want to do is eat." Being part animal, she should know.

Jessicana picked up the spyglass and resumed her original position. She stared at the waves with their hypnotic rhythm. Gazing into the distance, she saw that the two black Darvonian boats bobbed on the water, and she was pleased to see that they were going just as slow as her ship was.

Suddenly Roseabelle spoke, nearly making Jessicana jump. "Jessicana," she said, speaking softly. "Do you think my mother's going to be all right?" Jessicana instantly felt guilty. Here she was just minding her own business, while Roseabelle was thinking about her mother. Jessicana was impressed by how well her friend hid her feelings.

Jessicana walked up to Roseabelle and squeezed her hand. "I don't know, Roseabelle. But as long as we're doing our best, Danette will be just fine."

Now she had to convince herself to believe it.

TWO MORE DAYS PASSED ON THE OCEAN, AND THE THREE friends took turns alternating between resting, steering, and keeping watch for any signs of danger as they steered toward Metamordia. The ocean was relatively calm, and Astro was glad they didn't have to pass through Blackwater Sea. After all, his definition of fun was not sailing through deadly black waters where only death and danger awaited.

Only hours earlier, Jessicana had spotted with their spyglass the fight between Danette's ships and the sneaky

Darvonian fleets. There had been cannons and bright flashes of Dragocone Rays, but the fleets had retreated farther into the distance and she couldn't see them anymore.

Astro glanced toward the trapdoor. He was amazed that during this whole time Moonstar had been asleep. Lucky animal. While everyone else was fighting, the creature was taking a nice long nap.

Right now, Astro was at the steering wheel, clenching it tight, peering straight ahead. He had counted that a week had now passed and his stomach wobbled a bit. Both of his friends were extremely lucky—Jessicana could get off the boat at any time and fly in the clouds for a few minutes, and Roseabelle could transform into a dolphin and swim freely. Astro didn't have the freedom to get off the boat at all, and as a result, seasickness was starting to bother him.

"See anything?" he asked Roseabelle, who was standing near the boat's railings.

"I can't tell," Roseabelle mused. "There's a lot of mist up ahead but we've traveled so far that Metamordia's bound to be close."

Astro turned back to steering as tiny crystal waves lapped at the hull. He honestly didn't know if they could handle being out here for much longer. They were already running low on food. What if they had completely missed Metamordia? No, that wasn't possible—the spyglass could see through enchantments.

"Wait!" Roseabelle exclaimed, lengthening the spyglass suddenly.

"What is it?" he asked.

"Nothing good," she said and held the instrument toward him. Astro snatched it and held it to his eye, looking for anything strange. All he could see was open water and an enormous mass of white fog. Squinting, he noted that the only thing beyond the fog was an endless sea of blue.

"I don't see anything," he said.

Roseabelle took him by the shoulders and jerked him to the right.

"Look closer," she insisted.

Astro did, and just as he was about to put the spyglass down, a blur of darkness flashed past his vision. "What was that?" he whispered to himself. The boat suddenly shuddered, and Astro nearly dropped the spyglass.

Jessicana came up through the trapdoor, rubbing her eyes. "Something wrong?" she asked sleepily.

A horrible grinding split the air and Astro winced. Yikes! What was that? He gripped onto the side of the boat with one hand and peeped through the spyglass with the other. His mouth agape, he saw what lay ahead of the boat.

Dark twisted rock spires and clumps of enormous boulders rose majestically out of the sea like giants. Astro wondered if the boat was skidding on pieces of rock right at that moment. He realized with a start that the spyglass was no longer extended at all—the spires were right in front of their eyes. They had been too busy looking way ahead to see what was right in front of them.

"We've got trouble," Roseabelle said.

Astro put down the spyglass and saw their boat barely miss a towering black rock spire.

"Where'd Metamordia go?" he asked urgently.

"It has to be beyond this rock," Jessicana said. "This is another Darvonian trick. Remember last time? We had to make it through that cloud of fog in Blackwater Sea to get to Darvonia. There's always an obstacle to pass. This one just happens to be crazy-looking rocks jutting out of the ocean. The Darvonians don't want anyone finding their way to the third island, that's for sure." Astro couldn't see very well through the mist that was sticking to the sides of the boat—the rocks seemed to pop out of nowhere.

"We have to steer out of here!" Astro exclaimed, reaching for the controls. There was no way they'd survive going through there. Their boat would be demolished and they would be stranded.

"Wait," Jessicana said, taking the controls first. "The Darvonians designed it like this. If we veer off course, we'll have to go through a different obstacle. We'll never get to Metamordia. Blackwater Sea is full of too many surprises. We have to go straight through."

Astro stared. Jessicana was absolutely right. "Kinetle's cloak, sometimes the Darvonians are so clever it hurts," he muttered.

"We need some sort of protection for the boat," Roseabelle said and instantly dashed off.

"Where are you going?" Jessicana called, but Roseabelle was already below deck. The boat tipped slightly as the hull scraped against a rough piece of submerged rock. Astro grabbed onto the stern, dropping the spyglass. It rolled around on the deck.

"Watch out!" he yelled at Jessicana. Yanking her down, they watched as a spire of rock, jutting out from a monstrous boulder, appeared where her head had just been.

"Thanks," she said, giving him a quick smile. Roseabelle came racing back .

"Get down," Astro said, worried that more rock spires might appear. "What's your plan, Roseabelle?" It wouldn't be long before the jagged rocks sliced through the wood of the boat like putty. If Roseabelle didn't have a plan, it seemed like they were done for.

Roseabelle was holding the trutan in her hands along with a bottle of ink and a quill. As she was running, some of her ink had spilled on the wood, staining the deck purple. Astro noticed her hands were shaking uncontrollably.

"What should we draw?" Jessicana asked.

"Wooden planks," Roseabelle said. "And tools. We're going to need to patch up any holes these rocks might make."

"Can't any of your powers help with the Stones?" Astro

asked. Although the trutan was better than nothing, it wasn't as fast as the Stones of Horsh. Eventually, these rocks would get the better of them and their boat would sink.

Roseabelle pondered the question for a moment while Jessicana began drawing frantically. "Telekinesis," she suddenly burst. "Of course! It'll take a lot of effort though. I might be able to move the rocks away from the boat with my mind. Astro, you man the sides of the boat and chop off any rocks that come near us with a Dragocone Ray. Jessicana, you keep drawing." Roseabelle took her position at the front of the boat and Astro dashed below deck to find a Dragocone Ray. Avoiding the puddles of water, all he could think was, *This had better work.*

CHAPTER 8

Metamordia

ROSEABELLE STOOD AT THE STERN, FOCUSING HARD AND warming up her mind. Beforehand, she already knew that this was going to wear her out, maybe to the point of total exhaustion. But it didn't matter. Her friends' lives were in jeopardy, and this was the only way they would make it to Metamordia.

This was the only way they would make it *alive.*

Shadowy shapes leered at them from above, jagged rock spirals sticking out from different angles. As a cluster of enormous boulders appeared, Roseabelle swerved the boat to avoid them. Glancing up ahead, she could see piles of loose black rock jutting out of the surface.

Clenching her teeth and clearing her mind, Roseabelle focused on the rocks, blotting out every other sound, every other movement. She made a motion with her arms, and the cluster of rocks wobbled slightly. "Come on," she muttered, thinking of her father on the other side of this stone graveyard. "He's just past this point. Come on, Roseabelle, you can do this. For him. For them."

Grunting, body pumping with adrenaline, Roseabelle lifted four of the rocks mere inches in the air. They skimmed the water and plopped into a different part of the ocean, where they disappeared below the surface. Face red and breathing heavily, Roseabelle focused on the other clusters of rocks that lay in their path. As they approached a second pile, she panicked, realizing she couldn't do it. Her mind was sore from the exhaustion of the previous lift.

"Brace yourselves!" she yelled as the boat headed dead on toward the rocks. Just as they were going to hit, Astro ran up behind her. With a quick downward swish of his Dragocone Ray, the rocks split into numerous pieces and sank to the sea floor. "Thanks," she said.

"Don't thank me yet," he said with a worried grin. At that moment, the ship slid into a cloud of white fog, and Astro and Roseabelle looked at each other nervously.

"The spyglass can see through this fog right?" Astro asked.

Roseabelle nodded. "Give me the Ray. Use your lightning but don't hit the water. With the combined Telekinesis and weapon, I should be able to move the rocks out of the way in time. We can't afford another blow."

Astro handed Roseabelle his Ray and slid off his silk gloves just as another rock spire dug into the ship's wood. He could hear Jessicana's triumphant shout as she finished patching the previous hole—then her groan as she realized there was another one.

With the Dragocone Ray gleaming brilliantly, Roseabelle could see relatively well through the fog, and with the spyglass, so could Astro. A jagged rock spire jutted from the side, and she hurriedly slashed through it, the rock splashing through the water. Astro's lightning severed the boulders so quickly that a path soon appeared, free of the rocky dangers. Astro cheered in delight as the fog and debris ahead of them cleared to reveal a pristine ocean free of obstacles. He exchanged a high-five with Roseabelle.

And then all the glee drained from their faces. Up ahead, as though in slow motion, a towering mass of smooth black obsidian popped up from the waters. Roseabelle's eyes widened, and she hit the deck. Acting on instinct, Astro grabbed the Dragocone Ray and flung it at the spire. As the Ray came into contact with the rock, a burst of fiery energy emitted, sparks flying in every direction. The rock was severed from its position, cut jaggedly and glowing bright red. The spire sank into the sea, causing monstrous waves to wash over them.

Several moments later, Roseabelle looked up—coughing and sputtering from being completely doused. Her heart was beating faster than usual. "Nice thinking," she said to Astro. He was kneeling beside her, equally soaked.

Jessicana came running up, panting. "I finished," she said. "But that was *not* easy. Below deck is pretty much ruined. We still have our supplies—" She was cut off as the three were almost blinded by white light.

Blinking and shielding their faces, they realized the fog had cleared and sunlight had poured into their view. But that wasn't all they saw. Jessicana leaped in her excitement and gripped the wooden railing of the boat, and Roseabelle let out a huge sigh. "Amazing," she gasped. Beside her, Astro's eyes nearly popped out of his skull.

The island before them was lush, with green grass growing everywhere. A glistening crystal waterfall gushed from a smooth brown cliff, and rolling hills were complemented by trees that grew rich green leaves. It was nothing like Benotripia, yet it shared the same exotic beauty.

"Metamordia," Roseabelle gasped.

Beside her, Astro took in the amazing sight, then frowned, running a hand through his spiky black hair. "There are no people. Isn't that a little strange?" Jessicana shrugged. From behind them, Moonstar suddenly bounded up and out of the open trapdoor. "So now he wakes up," Astro said, groaning playfully and the animal obediently slunk next to Roseabelle, purring softly. She patted the animal's head and bent down next to him, her mind whirling.

"And what have you been doing all this time?" she murmured, petting his smooth black-and-red fur.

The boat thudded against the shore, bumping against the sand. Roseabelle turned to the group. "Jessicana's patch-ups won't last for long and the Darvonians are close behind us. We're going to have to abandon the boat and start looking for my father straightaway."

"I'll scout for anything suspicious," Jessicana volunteered, and Roseabelle agreed wholeheartedly. If they were going to explore an abandoned mystery island, a bird's eye view would be helpful.

Astro took the spyglass from her and peered into it. "We really have to hurry! The Darvonians will be here in a matter of minutes."

"What?" Roseabelle exclaimed. That couldn't be true. Hadn't the Darvonians been way behind? She peered at the ocean, putting a hand over her forehead and blocking the sun from her eyes. Sure enough, the boats were moving swiftly toward the three friends, easily tracing the path Roseabelle and Astro had blasted.

"Hurry!" she said. "Astro, grab our supplies. Jessicana, scout the area. I'll take Moonstar and start searching in the trees." Roseabelle hurriedly surveyed the island, then pointed to a large brown cliff in the distance. "We'll meet there. Now go, go, go!"

"Good luck," Jessicana and Astro said at the same time, then all three of them scurried their separate ways.

* * * * *

JESSICANA IMMEDIATELY TRANSFORMED INTO A PARROT AND fluttered away, soaring high above the green treetops, swooping through the clear blue sky. She tried to stay within the white fluffy clouds so the Darvonians wouldn't see her.

Metamordia was enormous. But as Jessicana flew, she could see no signs of natives living there—and no Darvonians either. There was, however, an abundance of animals creeping, crawling, and flying about, so she knew that the island wasn't deserted. Looking down, she could see Roseabelle and Astro panting as they ran after her, crashing through masses of rich green bushes and trees.

Jessicana landed swiftly on the smooth brown cliff, ruffling her wings anxiously. Where could Magford be imprisoned? This island definitely did not look as though Darvonians had taken over it. She wondered if the Darvonians following them had landed on the island yet. The thought sent chills tingling down her spine. Parrots didn't seem to be common on this island. What if they recognized her for who she was?

Surveying the island, Jessicana compared Benotripia and Metamordia. It was strange how two things could be so different yet so amazing. Listening contentedly to the rush of the crystal waterfall, she marveled at how different it was from the one that had guarded the Stones of Horsh. This water was so clear and so pure, Jessicana could see straight through it.

She swooped down and looked through it, then squawked in surprise.

Was that a black stone behind the waterfall? Jessicana inched closer to the perilous rush of water, her sharp parrot eyes scrutinizing the waterfall. Beyond the falls, a strong sheen of black stood out. Her curiosity shot sky high.

Taking a deep breath, Jessicana flew straight through the water. Her wings became waterlogged and she gasped for breath. Transforming back into a girl in midair, her fingers latched on to a sharp protruding black rock.

And then Jessicana realized what was behind the waterfall.

She saw a wall of black stone with a small ledge precariously jutting out. Jessicana was relieved to see that no Darvonians or Metamordians were around to witness or report her being there. At least, she didn't see anyone.

Her blonde hair was soaked, and she figured she had better let herself dry off or when she transformed, her wings would be waterlogged. Jessicana found handholds and footholds and descended the wall of black stone carefully, looking around for anything unusual.

Her hand slipped and she caught herself, a small shriek escaping her lips. That was close. Even though she could transform into a parrot, flying with wet wings wouldn't be the greatest option. She'd probably have to walk back. Grasping onto the slippery rock, she cautiously descended a bit more, forcing herself not to look down.

Suddenly Jessicana found her foot swinging in midair as she searched for a foothold. Her stomach leaped into her throat. Did the wall of black stone end right here? Peeking down, she looked over the terrain.

Although the wall continued down, she could see an open crevasse right below her. She was glad she was used to heights; otherwise, she might have fallen the twenty feet to the ground. Carefully, she lowered herself using only her arms, her hands shaking uncontrollably, searching for a lower foothold. But she couldn't find anything, and her feet dangled in the open air.

Jessicana had to get around this certain crevasse or she knew she'd never make it to the ground. "I should've gone back to find Astro and Roseabelle," she said to herself, taking a calming breath. But already her sweaty fingers were slipping from the ledge. "No, no, come on. Keep yourself up," she whispered. As she grasped for a better handhold, her hands slipped, and she plummeted toward the ground, her stomach leaping into her throat.

And then she stopped. Jessicana realized with a *thump* that she'd landed on solid ground. She looked up and recognized the spot she'd been positioned at—only four feet above where she was now. Yet she was still surrounded by black stone. She'd landed on a flat ledge, overlooking the rocky pool that the waterfall gushed into.

Turning her head, an astounding sight awaited her gaze. It

was an archway, tall and outlined by stones, fitting completely into the black cliffside. Jessicana observed the ledge she was standing on. It was particularly wide and rather thick. She jumped carefully on it a couple times. Obviously, it could hold a lot of weight.

Deciding she'd wait for Roseabelle and Astro, Jessicana sat down on the ledge, suspecting that if she went to try and find them, she might lose this particular spot on the waterfall. It was rather discreet. Finally, she saw a blurred shape through the waterfall. "ASTRO! ROSEABELLE!" Jessicana shouted. She repeatedly yelled their names until her voice became hoarse. A few moments of silence passed by.

There was a flash of silver and Astro stepped out from the torrent of water, coughing and sputtering. Jessicana doubted he'd ever be dry again. "Jessicana?" he asked. The two remaining backpacks—one had been lost in the rock spire graveyard—were slung over his shoulders.

"Up here!" she called. A few seconds later, she spotted a blurred shape nearing the waterfall once again. "ROSEABELLE!"

Jessicana rubbed her sore throat. Roseabelle eventually emerged with Moonstar by her side. The animal shook his fur out, sending droplets of water in every direction. Roseabelle squeezed out her mess of saturated locks and a stream of water erupted from them. "I never want to be wet again," she sputtered.

"Never mind that. I found some sort of tunnel!" Jessicana announced. "We can hide here and figure out a plan to find Magford."

"Great, but how are we going to get up there?" Astro asked. "We can't exactly fly like you." Beside him, Moonstar scaled the rock with bounding leaps, causing Jessicana to jump as he landed on the ledge. "And we aren't wild animals," he added, glaring at Moonstar.

Jessicana thought for a moment, tapping her chin. Suddenly,

she straightened. "Roseabelle, use your Fur Beam," she suggested, thinking back to when her friend had transformed into a giant hairy beast. "That way you can boost Astro up, then turn back to your normal self and we can help you up."

"What?" Roseabelle groaned.

Astro looked away, and Jessicana suspected he was trying not to burst out laughing.

"Oh, be nice, Astro," Jessicana chided and he turned back, biting his lip.

"Sorry, Roseabelle," he said, but Jessicana could see his mouth still quivering as he stifled a laugh.

Roseabelle sighed and moved to the corner of the rock wall where tiny rays of sunshine were seeping through. She rolled up her sleeve and held up the sickly yellow spot on her elbow. A bright flash of light nearly blinded them, and Jessicana clapped a hand over her eyes.

"Please look away, Astro," Roseabelle's deep growly voice stated, and he obediently did what he was told. Jessicana's eyes opened just a crack. Sure enough, her friend was a couple of feet taller, covered in fur, and had gnarly claws. Astro tried to close his eyes and stumbled toward her but ended up smacking into the black wall of stone.

"A little help here?" he asked. Jessicana guided him verbally over to Roseabelle. "I think I'm permanently blind."

Jessicana giggled. "You'll be fine, Astro!"

With Astro riding piggyback, Roseabelle moved from her crouched state and into her full height. Astro blinked, opened his eyes, and climbed off her back onto the ledge next to Moonstar. Below them, Roseabelle shone her yellow spot in the sun again and reverted back into a girl.

Moonstar waited patiently for them as Jessicana tapped her chin thoughtfully. "Hey, Astro, grab onto my ankles and lower me down. I'll help Roseabelle up."

"What?" he asked. "It's too far down. Can you even reach her?"

Jessicana scrutinized their surroundings and realized that Roseabelle was at least fifteen feet away from them. Astro was right; it wasn't going to work. She glanced down at her ring, pushing the Grapplegore's emerald button. Instantly two ropes sprang, one dropping toward Roseabelle. "Hold on!" she shouted.

Roseabelle tied the rope around her waist, then began to scale the rock. Jessicana assisted her climb by pulling on the rope as much as she could. Roseabelle ascended rather smoothly, although she tripped a couple of times. Thanks to the Grapplegore, though, she stayed clinging to the rocky cliff side.

Roseabelle made it up the cliff and untied the rope from her waist. "Thanks, Jessicana," she said, out of breath.

"Are the Darvonians close behind?" Jessicana asked.

"They're on the island near here," Astro reported. "We need to be careful; I had a close call. When I was leaving, they were just docking on the edge of the island."

Abruptly and without a single noise, the animal slunk into the shadows, disappearing into the tunnel hole. Jessicana's eyes widened in alarm.

"Moonstar, come back here!" Astro hissed but the creature just kept on going.

"So, we follow?" Jessicana asked, glancing skeptically at the darkness that awaited them.

"We follow," Roseabelle agreed and stepped ahead, weapon at her side.

CHAPTER 9
Darvonian Caverns

Stepping into the pitch-black cavern, Roseabelle and her friends followed the pattering of Moonstar's light steps. Pebbles crunched underfoot as they walked, and she winced with each noise. As if reading Roseabelle's thoughts, Jessicana said from behind, "Try not to make as much noise."

Moonstar abruptly halted in his tracks, and Astro nearly tumbled over him. There was a faint echo and Roseabelle stopped, nervously glancing into darkness, but she couldn't see anything. Taking a cautious step forward, she found her foot hanging in thin air. Was this some sort of precipice? She stared accusingly at Moonstar. "This leads off a cliff edge," she said. "What are you trying to do, Moonstar?"

In response, he pushed her forward a bit, and Roseabelle yelped, then realized her foot had touched a solid surface. "It's a staircase," she muttered to herself in relief. Moonstar moved past Roseabelle and continued down the stairs. The three friends descended after him. But as the distant sound of rushing water faded, new noises flooded over them. It was the clash of wooden wagons and the simmering of lit torches.

As they reached the bottom of the staircase, a vibrant amber glow washed over them, and they all stopped short.

They had just entered a clearing, illuminated by dim torchlight. But it was enough to see that they were no longer alone. Hooded figures pushed stone vehicles forward on wheels, and the murmur of chatter and conversation echoed in the tunnels. Roseabelle could see smoking pits from where various lights danced, and the three friends, all at once, exchanged wide-eyed glances.

Darvonians.

But that wasn't the freakiest part. Relaxed and lying near the entrance was a monstrous creature with soft green skin and an enormous shell. Webbed nets lined with spikes covered its shell, which connected to a large head, wrinkly and gray. Its legs were short but thin and packed with muscle.

Luckily, the creature's eyes were closed.

Roseabelle, Jessicana, and Astro exchanged alarmed glances. Roseabelle hesitated. It wouldn't be wise to sneak past this creature. Where were they going? But they couldn't just abandon Moonstar. And besides, if he were seen by the Darvonians, they would be suspicious. Feeling a bit reluctant, she crept past the creature with Astro and Jessicana close behind. Roseabelle tried to keep calm, hoping that the animal wouldn't wake up. If he did, they would be done for.

The truth hit Roseabelle hard. The Darvonians had clearly been here for years, using this place as their secret hideout. But for what? And where were all the Metamordians?

Before any of the friends could talk to each other, Moonstar purred quietly, so soft that only they could hear. Then he darted behind a stack of tall barrels a few feet to their left, leaping into open sight for just a second. "Moonstar!" Jessicana whispered loudly, but the animal stayed where he was, shooting a pleading glance at Roseabelle.

"We need to follow him," Roseabelle whispered. They

couldn't just stay here, crouched in a big huddle, waiting for the Darvonians to find them. "He knows what he's doing."

Rolling and ducking, Astro dashed behind the barrels, and Jessicana followed. Roseabelle crept after them, glad they had the cover of darkness on their side.

They continued traveling discreetly in this manner, Moonstar leading the way, and the three friends clambering after him. Luckily they'd had some experience keeping quiet before, and didn't make any suspicious noises. Leaping from one obstacle to the next, they managed to stay hidden in the shadows.

And then Astro's foot clanged against a metal shield resting on the ground. Roseabelle froze, heart pounding, as the clamor of hushed conversation suddenly halted behind them. But after a few painstaking seconds of suspense, the Darvonians resumed their work.

Not much security, she thought. She dug in her pack silently, withdrawing a sheathed sword that she had borrowed from Astro, as Moonstar directed them to a stop at a black stone wall. Up ahead, Jessicana pulled out a Spidegar, and Astro armed himself with a Trapita, a rod with three blades lined on it. Any moment they could be discovered, and they had to be ready for an attack.

Roseabelle saw the creature take another step forward. Up ahead, Jessicana took in a sharp breath. Roseabelle blinked a couple of times when she realized that Moonstar had disappeared. One minute he'd been there, right in front of them, and the next he had melted into the shadows.

"Where'd he go?" Astro muttered frantically and crawled forward. Then, Astro was gone too.

"It's a portal!" Jessicana realized, keeping her voice low. "Come on." She moved forward and then vanished from sight. Roseabelle winced, glancing back. Well, what did she have to lose? She could only hope that on the other side, her father really was waiting.

Inhaling deeply to calm her nerves, Roseabelle stepped forward as a light-headed, dizzying sensation enveloped her.

When she opened her eyes, she only met darkness. "Roseabelle?" said a voice to her right. *Jessicana.*

"Where are we?" she asked. A silver-blue glow flared inside the room from Astro's crackling fingertips. Roseabelle could now see that they were in some sort of black hall. The worn stones they stood on were covered in slash-and-burn marks, as though weapons had been forged here.

"Moonstar went this way," Astro's voice said. With the small amount of light, she could see his faint outline. "Everyone okay?"

"Yes," Jessicana said, and Roseabelle echoed her.

"This way," Astro said, and the girls made an effort to follow his footsteps, because he was the only one with light. Roseabelle scanned their environment, taking in every little detail in case they needed to make a quick getaway.

"He's stopped," Astro reported.

Roseabelle put a hand on her sword. An eerie feeling sent chills tingling down her. Could it be possible that someone was watching them? "And now he's turning a corner and—" His voice broke off in the empty blackness. Jessicana crossed over to him, treading lightly.

"What—" Jessicana tried to say, but Astro clapped a hand over her mouth. Roseabelle swallowed and quickly caught up with her friends. Obviously, something unpleasant was right there.

Astro slowly took his hand from Jessicana's mouth. By the light of his crackling fingertips, Roseabelle could see a long corridor with at least six metal doors guarded by a mass of about twenty Darvonians. Fortunately, Jessicana and Astro had been whispering, and the Darvonians hadn't been really paying attention. It was clear that they didn't expect intruders to find their secret hideout, maybe because no one had ever showed up that they'd needed to fight. Roseabelle again wondered just how long the Darvonians had been secretly encamped down here.

"We need to get into the open and knock them out," Astro mouthed. Roseabelle shook her head. They were three kids against twenty grown Darvonians. Even with their powers, it was a challenge. And if even one of the Darvonians escaped, they would be in serious trouble.

"No," she mouthed back. "I have a better idea."

Bending down in the dirt, she drew a diagram with her finger, outlining the plan. Slowly, her friends' faces lit up.

A few minutes later, they were all ready, each standing in a different position in the corridor. Jessicana had a Spidegar from Astro's pack and was crouched at the far end of the hall, around a corner. Roseabelle herself waited at the opposite end of the hall in the same position, her sword ready.

Astro, lying flat on his stomach, looked to Roseabelle, who nodded. Suddenly a stream of silver blue lightning flew from Astro's fingertips—right at the Darvonian guards.

Lightning crackled in every direction. It was just as Roseabelle had predicted—pandemonium. Already she could see six Darvonians lying unconscious. Their armor had protected them from further injury. Another Darvonian who had escaped the brunt of Astro's attack raced out of the corridor blindly, frantically attempting to get out. Jessicana quickly wrapped him in the webs of her Spidegar, entangling him fully. Astro shot a separate bolt of lightning at him as well, and soon the hooded figure was out cold.

In a matter of minutes, all twenty Darvonians were face-down and unconscious. Standing, Roseabelle quickly searched them, but found no keys. "Do you think my father is behind one of these doors?" she asked, and Jessicana shrugged.

"Most likely. Moonstar seems to know what he's doing." Inspecting the doors closely, Roseabelle took a few steps back. They were made of a certain kind of metal and had no barred windows to look inside. But to her left, Moonstar whined and crouched at a door at the end of the corridor. It was tinier than the others, with no keyhole.

"How do we get in?" Astro asked.

Roseabelle sighed, wondering what she could do and which powers she could use. Dust Draining? It would have no effect. Fur Beam? It could be useful, but there was no sunlight here to allow her to morph. Telekinesis? There was no way she could remove a door that heavy.

Suddenly, the trio heard the faint echo of voices from behind them, and they exchanged worried glances. The Darvonians must have heard the commotion. They had to get inside before they were found!

Moonstar clawed at the hinges. Astro dug in his pack, then began hacking at them with a Dragocone Ray. The metal began to dent slightly, but even the force of a powerful weapon couldn't break the hinges. "Wait," Astro said as he dug in his pack again and brought out a heavy Flame-hurler.

"But that could cause an explosion," Roseabelle protested as he loaded extra force ammo onto the Flame-hurler and leveled it at the door.

"What if Magford's behind the door?" Jessicana pointed out. "And if the Darvonians come through, we can't lock the door on them."

Astro sighed. "You're right." He slid the Flame-hurler back inside.

Roseabelle studied the hinges frantically as the sound of clonking heavy footsteps became even louder. She noticed something on the silver hinges. "They have slits!" she exclaimed. "Astro, shoot your lightning between the openings in the hinges."

"What?" Jessicana exclaimed.

"It'll work," Roseabelle assured them. "It'll break the hinges open, and once we're in, we can bar the door from the inside. We have to be quick, though. I can use my telekinesis to help too."

"Well, it's better than exploding everything," Jessicana agreed. They took a step back to allow Astro to step forward. Quick as a flash, three bolts of precise lightning shot through the hinges and the door fell forward. Just before it hit the ground, Roseabelle clenched her teeth and froze the door in midair with her telekinesis, strength draining from her limbs.

Astro and Jessicana raced forward to grab the door, and they caught it inches before it hit the ground. "Go!" Astro urged. Roseabelle leaped past them into the dank musty interior of, hopefully, where Magford was being held.

Moonstar followed her, trotting alongside obediently. "You okay?" Roseabelle asked as Jessicana and Astro lifted the door back into its proper place.

"Yeah," Jessicana said, brushing her blonde locks out of her face. "We'll stay here, just in case the Darvonians try to enter." She touched Roseabelle's arm. "Good luck."

Roseabelle smiled. "Thanks." Swallowing her fear, she turned the corner, ready to face whatever would come next.

CHAPTER 10
Tropjyle

ROSEABELLE REALIZED THIS CELL WAS A LOT LARGER than a normal one would be. It wasn't just a single room; winding corridors, fake doors, and windows twisted all around her. Moonstar rubbed against her leg. "How do I find him in this place?" she whispered, and the animal bounded forward. "Wait up!" she called and ran after Moonstar, following him through rapidly twisting passages.

Moonstar stepped into an even darker room than before, and Roseabelle cautiously followed, an unexpected flash of friendly warmth filling her being.

The room was full of scrolls and ink, the pleasant aroma of a library drifting in the air. A few rugs lay on the floor and a small bed was pushed in the corner of the room. In the center of it all was a man dressed in a ratty brown shirt with raggedy pants and worn sandals. His back was facing her, and he was writing furiously on a piece of trutan with an ink-tipped quill. What Roseabelle noticed most of all was the large mop of curly red hair spread all over his head. A dirty black chain was connected from his ankle to the wall.

Hearing her hesitant footsteps, he turned around. He had a red beard as well, Roseabelle noted. His eyebrows scrunched together. and he bore a striking resemblance to Dastrock. "Huh. Didn't know they sent IBs down here anymore." His voice was warm but firm and gentle at the same time. Roseabelle grimaced at the mention of IBs—the term stood for Imitation Benotripian, Darvonians who resembled Benotripians.

Roseabelle took a few steps closer and incredible warmth filled her chest. Could it be? She had to pinch herself to make sure that this really wasn't a dream. "It's really you," she said, a relieved smile spreading over her features. Magford had gone missing when she was very young, and Danette had been left to rule Benotripia all alone. All Roseabelle's life she'd dreamed about what her father would look like, and here he was, right in front of her.

"Sorry, I don't think we've met before. As I told Sheklyth, these scrolls aren't really worth scouring. No information for you here." Magford talked to her, turning back around and Roseabelle understood. Of course. The last time he'd seen her was when she was two years old.

"I'm not an IB," she said, taking a tentative step closer to him.

"Metamordian then? Fellow prisoner?"

"Not exactly. My name's Roseabelle." She didn't know what else to say, desperately hoping he'd remember her name.

Magford slowly pivoted to face her, his expression mesmerized. "Now that's a name I haven't heard in a very long time." Roseabelle swallowed as he took a quick breath. "I can see Danette in you . . . that face . . . and that hair . . . It's not possible . . . Roseabelle?" He said each word slowly as if he was staring at a ghost.

Roseabelle choked back tears of happiness and leaped forward, embracing her father as he looked into her face, shaking his head in disbelief. "I-I've been thinking, dreaming about you ever since they took me away from Benotripia," Magford said, holding Roseabelle close. "I can't believe it! You're really here! I—" His voice broke off, trembling with emotion as they hugged each other. Roseabelle closed her eyes, solidifying this moment in her mind and vowing to never let it go. They held on for a long time—it seemed like years to Roseabelle.

They broke apart and Roseabelle stared at all of the objects around them. "I don't get it. Why do you have all these scrolls and furniture?"

Magford chuckled and gestured to the chain on his ankle, which Roseabelle realized was actually extremely lengthy. Part of the black links coiled in an enormous pile. "They let me roam around free in this entire maze. It used to be a lot of junk, kind of like a storage area. I turned it into this." He gestured to the room. "And of course, my power of supersonic speed did help."

Roseabelle stared around in wonder. "Wow, you really did make some amazing things. Why didn't they confiscate all this?"

"They were hoping I'd write some secret plans on the parchment, maybe give some clues to what the Benotripians were planning, communicate with the outside world. I knew too much, you see. That's why they brought me here. And ever since, they've basically forgotten about me, except for a few occasions." Magford shook his head. "Roseabelle, you've put yourself in grave danger by coming here. How did you get here?"

Just then, Moonstar appeared, melting out of the shadows, and Roseabelle jumped in surprise. She'd completely forgotten the creature was even there.

"Of course." Magford laughed and Moonstar tread up to him. The man stroked his ears. "The last thing I told this little guy was to find you. I can telepathically communicate with animals, you know."

"You can?" Roseabelle asked, astonished. Danette had really never talked about Magford's abilities.

Magford nodded. "He probably was a stowaway on a Darvonian ship or something. We share a special bond—Moonstar has been my personal companion for a very long time. He's a Sheilvoh, part of a rare species with extraordinary powers." He shook his head. "But why didn't Danette stop you from coming? How did you even leave Benotripia?"

"It's a long story and we'll get to that later, but we need to get you out of here," Roseabelle said. To her horror, the clashing of metal and sound of angry yelling echoed in the caverns. "The Darvonians found us," she whispered. "Of course they'd know to look here." She circled around the chain. "What are your other powers?" she asked, examining it closely.

"Shadow tumbling, camouflaging myself into my surroundings, Bubble building, lots of others too. But none can get me out of this chain. Believe me I've tried. And besides there's no way I could get past the Tropjyle."

"Tropjyle?" Roseabelle asked, inquisitive.

"The monstrous reptile guarding the front," Magford pointed out. "It can hurl its nets at lightning speed and the barbs attached to those things are deathly poisonous. You get caught in one of those, and it's all over."

"So obviously, don't wake the giant monster," Roseabelle said, taking a shaky breath. Her eyes drifted back to the chain. She knew a sledge hammer or a large axe should cut it, but she didn't have the time to draw one on the trutan. Wait a second. "What's this chain made of?" she asked.

Magford grasped her shoulders. "Roseabelle, you need to leave now. Shadow tumble out of here! I don't matter. You can come back later."

"No, I can't," she said. "I can't leave my friends behind."

"What? You're not alone?" Right on cue, Jessicana and Astro came bursting in, breathing heavily.

"The Darvonians found us," Jessicana wheezed. "We blocked the door with a few crates we found in a different room, but it won't last long."

"We need to get out of here!" Astro exclaimed.

"Astro!" Roseabelle said. She turned to her father. "Do you think lightning would slice through the chain?"

Magford raised his eyebrows. “Uh, lightning?”

“Quick, Astro,” Roseabelle said, glancing at the other passageways. “It’s worth a try.” Astro bent down and carefully examined the chain from Magford’s ankle.

“Look away!” Astro announced and everyone shielded their faces. There was a flash of silver and blue, and the chain thudded to the ground. Magford quickly gathered up his scrolls in a bundle, tucking them under his arm.

“Thank you,” he said to Astro. “Are you armed with weapons?”

Astro nodded and quickly handed Magford double swords. “How do we get out now?” Jessicana asked frantically. Roseabelle quickly slung her backpack from her shoulder and set it on the ground, rummaging inside. Just then they heard the door knocked over by the furious Darvonians.

“I have an idea,” she said. “Obviously our cover’s blown, so we can’t use the element of surprise. That means,” she continued, withdrawing a Flame-hurler from her backpack and loading it with ammo balls, “we need to cause an explosion.” She grinned at the shocked Astro and Jessicana. “Everyone back!”

She pulled the trigger and three missiles shot straight at the metal wall, exploding in a mass of fire and smoke, shaking the entire room. Coughing, Roseabelle squinted through the smoke. Sure enough, a gaping hole had been blown into the wall, revealing the Darvonian hideout they had been in earlier.

“Run!” Astro yelled as the Darvonians in the hideout brandished glowing weapons. As Jessicana followed him, Magford glanced at Roseabelle, shaking his head.

“When did you grow up so fast?”

Then they plunged into battle. Roseabelle reached into her pack, retrieved a spear for herself, and zipped it closed. Astro was rapidly shooting lightning bolts at a group of Darvonians and Jessicana was jabbing a Thepgile at two hooded figures, holding them back for now.

As a Darvonian thrust a Trapita at Roseabelle, she blocked

the blow with her spear, throwing him back against the wall. She ducked as another one swung a Dragocone Ray at her, rolling and thwacking him in the legs with the spear, sending him sprawling.

Out of the corner of her eye, she caught a glimpse of her father. For someone who'd been cooped up in a prison for years, he fought extremely well. Jabbing, slicing, blocking, and thrusting, Magford battled against at least thirty Darvonians, using his supersonic speed. They tried to fight back, but whenever they swung at him, he was already in a different spot.

Suddenly a monstrous roar echoed through the caverns and everyone froze—Darvonians, Benotripians, and Magford and Roseabelle, who were Metamordians. By the light of the dim torches, Roseabelle could see a wrinkly head rise above the throngs of people, and she backed up slowly.

The Tropjyle had awakened.

The Darvonians instantly dispersed, but they were too late—the creature shifted its shell and five nets sprang out, catching a few cloaked figures in their grasp. It was obvious that the monster was feeling threatened and was now protecting itself.

Roseabelle noticed its feet were built for sprinting fast and she backed up. The Darvonians screamed as the creature released nets in every direction, trapping many figures. She had an urge to grab her friends and father and dart up the stairs, but the monster was blocking their path.

The annoyed Tropjyle's eyes suddenly locked onto Astro, and it advanced toward him. The monstrous footsteps shook the entire tunnel, rattling the ground and causing a cloud of dust to float down from the ceiling. The Tropjyle's piercing stare swept over them, and Roseabelle suddenly froze, paralyzed by fear. Several other Darvonians were suffering the same effect. It was obviously a quality this reptile possessed.

Roseabelle watched in horror as the monster thundered

over to Astro, rearing back and preparing to lash the lightning boy into its trap.

"Hey!" Jessicana abruptly yelled, waving her arms in front of the Tropjyle, and Roseabelle jumped, breaking out of the trance. The huge creature swiveled its head, eyes narrowing in on Jessicana. Roseabelle barely had time to wonder how her friend had gotten out of the Tropjyle's paralyzing effect, before the enormous foot of the monster rose over her. In its path toward Jessicana, the Tropjyle was ready to lumber right over Roseabelle. She leaped out of the way just in time as it came crashing down, sending her flying against the back wall.

The next thing Roseabelle knew, a sharp pain had pierced her skull and her head lolled back, her vision blurry and distant. A hand touched her arm and she struggled to focus her vision. "Roseabelle!" said a voice beside her and she blinked. Her father was crouching beside her, looking concerned. It took Roseabelle a minute to get her bearings before she could look at the battle playing before her. Astro and Jessicana were fighting the Tropjyle—lightning peppered the monster and a brightly colored bird circled it, pecking its leathery head. The creature shot numerous nets at Astro, but he dodged—unfortunately his sword wasn't so lucky. Roseabelle saw one net curl around the sword and wrench it from Astro's hand. The weapon clattered to the floor, wrapped up within poisonous barbs.

Jessicana dove away from the Tropjyle and zoomed toward Roseabelle, transforming back into a girl. "Roseabelle!" she exclaimed. She dug in her pack and brought out her mini potion kit. As a healer, Jessicana carried potions with her wherever she went.

The Darvonians had switched tactics and were coming toward them now, but Roseabelle was too dazed to say anything. Magford noticed something was awry and pivoted, slashing his double swords at the cloaked figures. He was like a whirlwind of fury.

Jessicana hurriedly mixed a frothy blue liquid and a white powder together, then shoved the contents into Roseabelle's mouth. Her senses immediately sharpened, and Roseabelle jolted up, warmth and energy trickling into her limbs. Moonstar suddenly leaped out from the shadows, sinking its knife-like teeth into the monster's leg and the Tropjyle howled. Roseabelle saw the Tropjyle's head retracting into its shell. It really was threatened now and was resorting to the only other way to protect itself. Another group of Darvonians was advancing on Astro, backing him into a corner.

"Thanks, Jessicana," she said and her friend nodded.

"There's no time to waste, come on, we have to get out of here!" Jessicana said.

A different throng of Darvonians rushed at the girls, and Roseabelle blocked one from striking with her Trapita and dodged another blow from a sword. Jessicana swung her javelin and knocked a Darvonian aside. The two then joined hands, running toward Astro.

But by the time they got there, his fingertips were crackling. The Darvonians who had ambushed him lay on the floor, out cold. Astro grinned and Jessicana muttered, "Show off."

The three of them turned toward Magford, and Roseabelle's blood ran ice cold. The Darvonians were closing in around him. To her relief, he sped around them—only to come face-to-face with another group.

"Dad!" she called. The word felt foreign but special on her tongue. She hadn't said that, well, in as long as she could remember, ever. "We need to get out of here!" Magford's gaze turned to the staircase and Moonstar raced between the Darvonians, bounding up the stone stairs.

"I'll meet you at the top," she promised her friends. Roseabelle dashed to a shadowy corner, closed her eyes, and pictured the shadow of the cave entrance.

In a whirling sensation, she was there, right at the top of the staircase. Magford, her friends, and Moonstar were rushing up the stairs below her. "Hurry!" she yelled. Her friends looked surprised at how quickly she had shadow tumbled, but they followed her advice, running up the staircase and skidding to a stop on the ledge of the cave entrance.

"Hurry, get on Moonstar!" Magford urged. "He can carry three kids your weight quite a long distance."

"How? And won't we just crash below? Wait—can he *fly*?"

"Not exactly," Magford said and touched Roseabelle's cheek. "Get away from here. I'll be with you in a few minutes. Trust me."

"Wait, back to Benotripia?" she asked, confused.

"No, Darvonia," he said. With that, he turned away. Jessicana and Roseabelle clambered onto the enormous creature. Roseabelle didn't exactly doubt that Moonstar couldn't carry them—he was huge—but he couldn't fly! Both of the girls heard the raging cries of the Darvonians close behind them, and Magford motioned for Astro to get on.

Just then, a Darvonian emerged from below, drawing a knife, and Roseabelle yelled, "Astro! Behind you!"

CHAPTER 11

A Plan

One second Astro was ready to climb onto Moonstar; the next he heard the clink of metal whizzing through the air.

Instinctively, he ducked and rolled. A dagger flew past just where his head had been, disappearing into the waterfall. A Darvonian stood by the staircase, completely hooded and holding a Dragocone Ray. Astro quickly dived for the Darvonian's ankle, tripping him, just as he was about to bring down the Ray on top of him.

The Darvonian landed in a heap on the ledge and Astro hurriedly jumped onto the animal. Worried, he turned to look back at Magford, who swung his double swords as he eyed the new attacker. Roseabelle's father then sank into the black camouflage behind him. Astro blinked a couple of times. If he hadn't been staring at Magford moments before, he wouldn't have known where he was.

"Moonstar will know where to take you! I'll catch up," Magford promised. As the Darvonians suddenly poured from the cave entrance, he began battling their Dragocone Rays, breaking their Trapitas in half, dismantling their Spidegars before they got a chance to even throw at him.

"Now, Moonstar!" Jessicana urged, and the Sheilvoh leaped off the ledge.

The wind whistled in Astro's ears, barrelling past him, an eerie whooshing sound filling the air.

The three friends screamed, closing their eyes as the ground came closer, but the impact never came. Astro opened his eyes—they were on the stone floor. This didn't make sense. He leaned over to look at the ground and realized Moonstar's paws weren't even touching the stone.

He's so fast he doesn't even touch the ground, Astro realized in awe. The three friends hung on as Moonstar carried them through the waterfall. The clear liquid came rushing down on them, and Astro coughed and tried to splash it out of his face.

Sputtering out water, Jessicana groaned. "Really?" Astro reckoned that was the third time she'd been soaked that day.

As they headed toward the ocean, Astro braced himself. Was Moonstar hiding some other secret power? Maybe he could lift a little higher in the air and fly? But as they left the ground, the friends felt ocean spray hitting their faces. It suddenly came to Astro—*Moonstar is so fast he can run on water.*

This was more exhilarating than anything he'd ever experienced, and he let out a whoop. Roseabelle reached out her hand to catch the salty sea spray, laughing as they sped across the ocean. It was unbelievable to be traveling so fast—Astro had never felt so free in his life.

But he suddenly realized he wouldn't feel free for long.

They were on their way to Darvonia.

Shadowy fog hung over Blackwater Sea as Moonstar sprinted across the water, the dark island coming within the three friends' view. "What if they see us?" Astro asked.

"I don't know," Jessicana said, tucking a strand of blonde hair behind her ear with a trembling hand. "But Danette and Dastrock should be safe, maybe hiding away. At the worst, they've been captured. The Darvonians would want them alive."

Astro could tell Roseabelle was trying to keep her doubt and fear hidden away. He put a hand on her shoulder. "It's going to be all right."

Roseabelle gave him a small smile but turned away, her muscles still tense. Moonstar suddenly put on a burst of speed as they neared the coast of Darvonia. Astro reeled backward, his vision blurring as Moonstar shot forward.

Moonstar skidded to a halt, and all three friends sprawled on the rocky beach, groaning. The Sheilvoh nudged them as if urging them to move on. Reluctantly, they all stood up and followed him to a small rock cranny, where an underground passage opened up.

The three friends sat down and broke out their remaining food, spilling two loaves and a collection of fruit on the ground. Astro gathered up all the food he could eat, completely famished. They had been so focused on rescuing Magford that they hadn't eaten in two days.

Suddenly from the shadows, Roseabelle's father appeared, and they all jumped back. Magford was covered in cuts and bruises, and his daughter gasped. "Are you all right?" she asked, leaping to her feet.

"I'm fine, Roseabelle," Magford said, embracing her quickly. "But, first, I must tell you what is going on. The secret I'm about to reveal is the reason the Darvonians captured me—I knew too much. So once I pass this information down to you, you must be careful. Understood?"

Astro's heartbeat picked up a bit, and he stared at Roseabelle's father with intrigue.

"What exactly do you know about the Dream World?" Magford asked.

Astro shifted in his seat, and his friends did the same as they exchanged glances. They recalled when Asteran, Jessicana's former trainer, had dropped a feather on the ground that Roseabelle had then picked up. She had entered into the Dream World. "Well, I accidentally traveled there a while ago," Roseabelle said, and Magford's eyebrows shot up.

Jessicana handed him Horsh's papers. "We found these in the ground near Astro's home," she said. "They looked pretty authentic to us and they had Horsh's mark on them, so we were certain the author was telling the truth."

Magford cleared his throat, looking over them. "Yes. These are mine actually."

"What?" Astro asked. Roseabelle's father was making no sense.

"Well, yes, they are Horsh's, but I excavated them from the ground. It's how I learned about the Dream World." Magford gestured to the point where the words stopped. "I smudged that over so the Darvonians wouldn't learn where the entrance to the Dream World was."

"So when the Darvonians captured you . . . ?" Astro began.

"Yes, when I found this they became incredibly suspicious. When they found out I had learned where the Dream World's entrance was, they came after me. Luckily I had already rubbed those words away and buried the trutan in a place I thought was safe." He raised his eyebrows. "How did you find this anyway?"

"Well, I fell from the sky and my lightning went off," Astro said, his tone nonchalant. "And then we kind of found it."

Roseabelle's father gaped at him. "Clearly, I've missed a lot over the past few years. Do you mind informing me a bit?" And so they did, telling Magford of all the adventures they had experienced, how they had rescued Danette from the Darvonians and how they had obtained the Stones of Horsh. Astro noticed Magford's eyes slightly moistened when they talked about Danette.

Jessicana withdrew the spyglass. "Is this yours too?"

Magford's eyes lit up. "Resourceful children! This is the Third Eye. It belongs to the rightful ruler of Benotripia—and it really is a useful artifact. I was scouting the Dream World, when they came. Moonstar was with me and I silently communicated with him that he should run back to Metamordia. I don't know what he was thinking when he found you, Roseabelle. Maybe he had sensed your presence near when he was out on the ocean, and traced you to Benotripia."

"So, where is the entrance to the Dream World?" Astro asked, but Magford held up a hand.

"I'd rather not say it out loud. Do you have the Stones?"

Astro reached into his pocket and patted the bloodred Stone. Jessicana nodded as well. Roseabelle slid her hand inside her tunic pocket, then froze. Frantically, she dug her hands into both her pockets, scrambling around, mouth agape.

"What is it?" Magford asked.

She held up her pocket and Astro saw a large hole in the bottom. "My Stone," Roseabelle exclaimed. "It's gone!"

Magford swallowed. "Well, that does present a problem." He slid his swords back into their sheaths. Drumming the hilts on the ground, he sat in concentrated thought for a few minutes. The three friends exchanged glances. They couldn't destroy the Dream World without Roseabelle's Stone!

"Wait," he said, flipping his swords into the air and catching them by the hilt. "I've got it! There's a high point in Darvonia where we could attract Roseabelle's Stone. Horsh originally wanted to hide them separately but it didn't work. All three are connected to each other. So if we touch those two together at a high peak, the third will magnetically float to it."

Astro grinned. "Awesome! Let's go!"

Magford shook his head. "It's not that easy. Darvonians will be patrolling everywhere. And it will be tiring for you two."

"We can fight through them," Jessicana said.

"We're a team," Roseabelle added.

Magford bit the inside of his cheek. "Listen, I can't just leave you here. You're children!"

"Yeah, but we've been through a lot," Astro said. "We rescued the ruler of Benotripia by ourselves. Now we just need to fight off a mass army of Darvonians. Plus we have a magical animal and a warrior dude by our side. We'll do just fine."

Roseabelle nodded. "Trust us."

"But is the entrance to the Dream World far from here?" Jessicana inquired.

Magford sighed. "It would be a three days' walk from here, maybe farther. But with Moonstar? A few minutes tops. We just need to evade a lot of Darvonians."

Roseabelle and Jessicana jumped to their feet, sorting through the backpacks and picking out weapons. Astro walked up to Magford. "Um, sir?" He pulled out his Stone. "Our Stones aren't working. It's like they lost their power ever since we left Benotripia."

To his surprise, Magford chuckled. "Horsh bewitched them to only exercise their power while in Benotripia or when near the Dream World. He didn't want the Darvonians to be able to use them freely on the island."

Roseabelle and Jessicana had overheard. "So, what will destroying the Dream World do to the Darvonians?" the daughter asked her father.

Magford put a hand on her shoulder. "Destroying the Dream World with the Stones of Horsh will demolish the Stones as well. Also, the Darvonians' power will decrease, their fear won't be as strong. They'll withdraw from Metamordia as the Benotripians advance on them. We'll free the people there." He gestured wildly with his hands as he spoke, and Astro could tell he was beyond elated.

Magford turned to the kids. "But the Dream World will be dangerous."

Astro frowned. "Why? Isn't it just empty?"

The Metamordian shook his head. "No, not exactly. Everything that that Stone has made disappear"—he gestured to Astro's jewel—"is in the Dream World."

Astro shook his head wildly and turned back to Roseabelle. Oh no, this was not good!

As Magford stepped ahead, Jessicana and Astro sidled up to Roseabelle. "You know what this means?" he asked her.

Roseabelle swallowed. "A lot of Darvonians will be in there?" she guessed.

"Well, that too, but Sheklyth is still alive!" Astro said. Roseabelle stared at her feet.

"We'll handle her," she said, forcing on a confident smile, but he could still tell she was beyond nervous.

"So we leave now?" Jessicana asked.

Magford seemed to consider it, then shook his head, pointing to the sky above. It was getting darker by the minute. "Darvonians relish the cover of darkness—it would not be wise. Let's stay here for the night." Magford nodded. "We leave tomorrow."

CHAPTER 12
Roarcaneum

MAGFORD SAT AT THE FRONT OF THE CAVE, HALF awake watching for intruders, and half asleep to get a bit of rest. Meanwhile, the three friends curled up in the back with Moonstar. Roseabelle had created sleeping rolls from the trutan, and Jessicana was curled up in one of them.

She couldn't believe everything that had happened—it was crazy. Brushing aside her mass of tangled blonde hair, Jessicana closed her eyes and made an effort to sleep. It felt nice to not be resting on a rocking boat that was being tossed about the waves.

Her fingers clutched tightly at her aqua blue Stone. Jessicana knew how important this was to the Benotripians. They might have their strong defenses but with the Dream World, the Darvonians could appear on Benotripia *behind* the defenses, catching the Benotripians completely by surprise.

Dawn broke the horizon, and they all breathed a sigh of relief that no Darvonians had spotted them during the night. They all sat down to eat milk and nuts, stomachs rumbling with hunger.

"All right," Magford said, tapping a finger on his mostly

bare chin. He had made an attempt to shave the beard off with a Trapita last night, which had left his beard a huge mess—all that remained was some ragged stubble. "Remember, we need to stay hidden. That's the key element here. This is life or death now. Stealth is the only option we have."

All of the friends gulped at the same time. "What's ahead of us?" Jessicana asked. "I mean, just the Darvonians themselves right?"

Magford grimaced. "I wish, but you know the Darvonians. Always full of surprises, whether you like it or not." He tossed each of them weapons: a Spidegar and javelin for Jessicana, a razor sharp Thepgile for Roseabelle, and a broadsword for Astro. "Weapons are great for defending yourselves, but you need to remember who you are—the Darvonians are all about weapons, fighting. But you are Benotripians, Metamordians. You have powers and you have them for a reason. So if you have to choose between weapons and powers, choose who you really are." He paused. "Now, let's find Roseabelle's Stone. Come on."

THE FRIENDS CREPT TO THE EDGE OF THE CAVE AND Magford motioned to the outside. The air was filled with thick black smog, and the landscape was as rocky as Jessicana remembered. "If we're lucky enough, the Darvonians won't know we're here." He took a step out into the open and his foot instantly squelched in a patch of dark mud. Magford winced. "I would just Shadow Tumble but none of you would know where to go."

"There has to be a specific spot?" Jessicana asked, and he nodded.

"Yes," Magford said. "Also, a single person is easier to overcome than four." He continued walking through the spongy ground, which was much like a marsh.

"That's strange. The ground was dry last night," Roseabelle remarked and took a step forward, following her father. Astro did the same. That was when Jessicana noticed black sludge reaching up toward Magford's ankles.

"Everyone," Jessicana said uneasily. "What are you standing in?"

Magford glanced down and his face suddenly went very pale. "Oh no."

"What?" Astro asked.

"We need to get out of here!" Magford roared.

The ground began to tremor a bit and Magford tried to squirm out of the sludge. Jessicana watched, helpless, as her friends struggled.

Jessicana frantically scurried around the cave, searching for something she could pull her friends up with. Her eyes landed on a piece of thick, dark wood lying in the back of the cave, and she scrambled toward it. Jessicana's eyes were wide. She had a slight suspicion of what was going on, but was too scared to think about it.

"Is this quicksand?" Astro yelled.

"Worse!" Magford said as Jessicana held out the piece of wood. Roseabelle managed to grab onto it, and Jessicana clenched her teeth, pulling back on the thick wood.

"Come on," Roseabelle grunted, and Jessicana pulled as hard as she could—but it wasn't working. She jumped when the wood broke in half, leaving a woozy Roseabelle still sinking into the sludge. All three of Jessicana's comrades were now knee deep in the mud.

"Try stabbing it!" Magford said.

Astro cocked his head to one side. "What are you talking about?" he asked.

"This isn't quicksand," Magford explained and did his best to worm out of the sludge. "It's a Roarcaneum, creature of the ground. And we've been caught right in his jaws."

"Try Shadow Tumbling!" Jessicana called out desperately, but Roseabelle shook her head.

"It won't work!"

Magford stared at Jessicana, his eyes wide and determined. "Jessicana, stab your javelin into the ground now! It'll get it to resurface and then you can fight it." Jessicana's pulse was beating rapidly, and she bit her lip.

"So the Darvonians did find us!" Astro said, scrambling to pull himself out.

Jessicana gathered all of her courage and looked all over the ground, holding out her javelin. Where was she supposed to attack the Roarcaneum? She'd read about these creatures in books before but they never specified where to stab them—that was the only way to get rid of them.

"Just do it!" Magford hollered as the sludge buried them shoulder deep. Acting on an impulse, Jessicana lifted up her javelin and drove it deep into the earth. The reaction was instant. The ground's radius around them began to vibrate. Jessicana stood her ground, trying to keep from toppling over, and yanked back on the rod of her javelin, breaking a piece of the shaft off. She pulled her javelin from the deep mud. An enormous shape withdrew from the earth, silver eyes glinting at Jessicana. It had a round head with slick mud dripping from its long neck. It also possessed a bulky nose with tiny nostrils, and its soft brown skin surprisingly camouflaged well into the earth. Roseabelle, Magford, and Astro were embedded in its head.

Then Jessicana saw the most bizarre scene she had ever seen. They were sinking right through the monster's head into its mouth! So that was how the Roarcaneum caught its victims.

Jessicana resisted the urge to squeak, and she took a step back. The Roarcaneum was undoubtedly huge—although it towered ten feet over her, part of its lower body was still submerged in the mud. The Roarcaneum stared at her, almost as if it was wondering if Jessicana was really worth attacking. On a sudden impulse, Jessicana suddenly leaped forward and hurled her javelin at it, but the sharp weapon bounced back against its hard coating of solid rock and soil. She yelped as the javelin came sailing back at her, flying over her head as she ducked.

"Hurry, Jessicana!" Roseabelle shouted, and Jessicana searched for the monster's weak point. It was protected by the earth, submerged in the earth. Then she saw its silver eyes staring past her.

Of course! The reason the Roarcaneum wasn't attacking her was because it couldn't even see her. Jessicana realized it had horrible vision. Its only weapon was to trap its victims and catch them by surprise. Her intellect took over, and she thought quickly, running all possibilities through her head.

Then it came to her. The Roarcaneum had to have an incredible sense of hearing to sense its prey above ground!

She dug in her pack, and the monster growled a bit as her friends frantically twisted out of the mush, striving to escape. Jessicana yanked out a Flame-hurler and loaded it with ammo. Roseabelle, Astro, and Magford were now neck deep in the slush. "Hold on!" she yelled and pulled the trigger.

Three iron balls of metal, electricity, and fire hurled toward the Roarcaneum, zooming right past it and exploding into a cloud of dark silver ash, raining down on the Darvonian ground. The earth monster, hearing the horrendous noise, jerked around to look. Unfortunately, the movement did nothing to release Jessicana's friends.

Jessicana gritted her teeth. The Roarcaneum, still startled from the commotion, kept looking all around for the noise. She just had to make more of it. Jessicana banged two swords together, but quickly dropped them. She attached a hook to an arrow, placed it in a bow, aimed, and shot. The hook embedded in the Roarcaneum's shoulder, and she quickly grabbed onto it as the Roarcaneum flailed about.

Grasping the arrow as tight as she could, Jessicana screamed as she was flung about. But seeing her friends above her rapidly sinking into the monster's head, she thought harder. *Think, Jessicana, think.*

Wait a second. I can fly! she thought. With not a moment to waste, Jessicana transformed into a parrot and zoomed up to her friends, wings flapping hurriedly. Astro had started hacking at the mud with his sword but that only resulted in bruising his arms as he tried to yank his weapon out of it. "Awk, use your powers!" Jessicana squawked loudly, and Roseabelle and Astro exchanged panicked glances. Jessicana transformed back into a girl in midflight and landed beside them.

Her friends were now shooting lightning bolts and hitting the Roarcaneum in the head with its own rocks. Magford's body had almost sunk through. Jessicana, keeping light on her feet so she wouldn't join their half-buried state, yanked Magford by his arms out of the mud, using all of her strength. She tried to not focus on the creature's height. She could maybe simply fly down but her friends couldn't.

As the Roarcaneum thrashed about, Astro managed to release himself, burning a hole around himself with his silver-blue lightning. He then turned to Roseabelle, digging her out as fast as he could. "Astro, a little help here," Jessicana groaned as she lifted Magford.

She fought to keep her balance as the Roarcaneum tromped around, following the many noises. She concentrated on not toppling over the edge even though the ground was shaking violently. "Astro, give me your pack!" she yelled over the monster's sudden roaring.

The lightning boy tossed it to her. Jessicana grabbed a Flame-hurler, loaded it up, and set it off. A single ball of ammo hurled toward the creature's eyes.

And then the Flame-hurler exploded in a flash of smoke.

Coughing and sputtering, a dark cloud of fog smothered them and Jessicana could faintly hear the wailings of the creature as it tipped this way and that. "Moonstar!" Magford yelled, but before he could continue, the Roarcaneum tilted drastically, and Jessicana tumbled through the air. Her vision clouded, her senses muddled—and then, suddenly, her limbs felt as though they were on fire.

An excruciating jolt of pain shot through her leg, and

Jessicana instantly sat up straight. She was positioned on the back of Moonstar, but she had landed wrong. One of her legs was sticking out at an odd angle. She cringed, her arms shaking.

Roseabelle and Magford appeared beside her, and Astro came plummeting down, flailing wildly. Roseabelle and Astro scrambled over to Moonstar and threw themselves on top of his back

Moonstar instantly sprinted away, and Jessicana clutched his sleek fur. As the Roarcaneum bellowed, she, Roseabelle, Magford, and Astro were carted across the rough Darvonian terrain, dark clouds blocking the sun.

"Won't it come after us?" Jessicana yelled over the sound of the wind rushing past their faces.

Magford shook his head.

"It's almost impossible to destroy a Roarcaneum, but the fortunate part is that it can't follow us," Magford said. "It's too grounded."

"But it wasn't there last night!" Jessicana heard Astro say, her energy seeping away. She managed to sit up. She was glad she hadn't been required to completely destroy the Roarcaneum. Jessicana hated hurting animals of any kind and only did it in self-defense.

"The Darvonians must have planted it, moved it somehow," Magford shouted back. "They probably were watching us from afar."

Moonstar raced up a dark hill, passing large walls of stones and hidden fortifications. They sped by Darvonian encampments, but they were traveling so quickly, the Darvonians couldn't see them, let alone stop them. Jessicana noticed Magford was staring intently at Moonstar, and she figured they were probably mentally communicating.

She glanced at her leg and winced, gritting her teeth. She hadn't broken it—Jessicana could tell due to her experience as a healer—but it still surged with pain. She gripped Moonstar's fur.

Moonstar suddenly came to a stop, and everyone was thrown off onto a patch of hard earth. Jessicana's leg hit a hard boulder, and she yelped. "Fortunate," she muttered, gritting her teeth as she pulled herself into an upright position. "Really fortunate."

Jessicana's fingers went to her deep tunic pocket where her blue Stone rested. She also took out some water from her pack. Her heart sank when she realized that most of the items inside had fallen out. But she still had her javelin and some leftover ammo from the Flame-Hurler. A needle-like pain shot through her leg again, and she dug through her tunic pockets as her face twisted in a grimace. Where was her potion kit?

Jessicana caught hold of a tiny metal container and pulled it out to see her emergency potion kit. Of course, it wasn't her full collection of potions and herbs so she couldn't heal fully, but at least the kit would fix her leg a little bit. She dipped her finger into some gray paste and swallowed it, shivering at the grainy taste. That should do it.

Magford helped Roseabelle up, and then Jessicana who gladly accepted his hand. Astro popped to his feet. They were standing on a tall rocky hill, and Magford nodded firmly. "Listen closely, very closely. Astro and Jessicana, you must take out your Stones and press them together. Their power will attract Roseabelle's Stone." He took a deep breath. "Meanwhile, I'm going to distract the Darvonians."

"What?" Roseabelle burst out, rushing to her father's side. Jessicana and Astro exchanged worried looks. Magford couldn't go into the midst of Darvonians—he could be caught again! He bent down on his knees to face Roseabelle and smiled gently at her.

"Roseabelle, from what you've told me, you've grown into an amazing person. You're an intelligent, brave girl, and I'm proud to call you my daughter. Once you obtain the Stones, follow Moonstar—he knows where the physical entrance to the Dream World is.

"You have to go inside, with your friends or alone, and go to the very core of the Dream World, avoiding Darvonians, creatures, whatever else may be there."

Roseabelle shook her head. "You already disappeared once. I'm not letting that happen again!"

Magford took her by the shoulders. "It won't. I'll come back, I promise. Dastrock and Danette should be fine, as well. I'll find them if I can. Be safe, be careful." Before they could stop him, he drew his double swords, offered them a half smile, and ducked into the shadow of the hill, closing his eyes and instantly vanishing. In a matter of seconds, he had Shadow Tumbled away without a trace.

"No!" Roseabelle exclaimed, and Jessicana touched her arm, smiling reassuringly at her friend.

"Come on," she said. "You can do this. Get the Third Eye. We don't know how the Stone is going to come to us."

Astro yanked the Stone out of his pocket and tossed Roseabelle the spyglass. She caught it in one hand and raised it to her eye. Jessicana cautiously withdrew her Stone and held it up to Astro's. The two glimmering surfaces pushed against each other.

For a moment, nothing happened. Jessicana shifted a bit. "See anything?" she asked Roseabelle, but her friend shook her head.

"No," Roseabelle muttered. Minutes droned on with Jessicana and Astro's Stones still pressed together.

Astro was about to open his mouth to suggest a new idea when Roseabelle suddenly perked up. "Guys . . . I see something . . ."

Jessicana grinned but it quickly faltered. The hill had begun to quake.

CHAPTER 13
The Chase

As the ground beneath him shook violently, Astro gripped his gleaming red gem. Gusts of air blew at the trio, and Astro squinted his eyes. Everyone's hair was tossed about in the wind. Out of the corner of his eye, he spotted Jessicana's tiny potion kit and most of their weapons fly away. He could see Roseabelle standing her ground as she clutched the Third Eye tightly in her hands.

Digging his feet into the soil, he raised a hand up to protect himself when suddenly it all stopped, and an eerie hush fell over the hills. Astro searched the landscape, and his eyes brightened when he saw a glittering object zooming toward them.

He glanced at his and Jessicana's Stones, the blue and red, and then back to Roseabelle's healing Stone flying quickly at them. He hurriedly caught it in one hand and gave it to Roseabelle.

"Why was there so much wind?" Jessicana asked.

"I'm guessing it was buried in the ocean floor," Roseabelle said. "Maybe the gravitational pull of the two Stones was so much it had to burrow itself out of there."

Moonstar had taken cover below the hill and climbed up

to meet them. Astro noticed that Jessicana's backpack had flown away, but luckily she still had her ammo, javelin, and, of course, her Stone. His pack had been lightly positioned on his back and still remained there. Roseabelle had managed to grab onto the Third Eye.

"Come on," Jessicana urged. The girls mounted Moonstar, and Astro was about to follow when a silver jagged disc sped past his head, barely nicking his ear. A Thepgile! He jumped in surprise and whirled around, protectively raising his hands in front of him.

"Astro," Roseabelle whispered. "Look."

He scrutinized the landscape closer and saw dark shadowy figures perched in trees and hiding below the hill. Darvonians.

There had to be hundreds of them, all armed with weapons. How could they have not seen them before? Astro shot a range of high-powered bolts at the line of the Darvonians. He mounted Moonstar when arrows flew past his head. Jessicana and Roseabelle had already jumped onto Moonstar.

"GO!" he yelled, and the Sheilvoh took off running, speeding past the throngs of waiting Darvonians. It was extremely lucky that the trio had Moonstar on their side. Astro figured that animals on Metamordia had powers as well, not only amazing speed but also incredible strength.

Jessicana glanced behind them. "They're not far behind!"

"It's all right. Don't look back, just focus on the horizon!" Roseabelle shouted back.

Ignoring her, Astro turned to see the Darvonians—but they weren't alone. His fingertips tingled when he saw the dark shadowy shapes they rode.

Shadow Horses.

Astro reasoned that the Shadow Horses had come from Metamordia but had been tainted by Darvonians so they could ride them. He clenched his teeth and held out his hands toward them. Enormous lightning bolts erupted from out of his fingertips.

Sure enough, pain flashed through his hands, and he tightly curled them into fists. "Astro—" Jessicana started to say.

"It's all right! I've got it," he cut her off. He wanted to reassure her, but Astro knew he probably wouldn't be able to shoot another round of lightning. The Shadow Horses radiated too much electricity, which overloaded him when he shot lightning. It also caused immense pain. Astro had finally resolved something. If the Shadow Horses were Darvonian, they would've known a long time ago. They had to have come from Metamordia.

Moonstar darted past rocky ledges and tall villages, bounding and leaping skillfully across the landscape. Astro, in the very back, nearly fell off twice. The Darvonians were still riding after them, but quite a few of them had stopped, which made Astro feel a little uneasy. What were they doing? He knew that the Darvonians wouldn't just give up. Up ahead, he heard Roseabelle mutter something. "What?" he yelled, his voice catching in his throat.

"Moonstar's taking us to Kinetle's castle!" Roseabelle shouted back. Astro saw that she was right. Kinetle was the ruler of Darvonia, Sheklyth's mother.

He felt the Sheilvoh's muscles tense a bit more, his pace gradually slowing. "Moonstar's getting tired!" he yelled. "He probably can't carry us much longer."

"I've got it covered!" Jessicana shouted. "I'll transform and follow you as best as I can." Without another word, she jumped into the air, transforming into a parrot midflight and soared above them. Although Moonstar was too quick for her, Astro could still keep sight of the tiny colorful dot in the sky that was Jessicana.

Moonstar traveled through the marketplace in a wild frenzy, knocking over carts and stands. Astro recognized it as the Darvonian courtyard marketplace they had come to while trying to find Danette, not too long ago.

"Is the door in the castle?" he shouted to Roseabelle.

"I'm not sure!" she responded. Moonstar swerved in the dark cobblestone path streets, leaping over surprised Darvonians. Astro tried to focus on their surroundings but everything became a blur as Moonstar gave an extra burst of speed. He thought he saw the enormous structure of the dark castle fly past him, but he wasn't sure. The next thing he knew, he was staring up at the foggy sky. He could hear Roseabelle groaning beside him, and Astro rubbed his head as a headache pounded into his skull. Beside them, Moonstar was lying on his belly, paws out in front.

Jessicana suddenly landed beside them and turned back into a girl. She wiped away the sweat from her forehead. "That . . ." she panted. "Was the most exhausting flight ever."

Astro wanted nothing more than to take a long nap. All the air was knocked out of him. He struggled to his feet. A silver jagged disc came swinging at him and he dodged it, the blade nicking his ankle, leaving a shallow cut. He looked back at the marketplace courtyard and saw cloaked Darvonians mounted on their Shadow Horses, cantering toward them. A few Darvonians had already drawn their weapons.

Roseabelle got to her feet, looking a bit woozy as well. "Come on," she said. "We have to get to the door, wherever it is." She put a hand on Moonstar's lithe form, and the Sheilvoh rose to its full extent. "Come on, Moonstar," she whispered in the animal's ears.

Moonstar seemed to sense the urgency of her tone. The Sheilvoh set off at a normal pace, and the three friends stumbled after Moonstar, who circled the vast perimeter of the castle. Behind them, the furious thundering of hooves followed. "They're gaining on us!" Astro shouted. He clutched his bloodred Stone, thinking how much easier it would be if the Stones worked in Darvonia.

Just then, a group of Shadow Horses, Darvonians mounted

proudly on top, veered straight in front of them, blocking their path. Astro stopped in his tracks as the Darvonians pointed their weapons at them.

They were completely surrounded. Again.

CHAPTER 14
The Invisible Door

Roseabelle let out a gasp when the Darvonians jumped out in front of them. Another group blocked their escape from behind. The Darvonians circled around them, enclosing the three friends and Moonstar.

Moonstar bounded back to the trio, stepping in front of them and growling. He purred softly, rubbing against Roseabelle's leg and nuzzling his horn against her pocket. What was he doing? She placed her hand inside, her fingers closing around the Stone and then the small spyglass. She carefully brought out the Third Eye. Maybe the Sheilvoh wanted to tell her something about it.

She put a hand on his head, then felt a rush of urgency directed at the spyglass. Discreetly, Roseabelle put the spyglass to her eye.

Something caught her vision—a brown object in the distance, floating in the air. A thrill ran through Roseabelle. Of course! It had to be the door to the Dream World, hidden by an enchantment to keep it invisible.

Roseabelle removed the spyglass from her face and stuffed it in her pocket before the Darvonians could notice it. She then peered past their enemies, seeing a cluster of jutting rocky stones from the path. Focusing intently on them, her mind lifted the boulders into the air behind the Darvonians.

Soft gentle breezes sifted through the area. The Darvonian in the front dismounted. "Where are the Stones?" the Darvonian asked, deathly quiet. Roseabelle recognized the voice—it was Heltonine, Sheklyth's younger sister! Heltonine turned to Astro. "It wouldn't be wise to shoot your lightning at us now." Roseabelle understood what she was saying. They were surrounded by so many Shadow Horses that the overpowering rush of power inside Astro could seriously injure him.

Concentrating hard on the boulders, Roseabelle used her telekinesis to lift them and lead them over to Heltonine. She felt Jessicana tense beside her. Roseabelle tried to block out all other thoughts from her mind as Heltonine carefully approached them.

"Fly," Astro whispered to Jessicana.

Roseabelle barely heard Jessicana's reply. "I'm not leaving you guys."

Roseabelle surreptitiously watched the boulders she was sneakily positioning above the Darvonians. Heltonine stopped a few paces in front of them, looking puzzled that the three friends weren't reacting to what she was saying. All was quiet as she surveyed the trio.

Suddenly Roseabelle tilted her head. The cluster of boulders hovering over the Darvonian's heads dropped, knocking the Darvonians to the ground. They remained motionless. Commotion instantly filled the courtyard. Jessicana quickly shot into the air as a parrot, but not before tossing Roseabelle her javelin and Astro some Flame-Hurler ammo. Roseabelle guessed Jessicana had quietly rummaged through her pack.

Because Roseabelle had kept the boulders behind the Darvonians before raising and dropping them from above, the Darvonians from behind hadn't seen anything at all. But now the Darvonians instantly reacted, and a dozen arrows rained down on Roseabelle and Astro. Roseabelle quickly sidestepped a cluster of arrows and swung her javelin to bat another away. Two others whistled past her ankles, and Astro quickly hurled some ammo at the group, which exploded into a mixture of dark fog, fire, and ash. A foggy wall rose up between Astro and the Darvonians. Roseabelle could hear Darvonians coughing and spluttering on the other side. "Come on!" she said, and Astro and she sprinted away from the throngs of Darvonians. Moonstar followed close behind, skillfully dodging all the missiles thrown at them.

Jessicana was already a few yards ahead. "Where's the door?"

"I saw it with the spyglass!" Roseabelle exclaimed, but Moonstar had already bounded ahead, leading them to it.

"Hurry!" Jessicana said.

"I think reinforcements are coming," Astro said, pointing upward. Darvonians had appeared on the buildings' balconies and towers. The sky began raining weapons. Roseabelle eyed the Dream World door and inside her pocket, her Stone began to vibrate.

"Do you feel that?" she asked, her eyes lighting up. "Of course! The Stones are regaining their power since they're so close to the Dream World's entrance!" They continued sprinting, thrilled at the sudden sizzle of energy in their pockets.

Suddenly a slew of arrows shattered the air around them. Roseabelle looked to see Darvonian archers shooting from the castle—the fog had cleared up and the enemy had spotted them. An arrow nearly hit Jessicana's leg, and Roseabelle felt one of the arrows nick her shoulder.

She saw they had two balls of ammo left, which Astro was holding. "Wait for it," he muttered as all three of them sprinted.

"Uh, Astro, I think you should throw that right about now!" Roseabelle's voice had a nervous edge to it as a Thepgile snapped at them. She quickly jumped out of the way as its owner reeled it back. They were running as fast as they could, following in Moonstar's tracks. Reinforcements had come, and Darvonians poured out of the castle at an alarming rate.

"Just a few more seconds," he countered as more Darvonians suddenly burst into view, with bows nocked and swords drawn.

Astro hurled one of the ammo balls at them, and a thick fog sprang up once again. Moonstar suddenly stopped and rubbed against something solid. Roseabelle raised the spyglass to her eyes, and she saw a room floating a few feet above them. Moonstar was rubbing against a pillar in the center that kept the room standing. A white door faced out of one of the room's walls, and she could see the glassy tube coming from it. A brown door led inside in the room.

"Hurry!" Astro shouted.

More arrows rained down from random directions; the Darvonians couldn't see it.

Jessicana flew up as a parrot and landed on a ledge beside the door. "Roseabelle, jump!" she called.

Bending her knees, Roseabelle focused and leaped, falling short by a few inches.

"I'll boost you up," Astro said, and Roseabelle quickly climbed on his shoulders. The smoke was clearing up; they didn't have much time. But as Astro stood up, she toppled over. He groaned. "Really, Roseabelle?"

Jessicana suddenly shook her head. "What am I doing?" she said incredulously. She withdrew her Stone, waved it, and a staircase appeared under their feet.

Moonstar leaped up and Roseabelle and Astro charged up it. Astro vanished the steps with his red Stone once they were safely positioned on the ledge. Jessicana threw open the door and they piled in, Roseabelle quickly closing it behind her.

Finally safe, at least for now, Roseabelle realized they had plunged into a tiny dark cellar, lit dimly by some torches placed on the wall. Roseabelle reached into her pocket and grabbed the glittering white gem.

"There it is," Roseabelle said, gesturing to the almost transparent door. On it were positioned three scooped openings, one for each Stone.

"Wait," Jessicana said as Roseabelle moved toward it. "Shouldn't one of us stay here? I mean what if the Dream World door closes on us and we're stuck in there forever?"

"Or worse, if Darvonians come down here and enter in while we're gone," Astro added.

"Or even worse, if something in there gets out," Jessicana continued.

"Or—"

Roseabelle laughed and put up a hand to stop them. "All right, I see your point. I'll go in alone." She swallowed, immediately regretting her words. "Once the Stones are in position, I'll quickly Shadow Tumble back to the entrance, so I won't be demolished with the rest of the Dream World."

"Are you sure?" Jessicana asked, coming up beside her friend. Roseabelle hesitated. She didn't know what was waiting for her, and the only thing she was armed with was the trutan and a javelin.

"I have my powers," she said. "I'll be all right." Astro and Jessicana nodded solemnly. "But if anything goes wrong, you have to destroy the Dream World."

"Don't talk like that," Astro said. "You can do this, Roseabelle. We believe in you."

Jessicana leaped forward and hugged her, and Astro gave her a reassuring grin. Roseabelle managed a small smile back. Even Moonstar rubbed affectionately against her leg.

Roseabelle crossed to the door and placed the white Stone inside of the door. "Wait," Roseabelle said and pulled out the trutan. She couldn't exactly do anything with it in the Dream World except lose it. "The Darvonians will come through the door, so use this to create anything you might need. They might've seen us disappear through open air and figured out where this room is."

Astro accepted the parchment. "Thanks, Roseabelle," he said. Together he and Jessicana put their Stones in the door, the gems clicking in place. The door instantly radiated a soft silver-white glow and it gently swung open, a soft mist flowing out of it. Roseabelle tried to peer ahead but all she could see was a glowing passageway. Astro removed the Stones from the door and handed them to her.

To their left, the door abruptly flew open. "Well, this is fortunate," a silky voice said. A Darvonian emerged from the shadows, followed by two guards dressed in cloaks. Roseabelle scowled. The fog must have cleared; the Darvonians had spotted them entering the room.

"Go, Roseabelle!" Jessicana urged. "Now."

The center Darvonian threw off her hood to reveal a familiar face. Roseabelle gaped. Of course! This Darvonian resembled an older Heltonine. It was Kinetle, ruler of the Darvonians. Roseabelle flinched and took a step backward, toward the open door of the Dream World. Her two friends were alone, cornered in a small room, standing up against three dangerous, fully-armed Darvonians. She couldn't just leave them!

Moonstar emitted a deep growl and sprang at one of the Darvonians. Okay, maybe they weren't so alone. "Roseabelle, go!" Astro shouted.

Roseabelle glanced into the Dream World.

"I can't believe I'm doing this," she whispered to herself and ran through the door to the Dream World. She left the door halfway open. It had to be left open or she wouldn't be able to come back. The last thing she saw was Astro, hurling their last ammo ball at Kinetle, and the room crackling with electricity.

CHAPTER 15

The Dream World

ROSEABELLE TOOK A DEEP BREATH; SHE HOPED HER friends would be fine. She looked down the passage of the Dream World. It was eerily quiet but she knew it wasn't empty. Roseabelle took a cautious step forward, amazed by all the mist floating in the air.

A light shone up ahead, and she continued down the tunnel, rounding the corner. An unbelievable sight greeted her eyes.

The landscape was dark and rocky—it mirrored Darvonia exactly, which was kind of scary. It stretched as far as the eye could see, and Roseabelle could even spot where she'd met Ugagush, Sheklyth's brother, for the first time.

When Roseabelle had traveled here in her mind, she had concluded that Darvonians gathered here, because she had seen Kinetle's son here. She had touched Asteran's feather and been instantly transported. She figured that the Darvonians made specific objects so they could meet here. So Darvonians could come here mentally but never physically. Roseabelle scoured the black sandy beach for anyone, but she saw nothing.

Except for . . . Her eyes widened when she noticed some black clad figures in the far distance, huddling in a small group. Those had to be the Darvonians Astro had vanished with his Stone. That meant Sheklyth was among them. The thought made Roseabelle shudder.

So where was the center of the Dream World? Roseabelle searched the sky but saw no clouds. The sky was just plain black, artificial, and unmoving. Roseabelle thought hard back to the conversation with her father about moving through the Dream World as quick as the wind. Was that really possible?

She pictured herself moving through the land as quick as the air. Instantly, an invisible force propelled her forward. Roseabelle's eyes widened and she imagined herself coming to a halt. Her actions obeyed her thoughts. "No way," she murmured, and her hand went to her javelin. There was a rocky black mountain beyond the group of Darvonians. It would make sense if the center of the Dream World was in there, because it was more prominent and large, but the mountain was miles away.

Roseabelle took a deep breath. The Darvonians would probably notice her if she sped by, but she had to hurry! She didn't have much time—Astro and Jessicana were still taking on the Darvonians back in Darvonia.

Imagining herself traveling at the speed of wind, Roseabelle closed her eyes and shot forward, an invisible hand pushing her. Her feet skimmed over the black grainy sand, and Roseabelle realized this place was almost a replica of Darvonia. Except for the looming mountain in the distance.

Her vision sped by in a blur. As Roseabelle shot by the Darvonians, she heard some confused shouts. She neared the mountain, clutching the Stones in her hands. They felt heavy in her tired arms.

Faster, she thought to herself. *Come on. You can do it!*

Glancing over her shoulder, Roseabelle saw distorted black figures chasing after her. Maybe they hadn't seen who she was but they probably were curious. She had to destroy the Dream World before they could get the Stones.

The Darvonians were traveling at the speed of wind also. Roseabelle saw the blurred figures following her, and she gritted her teeth, putting all her strength into reaching that mountain. She closed her eyes, thinking of Astro and Jessicana, her mother and father, and Benotripia. She had to get there in time!

She suddenly halted in her tracks, the force nearly toppling her over. She was already halfway up the mountain. Roseabelle spotted a boulder and ducked behind it just as the Darvonians shot right past. She counted two seconds and then once again emerged, speeding across the ascending black stone.

Her breath whipped out of her throat, Roseabelle peered up ahead to see the Darvonians slowing down, probably wondering where she had disappeared to—and then she passed them. She focused on holding onto the Stones and her only weapon.

Roseabelle focused on the mountain's peak and her face split into a wide grin. This was it. Benotripia was finally going to have peace! The solution was just moments away!

But a hard hand suddenly gripped her wrist. The combination of her intense speed and the abrupt pull on her arm caused Roseabelle to fling backward onto the hard ground. The javelin landed to her right and the Stones scattered all over the ground.

She instantly jumped to her feet, seizing the javelin and the blue and white Stones, but a pale hand grabbed the red Stone before she could reach it. Roseabelle looked up to see the group of Darvonians right before her, armed with shields, swords, maces, and other kinds of equipment. *Why did Astro have to make them disappear with their weapons?* she thought.

Her blood went ice cold when she saw who was at the front. A smirk was on her face and the red Stone in her hand.

Sheklyth, a black cloak encircling her, looked no different from the day she had betrayed the Benotripians.

Roseabelle immediately leaped forward with her javelin,

swinging at Sheklyth's hands and taking the Darvonian by surprise—she obviously hadn't been expecting Roseabelle to attack her. The red Stone fell from Sheklyth's grip, and Roseabelle dived forward.

As she lunged for the Stone, Roseabelle suddenly found the tip of a sword at her throat. She backed away, realizing that one of the Darvonians had caught the Stone. Sheklyth snatched it from him hurriedly.

"How did you even find out about this place?" Sheklyth asked, her intense eyes staring into Roseabelle's. Roseabelle had faced Sheklyth many times before—as a friend, as a new foe, and now as an old enemy. Sheklyth had been her former trainer going by the name of Shelby, pretending to be a Benotripian while actually spying for Darvonia.

"Give me the Stone," Roseabelle said slowly, readying her javelin. She didn't know what else to do or say; the Darvonians definitely outnumbered her. Up ahead, she could see the peak of the mountain. There was some sort of silvery basin—that was where she needed to go. She just had to get that Stone . . .

Sheklyth reached inside of her cloak. "You're too late, you know. The Darvonians are already here."

"What?" Roseabelle asked, her thoughts turning furiously. What was her former trainer talking about? Just then, Sheklyth took the opportunity to strike with a long dagger. Roseabelle quickly blocked the blow with her javelin. The other Darvonians attempted to approach them, but Sheklyth just handed the red Stone to them, most likely making sure she wouldn't lose it in battle.

Roseabelle drove the hilt of her javelin at Sheklyth, but the Darvonian sliced through it with her dagger, cutting Roseabelle's weapon in half. Sheklyth took another jab at her, and Roseabelle stumbled a bit but managed to sidestep it. "Face it, Roseabelle. You're beat."

Seeing her broken weapon, Roseabelle glanced at the Stones in her hand. Should she use them to conjure another weapon for herself? Roseabelle could only create, not summon objects with the blue Stone; otherwise, she would've tried to get the red Stone from out of the Darvonian's grasp.

Deciding against it, Roseabelle dashed to the side, ducking into the shadow of a large boulder. Before the Darvonians could reach her, she pictured a spot right behind the Darvonians and stomped her foot.

Instantly, Roseabelle appeared right behind Sheklyth, literally in her shadow. She wrenched the Stone from the Darvonian's grip, thwacking Sheklyth's fists with the pole of her broken javelin. As Sheklyth cried out in pain, Roseabelle darted up the mountain. She could hear heavy footsteps behind her and turned back partway, focusing on a particular patch of hard gritty earth. As the Darvonians advanced, she backed up the mountain, levitating a loose chunk of dry earth. She moved her head to the side and it splattered down on the Darvonians, knocking them to the ground.

Roseabelle raced to the top of the mountain and realized it wasn't a basin she had been looking at. Instead, it was an embellished silver bowl perched on top of a staff. This had to be it. Nothing else in the Dream World had beckoned to her like this object did.

She was about to place all three Stones in the bowl when a black arrow pierced her sleeve, slamming her arm against the bowl. Two of the Stones slipped from her hand and tumbled from view. Roseabelle glanced over her shoulder to see hundreds of Darvonians pouring from the passage into the Dream World, all armed with weapons. Fear penetrated her mind, fuzzing up her senses, and Roseabelle did her best to push it away. She was too close now to give up! There were hundreds of Darvonians, it seemed. Roseabelle wouldn't be surprised if they were streaming from every corner of the island.

Black-clad figures were zooming up the mountain. Roseabelle hurriedly slammed the red Stone into the bowl and watched as the silver melded around it. The gem had become part of the bowl. She bent down and stretched out her uninjured arm for the other two glittering jewels that lay innocently on the black sand. She grabbed the blue Stone and soon it was melded into the bowl as well.

One more.

Adrenaline pumping and heart racing, she reached for the third Stone. Suddenly, a piercing pain engulfed her leg. She thudded to the ground over the white Stone, face twisted in agony.

An arrow had struck her leg. Breathing heavily, she saw that the Darvonians were filling the entire top of the mountain. As one group surrounded her, another walked over to inspect the bowl.

Agony like she had never felt before racked Roseabelle's body, racing up and down her limbs in hot flashes of pain. She knew she had to get the last Stone. Where was it? She was too stricken, too paralyzed with stabbing pain to move. A part of her knew it was all over. The Darvonians had entered the Dream World and it had not been destroyed. All her friends' adventures and sacrifices had been in vain.

But as she stared vacantly at the ground, Roseabelle pictured her friends at the entrance, waiting for her to return, fighting just so she could succeed. Jessicana and Astro had always been there for her—she couldn't just abandon them now! Benotripia would be overrun if she did nothing. But what could she do? She was surrounded. Sheklyth had won.

Tears pooled in her eyes as Roseabelle recalled one more thing—she had finally found her father. If she survived the Dream World, her family would be united once again. The joyful faces of Danette, Dastrock, and Magford, all together—that was all she had wished for her entire life.

Roseabelle wanted to see her father again, wanted to tell him how glad she was to find him at last. She wanted to see her mother's face when she saw Magford. All the things she wanted now seemed distant, like a dream.

Here she was lying on the ground, helpless, wounded. But thinking about her friends and her family filled her with sudden warmth. Hope. It fueled her. It wasn't over yet. There was still time.

She'd been in dangerous situations before. Roseabelle knew she had to figure something out before the Darvonians found the other Stone and whisked it away.

Roseabelle heard the Darvonians trying to remove the Stones from the bowl, but it didn't work. Sheklyth's sharp voice struck her ears. "What's done is done, but the Dream World is still standing. Get the girl out of here! Is she dead yet?"

"Probably just in too much pain to move," a gruff voice responded.

Roseabelle's thoughts raced through her mind, and she shifted a bit. An arrow to the upper leg could be fatal if it wasn't treated right away. She could see the black arrow protruding from her, and the pain was growing more intense.

Out of the corner of her eye, Roseabelle spotted a gleaming object right near her foot. It was her Stone, radiating as clear as the noonday sun. If only she could get a bit closer to it. Gritting her teeth, Roseabelle shifted back a bit and ignored the pain.

She grunted. Her breathing became more shallow as she inched toward it and covered it with her feet.

"Retrieve the white Stone! Where is it?" Sheklyth hissed from above. Roseabelle forced herself not to panic.

Gathering every last ounce of strength she had, Roseabelle focused on the Stone, and it suddenly scooted over to her, settling beside her wounded leg.

She could feel it right under her leg, healing her. She heard the Darvonians scuttling around to find the Stone and knew that this was the opportune moment to strike.

Roseabelle sat up with a start, wrenched the arrow from her leg, grabbed the Stone, and quickly plunged it into the bowl before anyone had a chance to react. The silver instantly melded around it, and the ground began to shake.

"No!" Sheklyth shrieked. "Retreat! Retreat!" She lunged for Roseabelle, her eyes mad with fury. Roseabelle dodged her, ducking into the silver bowl's shadow. Trembling, Roseabelle pictured the shadow of the Dream World doorway.

Her body felt as though it were folding this time as she Shadow Tumbled. Roseabelle knew the Dream World was about to collapse on top of them. She was jolted back to the present as she appeared in the foggy passage with the door to the Dream World on her left. She had to get out before it was too late!

CHAPTER 16
Vanquished at Last

Astro and Jessicana were standing in the doorway, eyes wide. "Roseabelle!" Jessicana yelled and ran forward, grabbing her friend's arm and pulling her to safety. Astro then slammed the door firmly behind them.

Roseabelle toppled onto the floor, body weak with exhaustion, her mind still woozy from using the Dream World to travel so fast. How did her father do that all the time?

"Roseabelle!" Astro said, grinning wildly. "You did it!"

"We were about to come in after you," Jessicana said seriously. "Suddenly all these Darvonians appeared and we did our best to stop them but they pushed right past us. They were too greedy in pursuit of the Dream World. There were too many of them, there was nothing we could do!"

Roseabelle laughed and hugged both of her friends at the same time. "It doesn't matter. You guys were waiting for me! That's what matters!"

They heard a deep shuddering sound at the other end of the room, and the three friends looked over to see the Dream World's door slowly disappearing. It changed into a semi-solid state and vaporized into mist. "It's gone," Jessicana said softly. Astro let out a whoop.

Soon all of them were jumping up and down in their excitement—the Darvonians had been vanquished!

"Where's Moonstar?" Roseabelle suddenly asked, her eyes wide.

"I don't know!" Astro said. The Sheilvoh had stayed behind with Jessicana and Astro, but now was nowhere to be found.

"Roseabelle!" called a voice from outside. The stone muffled the sound and it was hard to make out who the voice belonged to.

Astro walked forward, staring at the stone wall. "Who is that?"

"Be careful. It could be a trap," Jessicana insisted.

"Hold on. It sounds like . . . my father!" Roseabelle said, grinning broadly.

"I'll blast through it," Astro said, striding up to the wall.

"But what about the Shadow Horses, Astro?" Jessicana inquired.

"I'm pretty sure they're gone," Astro said. "I don't feel overloaded with electricity or anything." He stretched forth his fingers and shot a range of lightning at the wall, peppering it with bolts. Jessicana and Roseabelle both took cover by dropping to the floor as lightning flashed across the room. It looked like Astro was engulfed in a radiating dome of silver and blue. Suddenly there was a white flash. Roseabelle shut her eyes, hiding them from the searing pain.

Jessicana tapped her on the shoulder and Roseabelle slowly opened her eyes to see a smoking crater in the wall and Astro standing beside it. He grinned and rubbed his hands together. "And that's how you do it, folks."

Jessicana coughed on the dust that was rising from the leftover debris. She rolled her eyes and stepped forward, picking her way through the broken slabs of stone. "And you said you weren't overloaded with electricity." Astro grinned sheepishly.

Roseabelle stood up and then stopped short in her tracks; on the other side of the hole in the wall stood three figures smiling at her. "Mom! Dad! Dastrock!" Roseabelle ran toward them, hugging her parents. She nearly plowed them over. She spotted Moonstar crouched beside Magford.

Danette immediately reached down to embrace her. "Darling, did you really—?"

Magford, who had stepped inside, nodded and grinned broadly. "She did." He shook his head. "Roseabelle, how did you do it? You took on hundreds of Darvonians!"

She smiled modestly. "Not really. I just put the Stones in a bowl. If Jessicana and Astro weren't here, I wouldn't have survived." She gestured at her friends and looked up at Dastrock. "I don't understand. What happened to you guys?"

Dastrock smiled. "Remember my power of making illusions? Well, once I received your mottel, which saved all of our lives, I made it look as though our ship was heading in a different direction. Then once we reached land, we abandoned ship and travelled to the Darvonian palace and saw Magford fighting some Darvonians so we joined in to help. The Sheilvoh led us here."

Magford thumped Dastrock on the back and Danette smiled at her husband, pulling him close in an embrace. "What about the Darvonians?" Jessicana asked.

Danette smiled. "Their leaders are now gone. Sheklyth, Heltonine, Kinetle—they were all overcome with the prospect of power, so they went into the Dream World. In fact, there are scarcely any Darvonians left. We have nothing to fear." Roseabelle glanced up to some debris in the air, a trail of where the Dream World had been.

Roseabelle felt all the worry, all the anxiety, and all the bad dreams about Sheklyth simply lift away, and she grinned at her friends. "Well, you know what this means right?"

"Let's go home," Jessicana said.

"And party!" Astro added.

All of them were so fatigued, so weary, that they burst out laughing. Right then and there, they plopped down on the ground, and Jessicana handed Roseabelle the parchment. Astro drew a rather sloppy meal on the trutan, and soon they were eating cheerfully and talking.

"Wait a second," Roseabelle said, turning to her dad. "How come Metamordia was so deserted?"

Magford sighed. "The Darvonians imprisoned all the people. They're stuck inside cliffs that dotted the island. As soon as you rescued me though, the Darvonians traveled to Darvonia, leaving the Metamordians unattended. I received word that they have gotten out safely."

"How do you know that though?" Astro questioned.

Magford shrugged. "Benotripia isn't the only island that uses mottels."

Roseabelle suddenly reached inside her pocket. "Oh no!" she said. "The Third Eye is gone! I must have dropped it in the Dream World." She expected Danette and Dastrock to be angry with her, maybe even a bit disappointed, but Danette just laughed and put an arm around her.

"Roseabelle, you are worth more than the most powerful magical relic in all of the three islands," she said.

Roseabelle's dream had come true right before her eyes. For once in her life, her whole family was reunited.

The smile she wore was brighter than a thousand suns. Or Dragocone Rays, for that matter.

Epilogue

Roseabelle sat at the kitchen table, her long red hair dangling down her back, partly tied back by a red ribbon. The blue dress she wore paled against her brown eyes, and she uncertainly glanced at the rainbow medal she gripped in her hands. It was the medal she had received for saving her mother; holding it always gave her a little bit of strength. Swallowing her fear, she slid it around her neck, the metal shining with a pearly radiance.

From the other corner of the room, Moonstar purred softly. "What?" she asked him teasingly. "Are you nervous too? I doubt it. I'm standing up in front of all of Benotripia today and being named." Moonstar just stared at her with his large golden eyes.

"He says you're being a drama queen," said a deep voice from the top of the stairs. Roseabelle looked up to see her father, Magford, wearing a long-sleeved white shirt and black pants made from Awnshneelia spider silk, one of the rarest and softest fabrics in all of Metamordia.

"I am not!" she protested and stifled a smile when Magford raised his eyebrows at her. "All right, maybe a little. But it's for a good reason. Weren't you a little worried too when you were crowned?"

Magford put an arm around her. "You'll do fine, Roseabelle. I'm so proud of you."

Just then, the front door swung open, revealing Astro and Jessicana. The parrot girl was dressed in a formal aqua dress and the lightning boy was in silver-and-black shirt and pants.

"You're going to be crowned!" Jessicana exploded, hugging Roseabelle. "You're going to be the ruler of Benotripia. This is so exciting!"

Roseabelle laughed while Astro grinned from ear to ear, his fingertips crackling with electricity. "Uh, Astro," she said. "Please keep your hands in your pockets. The last time you were in my house, we had some silver fireworks."

He grinned sheepishly and stuffed his hands in his pockets. "This is so cool, Roseabelle!"

Danette poked her head into the room. "You ready, Roseabelle?"

She sighed. "I-I think so."

"You're ready for this," Danette said. "You realize what today is?"

She nodded solemnly and Magford smiled. "Four years ago, this very day was when the Darvonians were vanquished."

Jessicana bounced up and down. "Come on, Roseabelle. You're ready for this!"

Roseabelle gave her friend a small smile. "But I'm not even Benotripian!"

Danette laughed. "Just because you were born in Metamordia doesn't mean you're not a Benotripian. You grew up here. It's all right to have two homes."

Roseabelle sighed. "All right, I guess I'm ready." Jessicana squeezed her hand and Astro grinned at her. All of them exited her home and scaled down the ladder. Roseabelle's eyes nearly popped open at what she saw.

People as far as the eye could see clumped together, some

sitting in chairs, some standing, eagerly awaiting her arrival. On the ground there was a glittering red-and-orange stage. Dastrock stood on top of it, holding an intricate scepter out of the same metal that her medal was created from. The rainbow colors glinted brilliantly in the sun.

The Benotripians cheered as Roseabelle descended onto the stage next to Dastrock, her mother and father following. Her friends stood at the left side of the stage, and Astro gave her a big thumbs-up.

Danette regally stood in front of the people as Roseabelle fidgeted behind her. She put on her biggest smile, warmth swelling up in her chest. Maybe she was nervous, but she was more excited. Danette raised her hand and the mumbling chatter instantly vanished. "We gather here today to honor my daughter, Roseabelle, who has gone above and beyond to serve Benotripia. She has bravely battled the Darvonians, defended her friends, and displayed endless courage.

"I am fully aware that the honor of becoming the ruler of Benotripia is normally bestowed to the heir when they are seventeen years of age. But Roseabelle is a different case at fifteen years old. She has given her all to Benotripia. Without her and her friends Jessicana and Astro, we would not be standing here today. Being a ruler is not about receiving; it is about giving. And these past few years, that is exactly what Roseabelle has done. So today, I bestow to her the Destiny Scepter—" Danette broke her speech as Dastrock held the scepter out in his hands, extending it to her.

Roseabelle looked at her mother and saw her kind face and intelligent eyes. She was smiling warmly, and motioning for her to take the scepter. She saw her father and uncle with identical grins on their faces and Jessicana and Astro, both beaming. Even Moonstar seemed as though he was smiling. Taking a deep breath, she spoke the traditional words: "I accept."

The crowd burst into roaring cheers, and Roseabelle took

the scepter and held it in the air. Jessicana and Astro raced to her, embracing her. "That was crazy!" Jessicana said.

"How were you so calm and collected up there?"

"I would have freaked!"

Roseabelle laughed. "Oh, please. Whenever I see you guys out there, I'm completely fine."

And truly and honestly, she was. Because finally, Benotripia was at peace.

Discussion Questions

1. If you could make up your own power, what would it be?
2. If you had the choice to live on one of the three islands—Benotripia, Metamordia, or Darvonia—which would you choose?
3. Roseabelle used her courage to venture into the Dream World, Jessicana used her potions and her wits to escape from the Darvonians, and Astro utilized his lightning to protect himself and his friends. Each of the three friends used their strengths to help each other. What are your strengths? How could you use them to defeat the Darvonians?
4. Why do you think Magford allowed the three friends to go after the Darvonians instead of making them stay behind while he took care of it?
5. What was your favorite part of the book? Why?
6. Do you think a Sheilvoh would make a good companion? Why or why not?

Acknowledgments

AT SEVEN YEARS OLD, I WROTE MY VERY FIRST STORY in a glittery purple notebook and spent an entire summer pouring out my imagination into it. Now, six years later, that story is published, I still have that notebook, and I'm now done with the entire Benotripia series. I can't believe I'm where I am today. Let's just say that I have a lot of people to thank.

Gratitude to my amazing family—Mom, Dad, and Ty—for supporting me in everything I do. You guys are truly awe-inspiring. The same goes to all three of my grandparents and every single one of my extended family members, especially the ones who dressed up as creepy Darvonians at my second launch party. I couldn't do any of this without you.

Thanks to Rachel Sharp for bringing the Benotripia characters to life with the out-of-this-world cover art and illustrations.

Also, to my crazy fantastic friends Erin, Samantha, Rianna, Frances, Sarajane, Marina, the three Ashleys, and Emma, for always boosting my morale and making me laugh. Thanks to Annabella, for being the perfect Jessicana.

I want to express deep gratitude to Ms. Kunz who first taught me the basics of writing and to Ms. Pearce for making my middle school experience positive and to Melia, for being so eccentric about my writing.

Jennifer A. Nielsen, Richard Paul Evans, and Frank L. Cole—thank you for being the most inspiring authors and people I've ever met. I'd like to show my appreciation to the Cedar Fort team for being so incredibly wonderful in all they do: Lyle, Angie, Alissa, Kelly, Rodney, and everyone else who has strived to make Benotripia a success.

And last but not least, love to my spectacular readers! Benotripia has been such a blast. Thank you for sharing and enjoying the story. Although the series is complete and I am already missing adventures with Roseabelle, Jessicana, and Astro, I have thoroughly enjoyed writing it. Thank you all for making my dreams a possibility.

About the Author

McKenzie Wagner is fourteen years old and has adored reading since she was four. Her love of books inspired her to write a book of her own, and she completed the first book of The Magic Wall series, *The Magic Meadow and the Golden Locket*, at age seven and the second book, *The Blue Lagoon and the Magic Coin*, shortly thereafter. With her new series, Benotripia, she has now expanded her writing to appeal to kids of all ages. She wishes to obtain an English degree and continue her path as an author. She currently resides in Utah with her mom, dad, and brother, Ty.

0 26575 17512 7